Sunshine in a Bottle

Indi has to submit to a wellness journey to inherit millions, whether she needs it or not...

Carolyn Finch

Enjoy Indi's journey to wellness!!

Happy Reading

Carolyn Finch

Copyright © [2022] by [Becky Lee Jenkins Smith writing as Carolyn Finch]

All rights reserved.

No portion of this book may be reproduced in any form without written permission from the publisher or author, except as permitted by Canadian copyright law.

Foreword

Dear Readers,

This is a first edition/first print run. This is one book of 200 only.

First of all! Please note: <u>this book is not intended to diagnose or treat any medical condition.</u>

If you need assistance in changing your eating or exercise protocol, please see a physician/dietician.

Also, the wellness journey (including the diet/therapy and preferred exercise) as well as the hairstyling references are my own experience; the rest of this book is fiction.

Thank you for your ongoing support. I appreciate every one of you!

Lots of Love,
Becky

Sunshine in a Bottle is for Peter.
Thank you from the bottom of my heart—you know why.

Chapter One

Antihistamines and Ammonia

My eyes sweep over the floor of thirteen hairdressers—oops—hairstylists. We aren't called hairdressers anymore. I'm showing my age in this industry.

Pressing my hands into my lower back, I realize my vernacular isn't the only thing aging me—my body is too. I thought about starting a diet to tackle these pesky sixty pounds that hurt my knees. Maybe Monday...

Pre-wedding season—eight-forty in the morning—already the scent of aerosol hangs heavy in the air. I can smell the hot rollers heating at my station. Blyss and Bloom books four weddings every Saturday from May to the end of September.

Esther, my business partner, my chosen sister—the girl who saved my life—is at the back bar washing out a highlight. I am the only one who knows her as Esther. We changed her name to Estee when we opened this shop together; in the nineties, when our bangs were so big that we had to duck to get into the salon.

My nose tickles and the top of my throat itches with allergies, distracting me from that happy memory. I reach for a double dose of antihistamines. My swollen fingers hurt as I slide a fingernail into the foil packet. I flex my knuckles to limber them up for the work ahead of me. Rooting around for an ibuprofen, I take that, too, to get rid of the inflammation that makes my ankles swell by the end of the day.

I am determined to get my health in order. I need to find a trainer.

Ugh... next Monday. Hmm, no, this time of year is way too busy.

I swallow the pills with ice-cold coffee that tastes terrible and watch the staff to make sure everyone is on time.

My phone distracts me from watching to ensure everything gets plugged in and ready for those first bridesmaids.

A text from my boyfriend, Ben.

Can't get through and haven't heard from you. Those idiots turned off my power. We'll have to have supper at your place. I'm not sure what you want to pick up, but after you get the food, can you pick me up? I need to borrow money for the power bill. Just until I get on my feet.

Love you, Ben.

I burn with frustration as I read the text.

Ben has been trying to get on his feet for the past two years. I think about ignoring this, but immediately, I feel guilty. I'd been there myself and had a helping hand. I E-transfer two hundred to his account. I wish I didn't know that his electric bill is exactly $198. It irritates me how I am expected to carry all the financial stress for my business, my home, and his.

When will he figure it out?

CHAPTER ONE 3

I shake that thought away. Ben will get it together. Of course he will.

I look over my book again, and once more, my phone distracts my sweeping gaze. A British Columbia area code covers my screen saver of a Belize coral reef. I used to fantasize about a trip there—it looks so perfect. I once yearned to travel, but just when I could go, Estee announced her pregnancy. She couldn't keep it a secret from the clients anymore since she had a few complications.

I couldn't leave.

I was the only person who could keep the business afloat in her absence, so I hired Elle to step in for Estee and maintain her clientele. I ran the business, and I shouldered everything.

As the years went on, I worked harder; put myself last, and the weight piled on. The thought of being in a bathing suit on a Caribbean Island became horrifying. I decided if I lost the weight, I would swim on coral reefs and—ugh. It never seemed like the right time. Just as I thought about booking a ticket, Estee had another baby, and the bulk of Blyss and Bloom's management landed on me—again. I told myself I didn't mind, and I worked harder.

The phone number from British Columbia flashed on my screen again. My heart pounds in anger because no good can come of the number on my screen. Tansy, my mother, has been in B.C. for the past ten years. I don't know where she was before that. I don't want to know. I haven't seen her since I was fifteen. The night that I—the night I never talk about—to anyone.

I have no time or energy for her chaos.

Utter chaos.

I block the number and smile as my screen saver comes back on. Salty water and sunshine—sigh! Some day!

I refocus on the work at hand; my eyes fixate like a laser beam on Alli's work station—empty.

Hmm. We require our stylists to be at least ten minutes early. I notice Alli slip in at the last minute. She looks exhausted, on the verge of tears.

I frown. Blyss and Bloom runs like a Swiss clock, and that is no accident. We've had amazing hairstylists over the years who just can't get to work on time, nor stay for their whole day. The worst of the divas think we'll bend the rules for them. We don't bend rules. Ever. Occasionally, Estee's eyes soften with sympathy, but I snap her back to reality. If they drag their drama to work, we fire them.

Alli, our junior stylist, came in just under the wire. I wanted to give her notice, but Estee said we should see how it plays out. I intend to keep my eye on her.

My first client, Ariana, has arrived, and it's time to work. I pull on my work cape that I feel hides the worst of my body. As I walk to my station, though, I carefully avoid looking at myself in the full-length mirrors. I know the location of every mirror in this salon and at home, and I trained my eyes to see only people—not me.

Not the truth about me.

I've got it all under control—except my weight. Actually, the list is a little long—Ben's employment, my weight, allergies, and the level of pain I work with are the only things I can't control in my life. It makes me feel helpless, and I hate that. I refuse to accept it and will distract myself until I can numb it later, after the last client goes home. I put all that out of my mind. Those thoughts are my personal drama, and there is no room for it here. Not now.

CHAPTER ONE

I focus on Ariana. My life will be consumed by whatever she needs before the wedding and on the big day. I wouldn't have it any other way.

The persistent phone number from British Columbia—a different one that I haven't blocked yet—blares across my cell phone screen. With a hard heart, I turn the phone over and get to work.

Chapter Two

Aerosol and Envy

I love Ariana. As much as a hairstylist can love a client, I love this girl. I'm desperate to hear her plans and how she's handling her prickly mother-in-law-to-be. Ariana is getting married on Saturday, and I am so excited for her. I can't wait to cheer her on. We are doing her pretrial hair for her wedding—again. We need to be sure we can execute that hairstyle flawlessly this coming Saturday.

I have been doing her hair since she was in Grade 8. I know everything about this girl. My heart swells with happiness at her excitement. As I section her hair, I wonder if it will ever be my turn. I shake that thought away.

This is about her, not me.

My hand stills for the briefest moment as I reflect on that thought. It's never about me, but that's for the best.

Love, marriage, family. I've seen the best and the worst behind this chair. I've lived the worst, and I'm skeptical—cyn-

CHAPTER TWO

ical—about the best. I've seen enough to know I am not risking my heart.

Love is messy. It's chaos. It's—a vision of the night that I left my mother. I stop working; I stop moving as the memory blindsides me.

Ariana doesn't notice.

"She's insisting on a different caterer because she wants vegan treats for her dog, whom she has insisted is coming to the wedding." Ariana rolls her eyes and throws her hands in the air. "A caterer actually exists with a menu for dogs. It's my day, and we're dealing with this lunatic and her insane dog—"

I snap back to the conversation at hand and drive the anger and hurt surrounding my relationship with my mother down; right down to the pit of my stomach. I promise to comfort that feeling with wine and lots of pasta later.

I laugh with Ariana and focus on the wedding crisis she lays out for me. Then, she shows me a new hairstyle on Pinterest for when she gets back from her honeymoon. It's a difficult one—a colour that is possible on only seven percent of the population. The picture makes me want to storm the halls of Pinterest and demand to speak with the manager.

Stop showing women the impossible!

I smile at her politely and say we'll work toward it. I put those thoughts aside because I can't wait for her big day.

As Ariana turns to leave, a shadow falls across her face. "What if you get sick? What would happen if you couldn't be here?"

"Remember, I worked for six weeks on a broken ankle, in a boot."

"Yes, I remember, but what if it's your wrist?" Ariana's eyes grow wide with fear.

"That's a good point." I can't have this girl terrified. "Elle, could you spare a moment?"

Beautiful Elle drifts across the salon to give Ariana a thousand-watt smile. "You're gorgeous!"

"Thank you." Ariana smiles back.

Ariana knows she's gorgeous, but I can tell she's happy to have it confirmed by an equally stunning human being like Elle.

I swallow my pride and ask for help. "Elle, just in case I break my wrist or have a heart attack"—I notice Ariana's face pale at the thought. Her eyes sweep over me, and I can tell she thinks I'm a likely candidate. Ugh! I mentally put my weight back to the top of my to-do list—"do you feel confident that you can do this updo on Saturday if something happens to me?"

Elle's eyes gleam in anticipation of the task at hand—not the wedding hair, but all the follow up. Elle knows as well as I do that she could buy a cottage at the lake for what Ariana spends on highlights.

"Absolutely." Elle doesn't blink. "But Ariana, why don't you come in tomorrow, and I'll put it up just so we're sure I can do exactly what you want?"

In other words, I'll get you in my chair so I can steal you away from Indi.

My eyes narrow, and I immediately check myself. There is no room for jealousy in a salon. None. I forbid it. Ugly green jealousy roars through me all the same.

"Oh!" Ariana's eyes shine with gratitude. "That's a great idea."

"That way Saturday runs super smooth, no matter what." Elle smiles at Ariana, then at me. "Is that okay with you, Indi?"

CHAPTER TWO

"I wouldn't have it any other way." I force a bright smile. Elle smoothly walks Ariana to her book and pencils her in.

"I think that would put my mind at ease." Ariana nods. She sighs with relief when her name is neatly written in Elle's column tomorrow first thing. "You don't mind, do you?" Ariana's eyes meet mine, and she doesn't look away.

"Not at all." I shake my head. "Elle is fantastic. It's good to have a backup, but I'll be here." I hug her tight. "I am so excited for you."

Ariana beams at me. "Okay. Deep breaths. I have to calm down."

"Yes, you do. Pick up some vegan dog treats and make peace," I advise as she makes her way to the door.

Ariana laughs and sweeps out of the hair salon just as the UPS man comes in with a big manila envelope.

"India Blyss?"

"That's me."

"Sign here, please."

I take the envelope and sign my name on his little electronic device, then hand it back to him.

"Have a great day." The UPS man quickly exits the salon.

I hold the envelope out to look at it. The return address is a law firm in Snow, B.C. My stomach clenches. Is this why the B.C. number is relentlessly calling me? My mother—correction, my crazy train-wreck-wrapped-in-a-time-bomb mom—lives in Snow, B.C. A fluttery panic beats around my heart as I clutch the envelope tightly.

Why is my mother sending me correspondence through a lawyer?

I don't like this. I don't like this at all.

Chapter Three

Carbohydrates and Compromise

I have a full book of work in front of me. I can't handle a crisis now, and if my mother is reaching out to me, it can only be for one reason. She's in trouble. She needs money, or she wants to reconcile, and I don't know what is worse.

Walking a client to the front door, Estee catches a glimpse of my face. "What is it?"

"An envelope from B.C. Registered mail." My hands shake with fury. I don't want to think about this. I don't want a thing to do with whatever chaos my mother is bringing to me. I have a monster of a day ahead of me. I can't be distracted.

Estee bites her lip. "What do you think?"

I see the slightest sign of a tell, her eyebrow arching just slightly.

"What do you know?" My eyes narrow.

"Not a thing."

She's lying, and now I'm terrified.

CHAPTER THREE

I tuck the envelope into my bag. "I think I have work to do. I'll read this later."

"I'll read it and filter it for you." Estee holds out her hand.

"Really?" I tilt my head, trying to see a trap of some sort. I remind myself that Estee wouldn't know my mom if she tripped over her. I'm being paranoid.

"Of course." Estee's eyes soften with concern because my hands are shaking. "I'll read it, and we'll discuss it tonight. Over supper."

Love for Estee rushes through me at the offer. "What about Craig?"

"He's fly-fishing with his brother tonight."

"The kids?"

"Happy with Grampie." Estee smiles as she thinks of her boys with her saint of a father.

"I'm supposed to pick up supper for Ben. I'll have to send something over."

"Oh, is Ben working today?" Estee asks sweetly.

Ben isn't working, but he has no electricity, and if I tell Estee that, she'll look at me with that judgmental face I don't like. She despises Ben and thinks he's freeloading off me. Estee doesn't understand that he's just trying to get on his feet. He had a bad upbringing. Like me.

I protect him from her judgments. "It's my turn to make supper."

"I see." Estee raises her eyebrow and sighs.

The unsaid *and when is it his turn?* is alluded to but not pointed out. I bristle and choose to ignore her tone, even though it makes me want to protect Ben more.

Why?

Turning our conversation back to the matter at hand, I look down at my phone.

It's lighting up with numbers from B.C. again. I turn it over.

"Tonight. We'll go out," Estee says.

"I'll need all the pasta and chocolate in the world."

"Italian then?"

"Yes."

—⁂—

I meet Estee at the restaurant at seven p.m. after sending a takeout supper to Ben, paid for it with my credit card. I'm tired—exhausted. My hands are already stiffening, my back aching, and my feet are so sore I'm grateful to sit for the first time in eight hours. At thirty-eight, I have twenty more years of work ahead of me—at least—and already I've had to cut back to eight hours a day instead of ten.

Estee's face is way too serene. She's read it, and whatever the contents are, she isn't surprised. I can feel a crisis brewing, so I order a big plate of pasta with extra cheese, extra garlic toast, and nine ounces of ice-cold Sauvignon Blanc—my favourite wine of all time. Estee raises an eyebrow at the food but says nothing. I'm starving, I am exhausted, and I am worried about the contents of the letter.

"You know, every day I say I'm going to stop drinking and eat better. Every night around four, I can't wait to dive into a bottle of Blanc like it's a life raft," I mutter as I devour the bread basket. I leave her one piece, but I happily slather salted whipped butter on the hot bread and nearly swoon with delight as it melts.

Estee laughs with me, but her laugh is forced. I can tell. She disapproves of Ben, my food choices, my glass of wine. Increasingly, her judgments irritate me. She married a saint.

CHAPTER THREE

Good for her. She was raised by a saint. I wasn't, and I have the triggers to prove it.

As the night I left my mother hovers in my memory, I take a big gulp of Blanc and put it aside.

"Just say it, Estee. What is it?"

"Indi, your mom has passed away. I'm very sorry." Estee speaks in a low, calm voice.

Shock washes over me, and close on its heels, guilt causes me to flash hot and cold. I didn't look after her—I left her.

"What did she die of?" I take another long swallow of Sauv to numb the host of emotions the word mother brings my heart.

"She had a cancerous tumour on her spine." Estee's dark eyes are soft with sympathy. "She chose not to have an operation because she would have lost her quality of life. She let it take her."

I can't think, and I'm numb from Estee's words. I thought I had shut off the part of myself that used to care deeply about my mother, but the care rises in my heart, and I shove it down. I am torn between so many conflicting feelings—I can't process how I feel.

I take another swallow of Sauvignon Blanc, irritated that the glass is now empty. I signal to the waitress.

"How much money does the estate want to bury her?" While I wait for the wine, I attack the new loaf of fresh bread, slathering it with extra butter.

"Indi, this is a twist we never expected..." Estee chooses her words carefully.

I hate when she does that. I feel like a toddler on the verge of a tantrum, and she's trying to placate me. "Just say it." I bite into a piece of garlic toast that provides comfort to my conflicted soul. I should be crying. I should be sad. I should not feel all this guilt and—I hate to admit it—relief. Immediately, I hate myself for that thought.

I wash down the salty, buttery bread with cold wine and wait to hear the news. I nearly swoon at the combination. I can survive any news armed with piping hot carbohydrates and ice-cold alcohol.

"Your mother left you a wellness clinic called Salt and Citrus Wellness. Its net worth is… well… just the property alone is worth a fortune… but she holds the most shares, so they want to explain everything to you in person."

My hand holding the wine stops halfway between my mouth and the table. Disbelief wings through me. This is impossible. When I knew my mother, she lived in a rented trailer with bare cupboards and no pillowcases. No way did she own a house, never mind a wellness clinic. This is a joke or a mistake.

"My mother couldn't manage a shoeshine operation, never mind a wellness center! They sent this to the wrong India Blyss." Relief settles on me. Absolutely a mistake.

"No, it's true, Indi. But there's a catch." Estee reaches for her drink and takes a fortifying sip.

"What sort of catch?" The anger comes roaring back. How badly is my mother going to complicate my life?

"You have to be there by Friday. The lawyer is some high-end tycoon who isn't available later."

"What do you mean by Friday?" My heart pounds with wrath. "Ariana's wedding is Saturday. I can't be there Friday." I set down my wine and attack the fettucine on my plate.

"In order to inherit, you have to be on site to sign the documents." Estee bites her lip.

"I'll go Thursday, sign everything away on Friday at six a.m. for the high-end tycoon, and be back in Manitoba on Friday

CHAPTER THREE

night. I'll get Lys to move my clients. But I will be here for Ariana on Saturday. That is nonnegotiable."

"Or Elle—"

"Ariana's wedding is far more important than this—whatever this is. She only gets one wedding." I straighten my spine and try to ignore the pain in my shoulders.

"You only had one mother." Estee's tone is reproving.

I don't like it. "Not true," I snap. "I had Phyllis." Estee knows my whole truth, and her sympathy toward me going to B.C. during wedding season irritates me. It's irresponsible. I have no patience for frivolity.

As if on cue, Estee looks up and signals to someone at the door. In walks Estee's mom, my foster mom, Phyllis.

On the terrible night I ran from my mother, the night I don't speak of, the police picked me up, frozen solid in the back alley of the trailer park. When they asked for my address, I gave them my best friend Estee's. Thankfully, Phyllis opened the door and took me in that night. Her care stretched to three years, but that's a story for another time. Back to Phyllis, who's just walked into the restaurant.

Phyllis is five feet two inches of pure mother. She still packs Estee and me a lunch if we stay the night. She has buttons with her grandchildren's faces on her purse. Phyllis doesn't think for a second that those precious babies are tacky pinned onto everything that will stand still. Phyllis works hard, does the right thing, and raised me with an iron fist from the age of fifteen. I may owe my biological life to Tansy, but I owe my current life and any success I have ever had to Phyllis. If one woman in the world could bend me to her will—Phyllis is that woman.

Phyllis notices the carbohydrates on my plate, and her lips tighten. A smart woman, she's picking her battles. I can tell.

"Indi." Phyllis leans over me and hugs me hard.

I'm glad I didn't have to stand. My feet are aching, and my lower back feels like someone hit it with a bat. "Yes." Tears prick at my eyes.

"I'm sorry, hon." Phyllis lets me go and sits down across from me.

"I'm fine." I take one more piece of bread. I wish I could feel my tension and stress ease. Nothing is changing in me.

Phyllis wastes no time. "I'm sorry, this is so shocking and unexpected."

"There has to be a mistake. Honestly. You, more than anyone in the world, know that crazy Tansy couldn't create a wellness clinic. This is absolute madness!"

Phyllis opens a file and hands me a picture of the clinic.

"Where did you get this?" I feel equal parts suspicious and curious.

"Tansy and I have been in touch since you left her."

"What!" Betrayal pounds through me. Phyllis is mine, not my mother's.

Phyllis shakes her head. "I'm a mom, Indi. Moms have a code. We stand together."

"My mother was never a mother to me," I whisper. My eyes meet Phyllis's, and hers soften with sympathy. "You of all people know the truth, Phyllis."

"Yes, I do. I know the whole truth." Phyllis watches me. "You don't."

"Then tell me." I cross my arms over my chest.

Phyllis shakes her head no.

I notice her permed-into-submission hair doesn't move. Estee and I have begged her not to perm, and she refuses to listen to us.

"It's not my truth to tell." Phyllis sips her water.

CHAPTER THREE 17

I burn with anger as Phyllis manages me. "Well, I'll sign everything away on Friday and be back Friday night so I can close this chapter." I shrug.

Phyllis squares her shoulders. "It's not that simple. She had investors, and you'll have staff members to consider."

I frown at them both. "What do you mean?"

"Your mother added another clause." Phyllis looks at Estee, who sips her cocktail.

I take a fortifying forkful of hot carbohydrates and cheese sauce. "What's that?"

.

Chapter Four

Betrayal

"You are going to be upset no matter how I say this, so I'm just going to be direct." Phyllis waits until the waitress hands me the wine.

Disapproval darkens her face, and I work hard to ignore it. I need some anesthetic, and this is the only legal kind. I pour it, take a gulp, and wait.

"Indi." Estee is concerned about how much wine I have consumed.

"I'll take a cab home." I put Estee's mind at ease. "What is the clause?"

Estee frowns and says nothing.

"You can't put it on the market right away. You have to run it for six whole months, and your mother laid out a wellness plan for you to complete in that time," Phyllis says.

White-hot rage swells in my heart, choking me.

I put down my wine and take a deep breath. "What?"

CHAPTER FOUR

"Salt and Citrus Wellness Clinic employs many people. There are investors who need to be taken into consideration. Your mother worried that a random buyer might not have the right vision."

I look at Phyllis furiously. She is talking about protecting people from losing their livelihoods if I do something rash—me, the person who survived my mother. Not only did I endure crazy Tansy, I flourished. How dare Phyllis!

Clearly not content to destroy my life while alive, my mother left one last way to create chaos—her will! How could Phyllis even think about presenting this plan to me?

"I can't leave my business here for six months, Phyllis... I can't." My jaw clenches. My tone hardens as I bring this madness to an end. "If she has investors, let them run it and keep me out of it. I'll get a lawyer."

"Indi, I disagree," Estee said quietly, and the betrayal compounds. "You can leave for six months."

"It's wedding season." I frown at Estee.

"I took three six-month maternity leaves."

"But you were pregnant, and there was time." I scramble to come up with reasons to stay.

"We can handle this." Estee isn't backing down, and I can tell she and Phyllis planned this conversation.

I'm stunned and horrified. They don't know how terrified I am to slide into any plan my mother concocted. "No, you can't."

Estee looks offended.

To avoid Phyllis's disapproval, I switch to water but continue to eat more hot bread—my trusty solution to emotional conflict. "When did you both decide this? I just got the envelope today—"

My heart sinks as they look at each other. They are mother and daughter. They have a bond I have never known with Phyllis, and I feel the loss so acutely I can hardly breathe.

"We all know that Elle is excellent. She did my maternity leaves. Move her to your clientele for the next six months." Estee sides with Phyllis.

My body shakes with wrath that is born from betrayal. They conspired against me.

"I kept us afloat when you were on mat leave. You were talking about cutting back." I hear the ice in my tone, and I can't stop it—can't gentle it. I'm hurt deeper than I can even acknowledge.

"I can do both." Estee's tone is firm.

"What if you can't?" More ice. More defensiveness. My mother's darkness is closing in on me, and I can't bear it.

"Don't sell me short. I can absolutely run the business I created with you." Estee's eyes narrow, and I can tell she's furious with me.

I don't care. Estee hasn't had my life. She's never known grinding poverty.

Between the two of us, I am the only one with the drive to keep it all going. Estee is a loose cannon. She could accidentally get pregnant. One of her kids could get sick. Elle could get sick. Anything could happen. I am the only one I can trust.

Phyllis and Estee look at each other across the table once again, and I can see it in their eyes. They want me to go. I am so hurt I can barely breathe.

"What about Ariana...?"

Phyllis leans forward. "You can come back for one week each month over the next six months to deal with a business emergency. Tansy wanted you to have six full months off, but

CHAPTER FOUR

I requested this on your behalf because no one wants Blyss and Bloom to suffer."

"However, I want you to take six whole months because you aren't well, Indi." Estee isn't letting this go. "You're in pain and exhausted all the time. Pick Ariana's wedding as your one week for the first month. You can work as much as you want that week, so any picky clients you feel you personally need to do can have that week with you."

"I—"

"We have amazing Elle to step in." Estee opened her purse. "Your plane ticket."

"What about Ben?" I know they both despise Ben and think I can do better.

Men don't look at me, though. Without Ben, I would be completely alone. It hurts to acknowledge that.

Phyllis takes a deep breath and lets it out slowly. "Ben is one of the biggest reasons I was on board with this from the beginning. I am not a therapist, but I believe you replaced the chaos your mother brought into your life with another form of chaos—Ben's. You chose him because he can't disappoint you. Dysfunction is normal for you in a relationship. You are codependent, my dear. Part of the wellness treatment includes learning what that is and how to rebuild you so you find the right man, if you want one. You don't have to have a man in your life, but if you do—it can't be Ben."

"So, it's not just hippie-dippie oils and rubbing me with weeds. I have to listen to psychobabble, too?" I can hardly see straight from fury. I can't believe two women I thought loved me can sit here and judge me this harshly. I want to say Ben just needs time, but I don't waste my breath. I look helplessly from Estee to Phyllis.

Phyllis brings out a purple book called Codependent No More, by Melody Beattie, with the image of a dandelion going to seed on the front. "Your therapist at Salt and Citrus, Summer, had a zoom meeting with me and Estee so she can get started on your process. She has prescribed this book for you to read before your first session. She recommended you read it on the plane. There is no time to waste."

"This is the most high-handed—"

"Indi." Phyllis is gentle. "Prove us wrong. Read it and give me a full report on how off our assessment is."

"I will." My eyes narrow as I hold out my hand and take the book from her.

"Your mother destroyed your life—for reasons you don't know. You are hanging onto resentments that hurt you. It's not healthy. We see it because you are living life behind a stylist's chair. Your business is amazing. You're amazing. But you're so busy that you aren't making time to live. You aren't engaged in real life. Your entire existence centers on Ariana's wedding. A client's wedding. Your boyfriend is a train wreck and is dragging you down with him. You need help, Indi—just like you did at fifteen. I helped you then, but it's your mom's turn now." Phyllis sips her water containing six lemon wedges. She gathers her breath and attacks me again. "Tansy is dead. She can't see or feel or experience anything now. All this anger won't hurt her. It hurts you."

Tears sting my eyes. "Ben just needs some time."

"Indi, Ben needs a team of specialists. He needs professional help that doesn't include you. You need to live." Phyllis holds my gaze with her own.

My teeth clench in anger. "Hairstylists don't run wellness clinics. Hairstylists use chemicals. We like fluoride in our toothpaste. They'll want me to swoon around and smell oils

CHAPTER FOUR

all day. This is harebrained. I'm not leaving for six months. I'm not letting my clientele go to Elle. I built that clientele for twenty years."

"Which means you deserve a break." Estee finishes her cocktail and switches to water with lemon.

I bristle at her self-control. I wish I had it. I don't.

"You can do this," Phyllis says quietly.

"I don't believe in essential oils and hocus-pocus wellness clinics!" I say mutinously. "I can't fake it."

"Of course you can." Estee leans forward and fixes her gaze on me. "You're a hairstylist. Let me remind you of your prowess at faking and mastering your facial reactions until you get the outcome you want. How many box dyes have we fixed?"

A smile twists my lips even as the weight of trying to figure out how to get out of this makes my heart pound. Estee is changing the subject so I can breathe. I let her, playing along. All hairstylists have a box-dye disaster to relate. Colour corrections are a universal rite of passage.

"Too many to count."

"They come in with long hair, and its level-five ash... they're desperate."

I nod as I remember many late nights fixing box dye. Many of those women we stayed late to fix are still clients. "We often cried with them."

Estee laughs, and I join her.

"But... I don't want to lose any length," Estee mimics every terrified client that does not know the process in front of them.

We howl with hilarity at the sentence that makes every hairdresser taking on a box-dye disaster cringe.

"My boyfriend likes it long!" I mock as we laugh so hard my sides hurt.

Estee shakes her head as her eyes fill with tears. "This should only take an hour, right? I have to work at five..."

We collapse into hysteria.

Phyllis smiles politely. She doesn't get it. She has never worked in the front-line trenches of box-dye colour correction. A person can't know the extent of the terror unless they've been there—in person. It's a special kind of calamity.

"You've faked a confident expression while waiting for the lighteners to work."

"Holding my breath, hoping the hair doesn't snap off."

Estee and I have locked eyes over countless colour corrections and soothed terrified clients with our words while we silently prayed for the toner to save us. That was twenty years ago, when we didn't have all the technology we have now—cutting-edge chemicals that do what we want them to do in the time that we allot them, which is why I love chemicals. They are stable. I wouldn't touch henna or natural colour products with a ten-foot pole. Natural means it can't really be controlled—it will follow its own path.

I like—hmm, not a strong enough word—I demand complete control in all things. Even Ben, with all his dysfunction, is under control. He needs me. I don't need him. I get no surprises that way. But the weight I carry for him is heavy. I look at the purple book and squint.

As Estee catches my eye again, I put that thought aside, and we can't stop laughing as she says one name, one horrible box-dye disaster that I will never forget—Marlys McNabb. The name takes me back eighteen years, and I am dying. Estee and I laugh so hard the other patrons smile at their tables. The

CHAPTER FOUR

looks on their faces say they can't tell if we might be lunatics. No one wants to tangle with lunatics.

My hysteria crumbles into silence as the full weight of what we have decided here settles on me. Am I really as bad off as they think? Have I been lying to myself? I'm curious.

"Indi, you're going," Phyllis says quietly, taking my decision away. "It's going to be okay. It's only six months. You can come back one week each month as you need, but once you get there, I think you'll see you need some time to heal and explore new things in life."

"I'm excited for you." Estee bands with her mother again.

Phyllis has a lot of sway over me, so I don't fight her. Once I have boots on the ground, I'll hire my own high-end tycoon lawyer to draft new documents, and I'll be back Friday night as if this hiccup never happened. Leave Blyss and Bloom for six months because of a harebrained scheme dreamed up by my lunatic mom?

No.

Absolutely not.

Chapter Five

Sunshine in a Bottle

I board the plane to Calgary, and after dosing myself with antihistamines, I'm determined to read Codependent No More so I can roll my eyes and text Phyllis to tell her it doesn't apply. As the plane takes off, I read and bristle with defense. By the time I get to page forty-one, the tears in my eyes have nothing to do with allergies.

I have a two-hour layover in Calgary, and I can't remember the last time I had two hours to just read. As I read, I weep, and I don't care who sees it. The book sends tentacles of new thoughts into my head that challenge my thinking, my beliefs, and I see Ben and my mother in an entirely new light. I weep through chapter thirteen, then my spine stiffens with new resolve when I reach chapter sixteen. I text Phyllis to let her know I read it and that she's right. It was life altering. I didn't read the last chapter about learning to live and love; I didn't read it because I'm not ready.

CHAPTER FIVE

With brand-new thoughts, I board a plane that looks like an enclosed toboggan with two props. It's so tiny they crammed us in like sardines. No amount of water and ibuprofen in the world could stop the pounding behind my eyes.

Stepping off the plane onto the tarmac at the tiny Cranston airport, I take a deep breath of Rocky Mountain fresh air. A short time later, I immediately lapse into an allergy attack so terrible I can't stop sneezing. Just when I think I have it under control, I sneeze again. The back of my throat itches, and the itch moves to the top of my throat and into my ears.

Ben's text message pops up on my phone. We need to talk. I lost my job this morning. I need a little cash to get me by.

Armed with new knowledge from that purple book, I realize Estee and Phyllis were right. I text back; I have every confidence that you will find a job that will work for you. As I am on my way—I stop. I don't need to give him an explanation. I delete the start of my sentence to explain why I am not sending money. I resume my text; I don't have any funds available for you, Ben. I itch to say we're done, but I would rather not in a text. As you know, my mother died, and I'll be back on Friday. We should plan for supper. Let me know where *you want to take me,* and I'll meet you at the restaurant.

Ben starts rapid fire texting me about how he has no money and what is he going to do? Text after text after text. My screen blows up with his chaos.

I take a deep breath and reply; I hope you find something that works for you, but I can no longer support you financially. Let me know where you want to meet on Saturday. I am turning off my phone now. I press the little button to turn off the phone, and the screen goes black. A profound calm settles over me. My shoulders loosen a bit—as much as hairdresser shoulders can.

The jagged snow-covered mountains take my breath away as I settle down to wait for my Aunt Truth in the Cranston airport, fifteen kilometers from Snow.

Through my bleary eyes, I see a woman wearing a flowery headband holding off a mane of grey-and-copper hair. Clothed in some sort of flowing skirt that might be pants—I'm not sure—she wears Birkenstocks on her feet. Her piercing blue eyes settle on me as I scramble for tissues in my handbag. I must have used them all. As she walks over, I think she is wearing hemp, or linen, something that has an uneven colour. I wonder if she may have made this outfit herself.

"Oh..." She flutters closer to me, her eyes wide. "Oh... my dear."

"Hi." I finally find a tissue and blow my nose.

"I'm not sure if those are biodegradable. Here you are." She hands me a stack of handkerchiefs.

I accept them gratefully.

Her eyes cloud with worry. "Oh..." is all she keeps saying.

"I'm Indi." I finally put all my tissues and her handkerchiefs in a Ziplock, pull hand sanitizer out of my purse, and squirt it on my hands. Allergies are a constant burden in my life. I have lived with them since I started hairdressing, and I am so used to it. I reach into my bag to give myself a double dose of liquid antihistamine.

"Oh." She shakes her head, and I think I see tears in her eyes.

I look at myself in the tinted window. I'm wearing an oversized dress and leggings for comfort. My shoulder-length level-seven-copper, level-nine-warm-blonde, and level-five-coffee-brown-lowlight hair is in order. The brown eyes blinking

CHAPTER FIVE

back at me have bags under them. I look exhausted, sure, but it was a long trip.

She seems distressed, so I treat her like a client and put the attention on her.

"Sorry!" I say cheerfully. "Allergies. I'm not sick. Promise. I'm Indi, and you are not my Aunt Truth, so who are you?"

She can't take her eyes away from me. "I see so much pain," she whispers, and she shakes her head, closing her eyes.

"Sorry?" I ask.

This woman is a nut, I've decided, a pretty but crazy nut.

"I'm Jet. I'm taking you to Salt and Citrus Wellness Clinic today. Truth couldn't make it. She had a situation." Jet closes her eyes, then opens them and fixes her gaze on me. "We can be a bit late. It's okay. We have to start now. Let me see your eyes."

"My eyes?"

"Yes, so I know how to help." Jet's hands flutter around me as if she wants to touch me, but she isn't sure where I hurt. Muttering to herself, she sounds like a cross between a Disney princess and a cuckoo.

I take a deep breath and let it out slowly. "I'm not sure I understand."

Tentatively, in the middle of the airport, Jet settles me into a chair. She reaches out, takes off my sunglasses, and looks into my eyes. I squint in pain as the sun blinds me. Jet puts her hands on my cheeks to move my face and see my eyes at different angles. I squirm under her scrutiny. Uncomfortable doesn't even touch it. I yearn to sink under the floor tiles.

"Oh, Indi. There is so much pain… so much inflammation." Jet closes her eyes as her fingertips move across my forehead. "Let me see your hands."

I extend my palms, and Jet shakes her head. Looking around at the other passengers, I'm convinced some will frown at us. No one seems to notice or care. An alarming number of headbands have taken the place of proper hair styling.

"I'm just going to touch you and figure out where all this emotional pain is radiating from. I can feel your distress," Jet murmurs as her hands draw across my face, over my sinuses, and under my ears.

Patchouli and another scent I can't place fill my nose. It reminds me of my mother, and I'm sick at the thought of the last time I smelled it. Jet notices, and her gentle hands drift to my tight-as-concrete shoulders.

"We're in the middle of the airport." I look around wildly, wondering if this crazy loon is going to come to her senses.

"It's okay. This is an emergency." Jet digs around in her hemp sack—because it cannot be called a purse—for something. Out comes a bottle, and she unscrews the top, then puts a drop in her hand.

I smell something that stops me from breathing. It's like oak trees and sunshine with a hint of mandarin.

At once, my mind races back to being eleven years old. I sat under a tree with my mother. All the other moms at the park opened coolers and handed their children sandwiches wrapped in wax paper. Not Tansy. She had a macrame bag of oranges and lay on the ground to peel the fruit with her thumbnail. Popping a segment of orange into her mouth, she sighed with pleasure.

She carefully peeled off the white pith and handed me a naked orange segment. "I'm spoiling you. The pith is good for you."

I popped the orange segment in my mouth and smiled as I bit down and the burst of citrus squirted into my cheek. I

CHAPTER FIVE

remember, with shocking clarity, lying beside her, looking up through the tree's foliage, and smiling as the sun filtered down through the funny-shaped deep-green oak leaves.

Warm memories of eating that orange with my mom on a perfect summer day flood through my heart. I remember her finishing her orange and lacing her sticky fingers with mine as she laughed. She said, "Isn't this the best day? This sunshine? This fresh air? I wish we could bottle it up and keep it. I would call it Sunshine in a Bottle. Wouldn't that be perfect?" She propped up her head on her hand as she looked at me. "Do you know why I named you India?"

I didn't.

"I was planning to run away to India when I graduated, but I got pregnant instead. I don't know where your father is, but you are my India." In a moment of rare tenderness, of normalcy, my mother traced my eyebrow with a fingertip sticky with mandarin juice. "I was running to India so I could have the sun. I crave the sun. But you are my sunshine, Indi. I love you, and I am so glad I had you." Tansy pressed her lips to my forehead for a kiss and repeated that she was so glad she had me.

My heart exploded with love for her.

Tears fill my eyes as Jet rubs her fingertips in the oil, then she stands in front of me.

"What is that oil called?" I am hoarse as I ask. It's not allergies this time. It's an emotion. How could I have forgotten that perfect memory? How could an essential oil, something I don't believe in, bring it back?

"Oh, this is Sunshine in a Bottle." Jet smiles, massaging the oil onto her fingertips to warm it.

I knew it. Before I ask the next question, I know the answer. I feel it all the way down to the ground. "Did my mother make that blend?" I whisper as tears fill my eyes.

"How did you know?" Jet asks, her eyes wide.

Tears spill down my cheeks. Tansy recreated the smells of that day into a bottle. She somehow achieved a goal I knew nothing about—a way to keep her sunshine with her. She missed out on India, but she had me and she had this perfect memory encapsulated in this bottle. My throat closes so tight I can hardly breathe.

"Oh, you're in so much pain," Jet murmurs.

You have no idea.

"I will address the worst of it, but we will do a full assessment when we have the meeting about your process. I won't be there, but this is pre-emptive... I'll have Tao see you right away." Jet mutters to herself about a raft of things that have been decided for me.

I feel like a wounded animal at the side of the road that she can't just leave. As everyone else in the airport rushes by, she has stopped to help this wreck.

"Uh... who is Tao? I am not sure..." I am a control freak, and this maneuvering does not suit me.

"Shhhh." Jet rubs her fingertips over my temples and across my forehead.

"What—"

"Sh." Jet shakes her head to silence me. "Breathe with me."

"I am not—"

"In," Jet demands, and I comply.

"Out."

I slowly expel the breath I feel I have been holding since the restaurant with Estee and Phyllis.

CHAPTER FIVE

"In." Jet moves from the front of me to the back. "Breathe in the sunshine."

The smell of my perfect day with my mother wafts around us. Part of me doesn't want to remember her and that perfect day. I want to nurture anger and resentment. I am walking away from everything; I remind myself. Every single thing. I need rage to stay sharp.

"Let the pain melt away," she murmurs as her fingertips move along the corded muscles in my neck. "Oh. Indi... so much pain. It's too much... too much for anyone." Jet keeps moving her hands over my tight neck muscles. "Breathe," Jet demands. "In and out. Come on. Keep breathing. In and out. Deeper."

The airport falls away. Everything falls away as I focus on my breathing that is completely in synch with hers. My entire world narrows down to her hands on my neck. Why do I care anyway? I don't know a soul here. I will sell and leave without a backwards glance. I'll be fine. These people will never see me again.

"This." Her hands stop on the right side of my neck, touching a muscle attached to my cutting hand. The muscle jumps under her ministration. "Why is this pain here? Is it work? Is it family? Is it financial stress? What is this pain from?" Her gentle voice in my ear commands me to breathe and address the cause of the pain. "Keep breathing with me... stay breathing..."

"I don't know."

I weep—not from the pain radiating to the top of my head and down my arm, making the three fingers on my right hand numb. That only usually happens during long hair highlights, but she has made it happen again. But I know I'm weeping from the smell of Sunshine in a Bottle—how that perfect memory is slicing through all my defenses, cutting through my resentments and anger.

It's not my truth to tell. Phyllis's words come back to me, haunting me. You don't know the whole story.

"Of course, you know." Jet digs her fingers into my muscle that seems attached to a deep well of sadness. "What is causing the pain?"

"I—"

"It's old pain." She smooths her hand over the muscle, then attacks it with fingers that feel like pincers. "It started when?" She demands an answer as her fingers dig deeper. "So old," Jet murmurs. "This hasn't been released in so long… Why is this pain here?" Jet's not letting go of the question.

I can't stop the tears from dropping onto the front of my dress. I want my sunglasses back, to cover this raw emotion, not have it open and exposed for everyone in the terminal to see.

Who am I fooling? No sunglasses are big enough to hide this pain as my face crumples. I bite my lip, hoping to hold off the tears as they continue to race up from the very depths of my soul.

"Cry, Indi. It's so cleansing. Let's cry this emotion out of you."

I burst into tears as her fingers press into the right side of my neck.

"Is it family?" Jet suggests as her words and fingers dig deeper.

She clearly has no intention of stopping this public spectacle until she gets an answer and is completely unfazed, as if women weeping in airports is normal. As if, on any given day in Cranston airport, women are massaging other women they have never met and getting to the bottom of pain they have refused to acknowledge for years. No, that's not true. I buried the pain under anger and fear and, yes, carbohydrates—and while I'm in full confession mode, Sauvignon Blanc. I weep harder, and part of me worries I will never stop.

"Breathe in sunshine and out darkness. Just breathe and name that pain."

"Loss." I sob. The word shocks me. I have no idea where it came from. Why loss?

"Yes," Jet whispers in triumph as she presses her elbow into the muscle and holds it there, forcing the muscle to relax under her pressure.

I surrender to the blinding white pain. The pain radiates everywhere, to the top of my head, down to my pinky finger. I cry, breathe, and let go of my defenses.

"Ah, it's letting go," Jet says softly. "Keep breathing in that sunshine."

I take a deep breath, and her elbow sinks deeper into the top of my shoulder.

"There we are. It's working. Keep breathing," Jet whispers.

I breathe with her, and what seemed completely ridiculous a few minutes ago is the only thing centering me in this world. I inhale again. In and out.

"We had a perfect day until the darkness came back—"

I gasp as she shifts her hands and presses where my skull meets my neck.

"I am helpless..."

"And," she breathes, and I breathe with her.

"I can't—"

"You can. I'm safe. You're safe here with me."

"The darkness came back, and I lost my childhood, the freedom that I should have had. I lost my mother."

Jet will not let go of my scalp. She presses harder. "One more. Breathe in the sunshine. Breathe out the darkness."

I feel the muscles give. Slowly, Jet removes her hands from my head. She rubs something into the muscle in the back of my neck and on top of my shoulder. Finally, I jump in surprise as she traces her fingertips along my eyebrows. She presses gently into the tops of my cheeks so my nose runs more, but I can smell the oils. The citrus undertone of the Sunshine in a Bottle drives through my clogged sinuses. Suddenly, my sinus clears a little, and I can move my neck better than I have in years.

"The pain is deep in you." Jet finally rests her hands on my neck and the top of my head, then gently removes them. "We have a twenty-minute drive to Snow. We'll look at the storefront, then Truth will take you to your mother's house and settle you there. You should have started this process years ago. You're in worse shape than any of us knew." Jet bites her full lip that I'm positive has never seen lipstick. "I don't know if six months will do it."

I decide not to argue about my plan to be on the next flight out of here. She seems like she is only half in this realm. "What shop? I thought it was some sort of clinic."

"Oh, Indi." Jet shook her head. "You know nothing of your mother's shop?"

"I left my mother at fifteen and never looked back." I hear the resentful tone in my voice. It's raw as it contrasts against the beautiful memories of eating an orange under an oak tree with my mother calling me her sunshine.

Jet reaches out and squeezes my earlobes between her thumbs and fingertips. Five minutes ago, I would have asked why. Now, I just submit to the ministrations.

CHAPTER FIVE 37

"You are angry. I feel resentment." Jet's eyes widen slightly as she moves her fingertips up my earlobes.

"Very. I have a perfectly good life I've built without her. I have clients and a business."

"But you are here now." The fingertips tighten on my lobes.

"Against my will."

"But you need this." The pressure on my earlobes intensifies, then she moves up my ears, pressing on points, then back to my earlobes. "Your liver," she mutters, and presses harder.

"I don't need any of this complication."

Jet looks at me hard and lets go of my earlobes. "She built it for women like you. She must have known—"

"Women like me?" Anger sharpens my tone.

Jet shakes her head. "Never mind. Let's go. Truth is waiting for you. I have to go, but you need Tao to start on your neck. Come on."

"I'm not sure I understand."

"You're a mess." Jet blinks. "I worry we can't undo all the damage. We won't know without a full assessment. There are so many chemicals."

"What chemicals?"

"You are a walking chemical!" Jet shook her head. She moved her hand to encompass my whole body. "Come on. There is no time to lose."

"I didn't agree to a process," I protest.

I was overwhelmed when Phyllis laid out the terms. I try to remember what she said.

Jet ignores my concerns as she leads me out of the airport and tucks me and my luggage—not one piece of hemp in the mix—into a massive Land Rover. The beauty of the Rockies strikes me as Jet crawls in by me.

"I am ovulating tomorrow, so the storefront is shutting down early today. I can't be there, and Truth wants to spend the afternoon with you. Sorry about that. I wanted to help you settle in, but I have a three-day window I can't miss."

"Um. You miss work for uh... ovulating?"

"Oh! Not typically, but we are trying to get pregnant... so I have to go."

"Go where?"

I have heard everything in the back room of a hair salon, but nothing as insane as this.

"The Tranquil Meadow." Jet tilts her head to the side as if I have lost my reason. "That's where I am trying to get pregnant. So, I will catch up with you next week, when the moon phase shifts." Jet pulls on her seat belt and readjusts the rear-view mirror.

Moon phase!

"Oh." I'm shell shocked at this maneuvering around the full moon, of all things!

"Great. I thought you might not understand." Jet smiled.

I blink at Jet. I haven't understood one speck of conversation since I left Manitoba.

Slyly, she looks at me out of the corner of her eye. "You don't seem the full-moon, tranquil-meadow sort."

"Jet, you can take that to the bank," I mutter under my breath.

Jet likely doesn't bank. Probably she has a hemp sack under her mattress.

Before she starts the engine, she looks at me. She could be beautiful if she had coloured hair and put on some makeup, if she took off that hideous headband and applied lipstick!

"I really wish I could be at the meeting for the process. I just want you to know that I hear you, and I will give you all my support. We should hold hands and really connect so you can feel my support for you."

"I'm okay." I hold up my hands to ward off more of her ministrations.

"Oh. I can see right into you. You're in the right spot for you." Jet ignores my thoughts and takes my hands in hers, then pauses for a moment.

I shift in my seat and can't believe Truth—my mom's twin sister, my aunt that left me to the wolves—sent this escaped mental patient to pick me up. Jet lets go of my hands, then places one palm on her heart and the other on mine. This is all way too weird and just—I don't know—it's too much.

"There." Jet takes a deep breath and lets it out slowly. She moves her hands between us as if connecting our hearts with an invisible string. She finally takes her hands away and turns the car key.

"Good thing you can see Tao. He'll get started on that neck..." She speaks in disjointed half sentences and turns her attention to the road.

Together, we go to Snow and the storefront of the Salt and Citrus Wellness Clinic. I try to remember to breathe in the sunshine and breathe out the darkness.

Chapter Six

Tranquil Meadow

I remind myself that this whacko, Jet, does not know what I've been through and a breathing exercise isn't going to make all my problems go away. Sliding the sunglasses back over my eyes, I look around the town square. Everyone is out and blinking in the sun at my arrival. Jet scrambles out of the Land Rover.

Near the front door of the shop, I see a man I wouldn't trust to pick up my recycling. He is tall, over six feet, I guess, and in desperate need of a haircut. A mess of grey-and-black hair escapes from the headband on his head. His inch-long beard has grey as well, and I'm equal parts distracted and horrified by his neck hair. He stands at the entrance to the essential oil shop and acupuncture clinic with a black dog of some sort sitting at his feet. Hiking boots and wool socks complete his ensemble. His broad shoulders strain the chest strap of his backpack as he pets his dog, who seems to smile.

CHAPTER SIX

He looks like a tough, grizzled soldier, like someone who did a hard tour and came home to live on a mountain to escape the memories.

An allergy attack starts in the back of my nose. I am allergic to his neck hair or his dog or both.

"That's Ford." Jet shoots me a quick grin.

"He needs his neck hair trimmed!" I mutter. I can't stop myself.

Jet's jaw drops in surprise. "You're exhausted from the journey. Once you get to know him—"

"Know him!" I shake my head. "He... has a dog."

The entire square sort of stops at my words. Ford tilts his head as he looks at me. I am noticing, too late, that almost everyone here has a big dog, hiking boots, and wool socks. The men anyway. The women are in headbands and hemp. I couldn't feel more out of place if I tried. I see no hair colour, no makeup, just a swath of greying locks and limp linen everywhere I look.

Jet stills. "Please tell me you like dogs," she whispers.

"Not really." I shift. I can tell Jet isn't sure how to handle this bombshell. I'm allergic to grass, trees, weeds, and obviously, cats and dogs.

Dogs are one more thing to look after, and they are not practical. They cost too much and take far too much time.

"I see," she says softly. "You're more distressed than I thought. Anyway, come along. You can meet the whole group."

Mountain man Ford takes a step toward me. "I'm Ford. I own the restaurant across the square here. I just want you to know how sorry I am about your mom." His voice sounds like an axe dragging through gravel.

He holds out his hand and engulfs mine when I shake it. The hand gripping mine is as rough as tree bark. His wrist has a bunch of beads wrapped around it with little tail ends that have curled a bit with age. The beads are all different colours. I've never seen anything like it, which shouldn't surprise me. Everything here is surreal.

I look up into icy-blue eyes with skin that crinkles at the sides. He not only needs his hair cut. He needs a bucket of SPF Fifty to protect his skin.

Jet stands beside me, and her face lights up as another neck in need of trimming exits the Salt and Citrus Wellness Shop.

"This is my husband, Leif." Jet's breath catches.

Leif stands by her, and Ford smiles warmly at them both.

"Well"—Leif can't peel his eyes away from Jet—"we better get going."

"Yup!" Jet slips her hand into Leif's.

A slice of sadness settles on me. I will never have a man look at me like that. I will never skip off to the Tranquil Meadow to conceive a child under a full moon. I had never thought of such a loony thing, but now that others are doing it, I wonder if I've missed out.

I put that thought aside. I can't handle a pet, never mind a baby! I had a fish once, and it was far too much trouble. Besides, I'm terrified of being a mother. I might follow in my mother's footsteps, and then where would we be? No. It's not for me. Three men have walked away from me for this very reason.

"Have a great day, Indi." Jet throws her arms around me. "See you when I'm back."

"Maybe text us to let us know you got to the... uh... Tranquil Meadow safely," I advise.

CHAPTER SIX

"Where we are going, there is no cell service..." Jet grins as Leif pulls her closer.

Leif looks like a Viking. I can't imagine what physical harm could ever befall Jet when in the company of her man, Leif.

A zing of envy and longing to have what she has stabs through me so hard I can't breathe.

"No data?" I gasp, covering my heartbreak of loneliness.

I try to imagine Ben and me skipping off to a Tranquil Meadow. The only thought I have is that he would need me to carry his backpack because his back is weak—and my neck is far too stiff to skip! I roll my eyes at the visual.

"We want to be sure our child starts life in peace and harmony." Leif leans down and kisses Jet on the forehead.

Jet looks up at him as if he were giving a sermon.

"So, we are going to the Tranquil Meadow." Leif's voice deepens.

Jet's breath catches again. Mine catches, too.

"We will return when the moon phase changes."

Leif, with his blond hair and big rugged body, speaks so reverently of the Tranquil Meadow that I'm actually intrigued. Ford nods as if this is all completely normal. We are adults speaking of Tranquil Meadows, ovulation, and moon phases as if we were discussing side salads or soup.

"Don't forget your fertility-phase oils," Ford reminds the couple cheerfully.

I catch a look in his eye. A look of longing? Longing tinged with fear. Odd. Why? Was he ever in the Tranquil Meadow to conceive a child? He's gorgeous, and a line of women would vie for the opportunity to carry his child, I am sure. I notice a wedding band on his left hand. Of course, he has a wedding band. He's rugged but very good looking—or he could be if he got a proper haircut and his eyebrows trimmed. I take a quick look at his ears. Yes. They could use some attention, too.

After assessing Ford's lack of grooming, I watch Leif and Jet gather their belongings and wonder if I have dropped into some sort of hippie-dippie movie for adults. Is a camera recording this, and will someone pop up and say you are on Candid Camera?

The happy couple, one ovulating and one manfully carrying two backpacks, take a trail to the left. I notice Leif adjust his load on his shoulders. Jet slides her hand into his. I think I need to read that final chapter about learning to live and love again. I put that thought aside. I'm not ready.

A truck pulls up, and Ford quickly helps the driver unload the heavy boxes so I don't have to. Ben would have shuffled his feet and wondered what to do. Correction; Ben would have been playing video games and had no idea I needed help.

I move forward to pick up a box, and Ford holds up a large hand. "No need. I've got it."

I did not know that men like this actually exist. Phyllis's husband Al was like this, but I thought it was just his generation.

I'm out of my depth. I haven't met a man like this in their natural habitat before. Even Estee's man is a stockbroker. He's polished. Nothing like the man in front of me.

"I hope a car is waiting for Jet and Leif at the end of that trail. Aren't they taking a vehicle?" I frown, determined to point out every potential problem with a happy couple making a human in a Tranquil Meadow. I don't like that I am picking holes in their plan, but I can't stop.

Ford puts down a box and goes back to the truck. "Oh, no... the Tranquil Meadow can only be reached by foot. They will hike in."

CHAPTER SIX

"What if one of them gets hurt? Or something happens? With no data—"

"A warden's station sits within the same pass. They can send a distress signal." Ford put the last box down by the shop's door. "You look surprised. Do people not get pregnant where you come from?"

"You make me sound like an alien from another planet."

"Well, honestly, whatever planet you're from has a lot of chemicals." Ford laughs as his eyes flick over my perfectly coloured hair—hair that would cost a mortgage payment.

"I'm a hairstylist." I bristle in resentment. How dare anyone with that horrific neck hair judge me!

"I know." Ford grins at me as if he can forgive my transgression.

I shake my head. "If I can find a pair of clippers, I'll take care of that neck hair."

"No way. I love it." Ford laughs again. "I spent years of my life confined in that box, and I'm not going back to that!"

Curious. I don't probe.

"Well, hopefully Jet and Leif are okay on the trail. It's all odd. I'm not used to this sort of… uh… transparency, I guess."

A tickle in my sinuses, probably from the cursed dog hair or all the trees, makes my nose run. Fir trees surround us. I'm not used to fresh air. I'm used to aerosol and air conditioning. Mortified, I quickly put a tissue against my nose.

Ford shrugs. "It takes some getting used to. I was all weird about it, too, until I was here a few months. It sort of rubs off and feels normal." Ford scratches behind his dog's ears.

His dog lays his head against the man's heavy denim-clad thigh, which stretches the soft fabric that looks like it has been through a war zone.

"For now, welcome to the Salt and Citrus Essential Oils Shop." Ford smiles at me.

My heart pounds in anticipation that has absolutely nothing to do with essential oils.

Chapter Seven

Patchouli and Sage

My eyes slide over the entire inside of the shop. I immediately feel a peace settle over me. The shop is bright. Rows of oils stand on the left. A big couch sits in front of me with reading material about how to use oils on the coffee table. And to my right lie different diffusers and jewelry so one can wear their oils, apparently. Behind all that is a massive desk with many oils, tea, and bath products. The storefront is a blend of modern and ancient. It's fascinating.

"This looks like an ancient apothecary shop in an airplane hangar," I murmur as I run my hands over the table's wood.

"Yes, Tansy had really detailed ideas about how she wanted people to feel. This is an extension of her clinic." Ford pets his dog, who lies at his feet.

"It's beautiful."

He crouches to rub the dog's belly, who stretches out and thumps his tail against the floor.

"You sound surprised."

"I think I am just totally speechless." I look around the shop, my eyes traveling over things my mother has amassed.

A tall, thin man wearing a white coat and holding a clipboard slips through a frosted-glass door. "Hello there." He walks up to me and holds out his hand so I can shake it.

"Hi."

"I am Tao. Please, come with me. Jet called ahead to let me know you need some work done on your neck. Truth will be here in half an hour. So, you have time for some acupuncture pain relief."

"I'm not sure..." I look at Ford, who's playing with his dog.

"You'll love it." Ford stands and moves behind the desk.

"I didn't agree to acupuncture. I'm here to sell a clinic and get through a funeral."

Ford smiles then turns his attention to a customer who entered the shop. The customer wants an aluminum-free deodorant, and I can't imagine anything worse. Ford promptly ushers her to a stand-up book case with various products. He seems to know about them all.

I put on my biggest hairstylist smile to cover my fear of needles. "Sure." I say to Tao—no need to be grouchy. It's not his fault I'm here.

"Have you had acupuncture before?"

"No, but can we do acupressure? I'm not so sure about needles."

Tao shakes his head as we settle into the little room. "You are beyond acupressure. You need something deeper." He puts two small rectangles of blue velvet beanbags on a desk between us. "Let me take your pulse."

I place my arms on the velvet, and he puts three fingers on either wrist, pressing each location.

"Let me see your tongue."

I stifle an eye roll and comply.

"You won't feel a thing." He presses on different spots on my neck, striking panic in me.

"I don't really believe in this stuff. I'm not so sure—"

"You can lie down here." Tao seems uninterested in my protests.

My entire body drenches in sweat as I crawl onto the treatment bed. Shame creeps over me as my arms don't fit on the narrow frame. I try to tuck my hands under my thighs. Instead, Tao pulls out little flaps and rests my arms on the extensions.

"You're sweating."

"I always sweat like this."

"During the day?"

"Yes."

"At night?"

"Yes."

"Hmmm." He moves to the tray table.

"What's wrong with me?"

"Just relax."

"But really, what is wrong?"

"Today I will work on balance and hormones. Is your period painful?"

First, I meet crazies getting pregnant on a full moon, and now this man is asking about painful periods. It's too much. "Yes, but that's pretty normal. I think that's normal, isn't it?"

"Nothing you're experiencing is normal," Tao says without judgment. "We'll fix the neck and female hormones first. Then we'll fix your allergies. I hope six months is enough," Tao mutters.

This seems to be a constant diagnosis.

"Where is the cramping pain during menstruation?"

"Right side."

"Hmm."

"How did you know about that?"

Tao smiles and continues his assessment. "Your pulse, liver, and kidney are stressed."

"That causes menstrual pain?"

"It causes much distress."

"Yes. I am stressed." These needles are frightening. I feel a cotton ball soaked in alcohol on the top of my foot and am scared to death of how a needle will feel there, so I babble. "I have had to leave my business—and my life—to come here. No one knows I'm not staying. I haven't broken the news to my aunt yet." I open up to this man I have never met before.

"Not that stress. Old stress. I'll have you sit up first, please."

These people are obsessed with the age of the stress. How do they know it's old?

I sit up, and he presses on my neck, making me cringe in pain as he feels around. These people are obsessed with my neck, as if it is the source of all my problems.

"Little pressure here."

Within seconds, I have pins in my neck just at my hairline. He twists them for a few moments, then leaves them there. I'm horrified. It's like bolts of lightning have been driven into my neck. He finally removes them and tells me to lie down.

"How much did Jet tell you?" I squint at him, then leap in shock as he slides a pin into my hand between my thumb and first finger.

"I don't need to talk to Jet."

Tao moves to my face, and I hold my breath as a pin goes in on the left side of my nose. Yes, a pin in my face. *I am dying for sure.*

CHAPTER SEVEN 51

"You have endured a great deal of suffering. I am so glad you are starting the process. We can help."

Old pain. Old stress. I wonder what this process is and if I'll survive it.

Chapter Eight

Truth and Consequence

Tao covers me in a very smelly oil he rubs on my neck after taking out the needles. I feel exhausted in a way I have never felt before. When I turn my head to the right, the pain is less—not gone but less.

"This was a very gentle first session. We'll do more next time."

Gentle! "Oh. I won't be here next week, but I appreciate your hard work." I adjust the collar of my oversized shirt.

"Not here next week?" Tao's eyebrows shoot up.

"No. I am giving up my shares, and I have to be back home Friday night."

"Really?"

"Yes. Really."

Tao makes a note on the clipboard. I don't know why since I won't be back.

CHAPTER EIGHT

I follow him back into the main shop. Standing in a shaft of light is my mother's identical twin, Truth. A burst of love and longing slices through my heart. The emotion is so powerful it almost staggers me. However, I forcibly steel myself. Truth doesn't deserve my love.

She wears a tie-dyed headband and a long dress, and across her body is a hemp sack like Jet's. She is earthy and beautiful, with lots of silver rings on her fingers and a stone at her throat. She looks like a magazine advertisement for boho clothing.

Memories involving her come back to me. I long for her and am furious all at the same time. It's too much. Tears form in my eyes. My heart beats hard with a feeling I can't place. A feeling of peace washes through me, like I'm home with her—the good parts of home, the parts I had forgotten when events forced me to leave, all the things I couldn't trust at the end. My heart seizes in my chest as memories flood me. I remember begging her to take me. I remember so many things that I can't breathe.

"Indi." Truth holds out her hands, and I step back.

I'm not ready to reconcile. The betrayal that rears up and consumes me drowns the love and longing. Anger, hurt, and resentment slice through me as I look at her.

I see it in her eyes. She gets it. Somehow, she is reading my body language like I'm reading hers.

"Indi, I am so glad to see you." Her quiet tone says she knows my emotional pain.

"I... It's hard to see you, Truth." I choke on the statement.

Truth's eyes fill with tears. "We need to talk."

"I have nothing to say to you." I'm whispering and don't know why. I take another step back.

"I'm here to take you to your mother's home and explain—"

"I won't stay at my mother's home. I have a hotel room booked." I turn on my heel and walk away from her.

"Indi. Please, I just want a chance to explain..."

I stop dead in my tracks as rage washes over me, and I try to tame it. I fail. Shaking, I turn to face her. "Explain what?"

The fury in my voice shocks her, and it horrifies me. I'm a professional. I deal with emotionally charged altercations daily. I can't believe how much wrath courses through me.

"I am sorry, Indi. I just want to speak to you." Truth steps back.

I see Birkenstock sandals under the hem of her long linen skirt. Typical. The Birkenstocks bring back even more memories I don't want. Everything is triggering me, and I can't deal with it. I don't have the skills to compartmentalize the feelings assaulting me.

"Don't manage me." The words hiss and tear from a place I can't seem to control.

"I have no intention of managing you. I want to help." Truth extends her hands as if in supplication. As if I have something she needs.

I have nothing for her. I have nothing for anyone. I'm spent.

My tone strips away the pretense that I will be civil. "You gave up every single speck of a chance to be part of my life twenty-three long years ago." My rage accelerates. "You left me. You left me with her, and I pleaded with you. I needed you!"

Truth's face falls. Tears form in her eyes. "Indi, I am so sorry. I can explain."

Customers enter the storefront, and both of us are professionals enough that we fall silent. Truth moves to help them. I guess Ford returned to his restaurant when Truth showed up. Her hands shake as she finds a lavender bag for one client.

CHAPTER EIGHT

I want the shoppers to leave so we can have it out. I think about calling an Uber but shake my head. No Ubers in this backwater!

Finally, Truth finishes the transaction, and the people leave. She locks the shop so we are alone, then turns to me. With no preamble, she launches into an explanation. "I had two children of my own the same age... and I had a brand-new breast cancer diagnosis. I wanted to take you—I couldn't. I had to battle for my life. I nearly died."

My eyes widen as her words penetrate the anger wrapped tightly around my heart. I feel sick. "I never knew."

"My husband left me and the kids a year into my battle. I was suddenly a single parent. I had to hire help to survive. I sent letters to you. I sent..."

My heart pounds as I process the truth. "I didn't read them," I whisper.

"Phyllis told me you didn't." Truth's eyes fill with tears. "I wanted you. I had to give up my kids at one point." Her voice cracks on that painful statement. "I couldn't battle cancer and take care of anyone. I wish I could go back and fix it."

"I didn't know." Tears gather in my eyes, and I try to blink them away. I have nursed this anger and grudge for so long. It's weird that the truth of the situation, the whole truth, causes the pain and anger to shift. "I didn't know about the cancer."

"That's why you're here, Indi."

"I don't need your help now." I shake my head and look away.

Suddenly, I see myself in a full-length mirror by a stand of hemp clothing and toothpaste without fluoride—a shock since I avoid looking in the mirrors in my salon and home. A woman I don't recognize stares back at me. A woman carrying at least fifty extra pounds, with a chip on her shoulder that weighs more than that.

"Not yet," Truth whispers. "You're not sick, yet. But we've been watching you for a long time, waiting for the perfect time... the time is now."

"I'm fine." I whirl on Truth.

It's not true. She knows it, and I know it.

Truth moves forward and places her hand on my shoulder. "We're here to help."

Our eyes meet.

"I look after myself, I don't need anything." It's a lie. Already, the one book written by a therapist I have never met has completely changed my thinking about Ben. I am certain I'm failing plenty of other directions.

"Your mother left a process for you, to help you heal."

"I can't."

"You can." Truth was not at all intimidated by my tone. "I want to reconcile with you, apologize for all the things you went through. You have been weighing heavy on my heart, and we need to resolve this, make amends, or I need to let you go in peace."

"So, you drag me across the country so you can say sorry to me? Wow! How convenient for you," I hiss.

"See what she built, Indi. You had to come here to see it." Truth doesn't back down.

"I have to bury her and get on with my life!" I roar.

Truth stands still. She doesn't back up. Her eyes lock with mine. "You have built an amazing business. I am so proud of your tremendous success, but are you happy?"

"Happy enough."

"Really? Besides your business, what are you racing home to be part of?"

CHAPTER EIGHT

There is nothing—absolutely nothing—in my life but clients, Ben, and the occasional supper with Phyllis and Estee's family, with Estee's children that aren't mine and never will be. I am stunned by the emptiness that engulfs me as I open my mouth to speak. I close my lips.

"You need to know everything." Truth stands so straight I want to scream at her.

My eyes fill with tears so fast I can't stop them. My nose tickles relentlessly. I'm allergic to this entire province.

"Come on. I'll take you to your mother's home. You don't have to stay there, but you have to see it."

I don't move. This is too much.

"If only to assess its value so you know how much money is coming to you—or know how much money you are turning down." Truth's eyes hold sadness.

"Truth, I will never step foot in my mother's house. Never. Not now, not ever." My hands shake.

I can't enter my mother's house. The memories will destroy me. I'm scared, really scared—terrified of unraveling, and of spiraling down. Fresh memories of the night I left her fill my head.

"We'll discuss it tomorrow," Truth says so quietly I have to strain to hear. She speaks as someone so centered in her life that she doesn't worry about asserting herself—as if she knows if she holds her ground, speaks her truth, the right people will listen and not disturb her peace.

I envy the stillness in her, a stillness that infuriates me. "Everything my mother touched, she hurt." The words spit from me so hard, so angry that I hate how I sound.

Truth rifles around in her bag. "She's dead."

I flinch at the word.

"This is a letter from her to you. She says—"

I hold up my hand. "I don't want to hear it. I don't care. I was done at fifteen. I'm still done."

"Indi. To move forward, you need the whole story." Truth's tone is soft. "You're here to bury your mother, but you are not up to the journey."

"What journey?" My eyes narrow. What sort of trick is this?

"We'll discuss it at the meeting."

"Sure. We can finalize the funeral plans, and I am on the next plane out of here. I have to be home by Friday night. In my bed by ten p.m." I cross my arms over my chest.

Truth says nothing, and for a moment, it's quiet between us. "Did you pack a bathing suit?"

My heart freezes in terror at the word. I haven't owned a bathing suit for two years. When my weight went over—never mind. "I packed pretty light." My voice sounds strangled.

"You'll need a bathing suit for the Hot Pools of Healing." Truth roots around in her bag for car keys.

"What are Hot Pools of Healing? Did I fly through a portal to another dimension? Am I still in Canada? What are these odd names for all this—"

"We run a wellness clinic, and we speak in terms that create healing in our minds. The Hot Pools of Healing are hot springs with strong sulfur. Sulfur is very cleansing."

"Why not just call them hot springs, then?" I grumble.

"We want your mind to associate them with healing. Recovery happens on different levels of the subconscious."

"I see." I have no clue what she's talking about, but if I admit it, they'll drag me to the peak of understanding or something equally insane.

"Do you have good walking shoes?" Truth brings me back to the present.

CHAPTER EIGHT

"No... I traveled light." I don't own walking shoes of any sort. I have work shoes and slippers. That's it. Suddenly, the thought makes me sad.

"Then we'll shop tomorrow for your gear. I couldn't shop for you when you needed it. I was sick. But I can shop for you now."

"Truth..." My throat tightens as I assimilate all this new information about my history.

Truth didn't abandon me because she didn't love me. She was battling cancer and raising two children alone. All the anger I held on to had oppressed me. Now, I feel unbalanced, raw.

"Yes?"

"What if no gear fits me?"

Truth's eyes soften in sympathy. "We'll find gear to fit."

The lump in my throat swells until I can't swallow it. "I had to take some medication a few years ago, and I gained forty pounds in a month. Since then—I couldn't get it off..." Why am I saying this?

Truth pulls me into her arms. "Indi." She holds me so hard that her body absorbs my trembling and shaking. "It's just weight."

"I can't stay, Truth. I'm here to see the lawyer and sign away the rights to this business. You or your kids will get it. I have a business at home. I'm leaving, and I won't be back until the funeral."

"Indi." Truth holds me at arm's length. "Don't make me call Phyllis."

My defiance crumples. I'm a thirty-eight-year-old woman who runs a successful business, and yet the threat of Phyllis is real. I take a deep breath and let it out slowly. "No need to call Phyllis."

Chapter Nine

Hot Pools of Healing

"You pick the pace, Indi. What you went through was terrible, and you never have to enter her house if you don't want to. I'll show you where it is. We meet with the wellness team this afternoon and the lawyer tomorrow morning, so you can get home in good time—to your salon, I mean."

My nose runs, and I quickly hold a handkerchief under it. "I don't need a wellness team." My cursed allergies take the sting out of my denial.

Truth shakes her head. "Okay." Tucking a soap and package of something under her arm, she holds the door open for me to exit. "Let's go so I can show you around the Salt and Citrus Wellness Clinic."

As we drive, I can't take my eyes away from the beauty of the place. I really can't. The Canadian Rockies are majestic, rugged, gorgeous. As the Land Rover turns a corner, we head

CHAPTER NINE 61

down a road lined by beautiful pine trees. At the end of the road is a two-story cabin with a shimmery lake right behind it. Cabin isn't the right term. It is a magnificent home built out of roughhewn logs, glass, and rock. The entire south-facing front has a deck on every level.

"This is it."

"It can't be." I catch a glimpse of myself in the window. My eyes are wide, eyebrows arched almost to my hairline.

"This is your mother's house," Aunt Truth says softly as she parks the vehicle.

I left my mother in a trailer; the door hanging by one hinge in a trailer park where we couldn't walk alone at night. I try and fail to understand how she got from that park to this mansion.

"How...?"

"It's not my story to tell, and as you said, you're not ready. So. This is her home. It has five bedrooms and four bathrooms."

"Why does she need so much space?"

"She ran wellness clinics for private clients who are very... um... wealthy. They wanted her, and they wanted a complete reset. She had a lot of friends in the wellness world who come and work at the clinic. Right now, we have an equine therapist, so her horses are here..."

"How?"

"Again, it's not for me to say. But this place is really stunning, so I hope, at some time, you feel comfortable to stay. I want to show you a treat."

"I don't know..."

"Please? It's really neat."

I follow her out of the Land Rover and around the back of the house. My back and feet are aching, but I try to ignore them.

My breath catches in my throat as I see the "backyard," though the term yard doesn't even begin to do it justice. Rocks and grassy areas surround two pools—not normal pools with straight edges.

An earthy smell assaults my nose. "What is that?"

"The Hot Pools of Healing. Tansy bought the place for this spring. She built her home and guest home around it."

"It's…"

"Try the water."

I trail my fingers through the water, and it is indeed hot.

"Some people have hot tubs, but she didn't want that. She lets anyone in the community use these pools for free."

"So, she partied with the community and got smashed every Friday night and called it decompressing?"

"No."

"I find that hard to believe."

Truth straightens and fixes her gaze on me. "Your mother never touched a drop after you left."

I stay still as I think about that. My eyes narrow as I don't believe her.

"Not a drop." Truth moves around to the side of the hot spring. "The pool over here is a salt pool. She used to swim in the salt pool every morning."

"Before walking a hundred kilometers."

"Yes." Truth grins.

The salt pool is at body temperature. I long to slide into the hot spring, but I have nothing to wear. I wonder where I could find a bathing suit my size. Surely, they must exist somewhere.

CHAPTER NINE 63

"I'll show you the guesthouse. Some of Tansy's friends are artists, and she offers residencies to local artists for week stays. Free."

"Wow."

"She thought you might not want to stay in her house, so we set you up there," Truth says softly.

The guesthouse is a three-bedroom bungalow made of the same rock and wood as the main cabin. The guesthouse has pretty nasturtiums, ferns, and ivy planted on the deck. Inside is a modest kitchen, a small bathroom, and a living room. I don't see a TV.

The master bedroom looks out over the pool, and it has a soaker tub big enough for two people. The king bed is done in cream-and-copper-coloured linens, and Truth flicks on a fireplace that warms the space. A terry cloth spa robe hangs by the spa tub and a stack of fluffy white towels.

Truth places the cotton bag and the soap by the towels. "This is our bestseller. Lavender and salts with a lavender bar of soap. It's *Tansy's Dream Soak*. It features three types of salt. This soak helps you sleep deeper. It supports proper magnesium levels in your body. You mom left you some things. We talked to Phyllis and asked your size. She has a swimsuit for you and a laptop."

"A laptop?" My ears perk up.

"Tansy told me you used to like to write," Truth says. "One of our artists in residence is a writer, and she left you a package of things all writers need—a pile of resource material on how to structure novels. The laptop has Scrivener and Word already loaded."

"What is Scrivener?"

"I have no idea, but all the authors raved, so you have it." Truth laughs.

"I haven't written for... hmm. The last time I took a vacation, I wrote every day, but I don't have time to write."

"We encourage writing here at the clinic. It's very therapeutic." Truth moves to the desk. "Tansy also left you a camera. We have photography clinics, which you are welcome to attend. Estee said you liked photography at one point."

I did. I love writing and photography. I never have time. A fist of tears tightens my throat as I look at the laptop and camera my mother left me. It touches my heart on a level I didn't know existed.

Truth leads me to the other room that looks out over the forest and a vast lake. The room is everything a person needs to be inspired. Beautiful photography on the walls, another fireplace, an enormous desk complete with paper, a laptop, pens, coloured pencils—I can't take it all in. I see a stack of different-coloured sticky notes of all sizes and get excited. Those sticky notes and coloured pens call to me.

I don't know what to say. It's like someone crawled into my head and heart and designed the perfect house and office for me.

"One author insisted on this." Truth pointed to a roll of paper. "They said they like to plot on paper."

"You're talking like this is even an option in my life—to come in here and write. It's foolish. I am not staying." I hate those words as they leave my mouth. This is a kind gesture, and old fears of being unworthy roar through me. So, instead of naming that fear, I act spiteful and mean. I don't like the person all this kindness has exposed. I don't like myself as I stand here and see this generosity, and I'm unhappy with the way I turned it down.

CHAPTER NINE

"It's getting late. I can take you for supper and drop you at your hotel, or I can cook supper here, and we can hit the hot spring before bed."

I don't believe it, but I honestly can't bear to leave.

I yearn to check out the laptop, to take pictures of the flowers on the deck with that new, fancy camera. The spa tub is so beautiful. My head wars with my heart. I want to stay mad, stay aloof, keep a distance between my carefully constructed life and the provisions my mother has offered me.

The warning bells ring, and I'm torn—very conflicted and confused. I never expected this kindness.

"It's okay to feel what you're feeling. She's not here, Indi. There is no catastrophe waiting to befall you."

I look at Truth and squint. "I am the only person I can trust because a catastrophe is always waiting to befall me."

"Not this time." Truth smiles.

I take a step back. Behind my salon chair, I am safe. I won't give that up—no matter what they have up their limp, hemp sleeves.

Chapter Ten

Codependency and Low-Carb Casseroles

I toss hundreds of dollars' worth of highlights and lowlights over my shoulder. "Staying tonight doesn't mean I'm committing to anything."

"Perfect." Truth nods. "I'll put a casserole in the oven. You've had a long day. I'm sure you want to be in bed early."

I do. But I'm curious about the Hot Pools of Healing—if it would help my neck. Then I could use that spa tub and whatever is in that little cotton bag by the tub. It smells like heaven.

Truth lays out a lovely meal—no wine, no garlic bread, no pasta, which I find concerning, and no chocolate. It's a simple meal of chicken and Mediterranean vegetables tossed in some sort of oil and spices—I recognize oregano—and covered in feta and olives.

CHAPTER TEN

After supper, Truth answers a phone call and has to leave. "I'm sorry! I can't do the Hot Pools of Healing with you. I have to go to the clinic."

"No problem. I'm tired and want to get a good sleep before the lawyer comes tomorrow."

"Right. I'll be here around eight so we can meet at nine. Your flight leaves at two, right? It's tight, but we can make it work."

After Truth leaves, I walk onto my veranda, and the moonlight shines down onto the healing pool of cleansing, or whatever Truth called it. The pool seems to call to me. I go to put on the bathing suit left for me and think it might be interesting to try out the natural hot spring—as a normal human being would call it!

I fight back disappointment as I struggle into the bathing suit that doesn't fit. I look at the size, and my heart sinks. It should swim on me. It isn't. I squeeze into it and then catch a glimpse of myself in the mirror. Ugh. My heart sinks to my feet. The mirror takes me off guard, and tears sting my eyes. How did this get past me? I work in front of a mirror. How did this happen?

I gulp down the tears. I might work in front of a mirror, but my eye is on my client. My focus is making sure that the client looks the best that they can so they embrace life and take on their next challenge, feeling their most confident.

Somehow, I stopped reaching for my next challenge. My mind races to the stack of books on how to structure novels. No. That's nonsense.

I stand behind a chair and watch life play out in front of me. Had I tricked myself into thinking I'm really living? Or am I living through other people's lives? When did I quit reaching for my dreams and goals? I was standing on the sidelines of my own life, behind my chair—safe. I need safe. Enough of that.

I step away from the mirror and go to the office to pick up the camera. I know how to create art with scissors, colour, and brushes. But I've been thinking about taking a photography course for years. I hold the camera in a hand that usually holds a comb. The weight of the camera surprises me. Slipping off the lens cap, I go out to the verandah. I hold the camera to my eye, then pull it away, frowning as I try to figure out how to use it. I have no idea. I find the power button and hold the camera to my eye again, but it has so many settings.

Disappointed, I put it back and pull out my phone to get a picture of the flowers on the deck. That's a mistake. Ben has left fifteen messages requesting money. Thinking of my purple book, I turn off the phone. I don't need to fix his chaos to feel worthy of love.

I can't believe a therapist I've never met sent that book, and every line seems to be written for me. Ben will never come to his senses or get his life together. Ever. Or if he does, it won't be because of anything I do. That thought is freeing on a level I never knew existed.

I feel light for a moment.

I wish I had wine to take to the Hot Pools of Healing, but all I have is a soda stream and citrus juices. I'll have a drink on the plane.

Narrowing my eyes at the bathing suit, I shrug. I'm out here in the wilderness with only my aunt around. What does it matter? I've tried everything to lose weight, and nothing has worked for me. I can't count every calorie for the rest of my life, and I'm too exhausted after work to workout on top of everything. A poor-fitting bathing suit isn't the end of the world. I'll head home after meeting with the lawyer without

CHAPTER TEN

a backwards glance, so it doesn't matter if someone catches a glimpse of me.

As I creep out onto the flat-rock landscape around the hot spring, I drop my robe to get in, and a deep male voice stops me dead in my tracks.

Chapter Eleven

Bath sheets and a Beached Whale

"I am so sorry," came the voice from the dark side of the spring, where a heavy rock blocks the moon light.

I scramble to drag my robe back on.

"So, so sorry!" The man chuckles as he comes into view.

It's Ford with the terrible neck hair and headband holding back who-knows-how-much long hair in need of a haircut. He swims closer and stands. I try to drag my eyes away from a broad chest with—no surprise—chest hair. He needs clippers and a professional, but he doesn't seem to care in the least.

Blinded by his muscles gleaming in the moonlight, I fight to get my left arm into the sleeve of my robe and cover my ill-fitting suit. I panic as I think of all the flesh spilling out of the suit in the most unflattering ways. Then—horrors—I slip! Sprawled out like a beached whale in every possible way one could be a woman and a whale, I struggle to drag my too-small robe around me.

CHAPTER ELEVEN

Ford quickly gets out of the spring to help me.

"No need. Enjoy your soak! I'm fine." I try to crawl away, but my knee holds me there. I want to die of mortification.

"I don't think you're fine." Ford moves athletically.

Of course, he's a natural athlete!

He's out of the hot spring and at my side in a moment. He's right—I'm not fine. I banged my knee, and my eyes smart with tears from the pain.

"I am so sorry. This is such an invasion of your privacy when you're grieving. I am just so—"

"No need to apologize." I hold up my hand as I try shrinking into the shadows. "I'm exhausted, so I will leave you to your healing-hot-spring—uh, whatever they call it—time."

I try to get to my feet without his assistance, but every time I get on all fours to haul myself up, my knee hurts even more. I curse myself for not joining a weight-loss program and sticking with it. Then I remember endless rice cakes and one-hundred-calorie snacks I would drag around in tiny plastic bags, and know I don't have what it takes to complete another weight-loss program—the endless input of calories and the call for will power. I had oodles of it until four p.m., when I started thinking about ice-cold Sauvignon Blanc, and by five, I was trying to finish my day. I was home on my couch by seven, diving into hot pizza and wine like a life raft, always promising to make better choices tomorrow. Years went by, and here I am, laid out on a slab.

Ugh.

"Here, let me help."

Ford holds his hands out, and I hesitate.

A fragment of the codependency book comes back to haunt me, warning me that many co dependents feel guilty accepting help.

Ugh times a million.

I tell myself to accept his help and stop being such a lunatic. Then my mind races with panic for a different reason. What if he's not strong enough to lift my carcass? What kind of damage would it do to a man's psyche to be emasculated like that?

I cannot lay sprawled out all night. I decide to risk it and put my hands in his. He hauls me up easily. He's very strong. I wish I could say I'm unaffected by the strength I feel in his hands. I wish I could lie and say my heart doesn't pound and my stomach doesn't flip.

I'm not a schoolgirl. I'm a grown woman in a too-small bathing suit and a tiny robe swooning beside a man. Ford, on the other hand, looks like the kind of person who bench presses kayaks for fun. I yearn for a bath sheet.

We stand very close as he supports me. The moon is so bright I see his blue eyes up close. At this vantage point, I realize we're near the same age—edging on forty. The skin around his eyes has creases. He looks like he's been outdoors a lot and forgets sunscreen. His big, solid body smells slightly of Sulphur from the hot spring.

"I live a quarter mile from here, just down that path." Ford waves in the general direction behind my guesthouse that's not actually mine.

The beads on his wrist catch my eye again, and I wonder what they're for. They seem out of character—a man like that with pink, blue, orange, and black beads. I can't figure it out.

He turns his attention back to me. We're so close I can see water beading on his heavy shoulders.

"Oh." My knees grow weak standing this close to a man—face to face. No cutting chair between us. It's uncomfortable and not my habit.

CHAPTER ELEVEN

I live behind a chair, a professional distance. I don't have a lot of male clients because I find most too disorganized to be in my rotation. But the clients I have are businessmen. They come every three weeks and are perfectly groomed and manicured. Their personal assistants contact me if they need to alter their schedule. They're that organized—or their assistants are. It doesn't matter which. They don't complicate my schedule. The male clients who can't keep appointments, I drop. Anyone who misses a couple of appointments gets dropped from my list—indefinitely.

I wonder if Ford gets his hair cut yearly. The thought is strangely horrifying and fascinating at the same time. That neck hair really is out of control.

"Your mother said to use the hot spring whenever I want. I should have asked you, though. I thought Truth was staying here alone. I want to apologize again. I'll be on my way."

"Listen." I hold out my hands in supplication. "Please use the spring whenever you want. It's totally fine. I'm not staying."

"Really?" He looks shocked.

"I can't stay here. I am actually furious that my mother planned all this during wedding season."

"Planned to die?" Ford tilts his head and frowns at me.

I open my mouth to speak then clamp it shut as I think. Unfortunately, fury tinges my tone. "We have been apart. On purpose. My decision. For a long time." My voice shakes. "That may sound insensitive. I am still kind of reeling from everything. I expected to pay for her funeral because I was pretty sure she would be homeless and living under a bridge by this point."

The words sound so harsh and terrible; I immediately want to bite them back.

Ford's eyes change. He takes a step back. "Oh."

I have never felt so judged by two letters in my entire life. That "Oh" said I'm the worst person he has ever met. He didn't say, "I can't believe you would leave your mother homeless under a bridge." He just nodded and said oh. As if he knows something about me now that he can't unknow, and he's sad about it.

I want to launch into an explanation, but I can tell by the set of his jaw, the way the muscles jump there, that he's shocked and completely unimpressed—maybe even disappointed—by my callousness. He gathers his towel and his bottle of water to leave. Shame crawls over me. I adjust my robe that doesn't cover me and look down. It doesn't matter. I'm leaving as soon as I can.

"So, I haven't decided if I'm staying... this whole thing... staying here, running a clinic I don't believe in... it all seems so..." I try to salvage the conversation, try to sound positive, and can't.

Ford holds up his hand, his face hard and set. "I'm going to stop you right there." As if thinking about how to choose his words carefully, he takes a deep breath and lets it out slowly.

To calm down?

He puts his towel around his waist and faces me. "I don't know much about your past with Tansy. It's none of my business. I do know that Tansy was in a twelve-step program and that she wanted to make amends with you. I can only imagine what you have been through. For me, though, I have to say that Tansy Blyss was one of the best women I have met, and I have met a lot of women."

As the moonlight illuminates the rugged features of his face and the powerful muscles in his arms and chest, I'm pretty

CHAPTER ELEVEN 75

certain he could have his pick of women at any time. The anger in his tone snaps my attention back to what he said.

"She has helped hundreds of people and was an inspiration. She was more than my neighbour. Tansy was like family to me. I'm so sorry you didn't know her once she was well." Ford takes a step back.

The easygoing bohemian I thought he was actually has a hard edge that's impossible not to respect. With that, he whistles, and his big dog comes bounding toward him. I open my mouth to speak then shut it.

"So, I think it's time to say good night. Come on, Jasper." Ford frowns at me as he summons his dog.

I hear the unspoken goodbye. Ford pats Jasper's head and slides on his shoes, leaving me standing by the Hot Pools of Healing. As he slips into the night and down the path to his home, a wash of fury flashes over me.

How dare he? He doesn't know me, doesn't know my story. He made an assumption and a judgment with no facts. I narrow my eyes at his very broad, retreating back. Soon, I can't see him. I stand by the Hot Pools of Healing on my own. Alone. Like usual. Well, except Ben. I have Ben and a business at home. Ben, with his weak back, video game obsession, and inability to hold down a job couldn't be called a man in comparison to Ford!

I try to drag the robe closed in front of me and can't. I don't feel healed by the Hot Pools of Healing. I feel misunderstood and furious. I harden my heart. I don't owe Ford—a person I only met today—an explanation. I don't owe *anyone* an explanation. What happened was between Tansy and me. Tomorrow, it will be between Tansy's estate and me. Then it will be Tansy's ashes and me. Everyone else can butt out.

Chapter Twelve

Forest Floor

I am so agitated by my altercation with Ford that I can hardly sleep all night. Finally, I get up and drink coffee as I wait for Truth. I will not step foot inside my mother's house. Never.

I will not take over the Salt and Citrus Wellness Clinic. I don't need a shark lawyer to say no to the whole mess. Within hours, I'll be out the door. My flight leaves at two p.m. Thank goodness.

I swipe my phone open to text Estee that I'll be on a flight at two, home by six, and ready for Ariana first thing tomorrow. I'll bring our favourite coffees. Immediately, I'm assaulted by text messages from Ben. I take a deep breath and let it out slowly. He can't believe he got fired from his new job. They are all idiots.

Honestly, the thought of dealing with Ben after dealing with Ford's assessment of Tansy is too much. I don't answer.

CHAPTER TWELVE

He hasn't asked me about the bigger issues I have today. I expect him to ask; how are you doing? Are you okay? I gave Ben enough to cover his rent yesterday. That has to be enough. I put Ben out of my head. Firmly.

Sipping hot coffee, I look out the window at the sink. The sun peeks up over the deep-green fir trees and shines across the lake. Again, I wonder how on earth Tansy ended up here, with all this beauty surrounding her. My nose stings, and my eyes water from allergies, so I turn away from the window to look for my antihistamines.

Grabbing my luggage, I glance longingly at the laptop open in front of a trio of floor-to-ceiling windows overlooking the lake. What would it feel like to write every morning as I look out over this amazing scenery?

I run my fingertips over the camera. I wouldn't have time to learn how to use it until after the wedding season—then it would be back to school, then getting clients ready for their colours to line up perfectly for Christmas.

Stepping away from the office, I leave the little bungalow to wait for Truth on the veranda of the main house. Everything in the yard is more beautiful in the early morning daylight. Big weeping willows provide the yard with privacy and beauty. The salt pool ripples, so I walk toward it to check the temperature.

Truth swims to the side to meet me. "Isn't it a glorious morning?"

"It is." My nose runs. I hurt my knee last night. My back hurts from the plane ride and sleeping on an unfamiliar bed. I try to make my swollen hands move easier by flexing them. Physically, I'm swollen and miserable. Emotionally, I'm already drained and exhausted. To make matters worse, I ran out of liquid antihistamine. I only have pills, which I need to take with the liquid to survive. Really.

So many flowers bloom on this property that I'm certain I will die from pollen poisoning. Blowing my nose for the nine hundredth time this morning, I yearn for an air filter and air conditioning away from the wilderness. I sit down at the table by the salt pool and wait for Truth.

"Sorry, I completely lost track of time. I always do that when I swim. The water is so perfect, and it will be such a beautiful day." Truth sounds like a motivational speaker.

Are people really like this?

Truth gets out of the salt pool and wraps a towel around herself. I envy the fact that my aunt, a woman seventeen years older than me, can wrap a bath towel—towel, not sheet—around herself and it covers her easily. I would need three sewn together. She shakes out her hair and sits across from me at the table.

I raise my hand to silence her look of concern. "I appreciate your efforts here, but I am going home."

Truth throws back her head and laughs. "I know." She reaches for her travel mug. "Do you need anything before we go?"

"The cottage had no bread for breakfast."

"Oh, right, I forget people eat grain. All I have are some berries. Would that interest you?"

It's like these people only eat what they can find on the forest floor. I can't wait to get back to pasta and wine.

"No, it would not." I honestly can't think of anything worse. "Don't worry about it. I'll be fine." I wipe at my streaming nose as I ignore Ben's frantic texts.

Truth pulls on a linen dress over her wet bathing suit, then adjusts a headband on her head. She pins her hair up and

CHAPTER TWELVE

seems to have no qualms about looking like she just stepped off a beach.

"Aren't you going to get... um... dressed?"

"Oh, I have clothes at the clinic." Truth waves away my concern. "I have a Pilates class at ten, then I'm taking a group of women on a six-kilometer hike this afternoon. So, I change a few times a day."

"Six kilometers?" I pale at the thought.

"Yeah. It's a beautiful hike. We walk around a lake, and it is so pretty I hate to come in."

"Isn't a wellness clinic doctors and diets?"

"No. It's a full approach to wellness."

"I don't know what that means. That seems rather broad." I squint at Truth because my eyes are so swollen by allergies that I can hardly see.

Truth uncaps a little bottle and rubs something on her face. I assume it's sunscreen—or some potion harvested from shamans in the Andes that keeps her skin perfect.

"We have a full team trained to deal with metabolic syndrome and type 2 diabetes. The clinic uses acupuncture, counseling, and various forms of exercise. Our clients can choose what suits them. We have a cooking clinic for people who have relied heavily on take out and now want to learn how to cook foods that will help them reach their goals. We roll with whatever our clients need and create custom plans to support them."

"And you think I have metabolic syndrome?" I do not know what that means.

"I'm not a doctor, Indi. I wouldn't dare diagnose you as anything."

Truth smiles, and I am suddenly suspicious. I'm pretty certain I have a syndrome of some sort just waiting to trip me up.

"We work with doctors. Your mother had many health conditions. As she was trying to deal with her mental illness, she took medications that caused her to gain a lot of weight. This clinic was born out of her wellness and weight-loss journey. Then, as people got on board and invested, it broadened. As we did four-week reset clinics, our clients wanted more. They wanted three-month clinics. Some wanted to live on site. So, we accommodated." Truth shrugs.

"Mental illness? I suppose I'm here to entertain some fantasy that she destroyed my life because of a convenient mental illness."

"I don't think bipolar disorder is at all convenient."

"What?" My breath stops in my chest.

Truth's gaze holds mine. "When your mother went into rehab for alcoholism, they diagnosed her with bipolar disorder. She quit drinking the night you left, she did intensive therapy, and she worked with addiction counselors."

"Bipolar disorder." Mistrust laces my tone.

"Yes. A very difficult diagnosis." Truth's tone is quiet. "Once she understood how to treat it, all she could think about was explaining things to you."

I'm overwhelmed by this knowledge. I still look back on the night I left with intense pain, but somehow, knowing her diagnosis makes everything slide into place. Everything suddenly makes sense. "I didn't know," I whisper.

"It doesn't erase what happened to you, Indi. Nothing can take away the fact that you've survived a hard life. But she wanted you to come here so you could have a break and find out the things you didn't know, so you could heal—not just physically, emotionally, too."

Silence falls between us for a moment as I process the information.

CHAPTER TWELVE

I change the subject. "How on earth did you fund this?" My aunt doesn't look like she works with the mafia.

"Oh, Indi." Truth grins at me and releases a laugh that seems to come from her feet. "We never worried for a second about money. We worried about people, and the money took care of itself."

That statement stops me in my tracks. It's exactly how I funded my salon, though Phyllis and Al helped us at the beginning. I often wonder where Phyllis got the money, but when I ask, she just laughs and says that's what banks are for. If I wanted to expand, I could tell a few clients, and I would have investors in a heartbeat. I never worry either. Work at what I love. Work on who I love, and everything else takes care of itself. I look at my aunt with renewed interest.

"Full disclosure; Tansy was in a rehabilitation center and became close friends with a very troubled young woman. She could tell the girl was on the verge of suicide, and she intervened. The grandmother of the young woman was wealthy and wrote Tansy into her will. The young woman recovered and works here with us. When the grandmother died, she left Tansy enough money to build a wellness clinic for people like her granddaughter. So, Tansy started Salt and Citrus Wellness Clinic with that money," Truth said simply.

"Now, since we've been running this so long, we have artists who do day clinics with people. We had a writer last week who came in to spend a day showing how to write a memoir. She donated half her fee to us. Writing is tremendous therapy. Our investors would love a writer-in-residence program that helps people write their soul journeys. We find many people need permission to stop the grind and really explore a creative outlet. So, it's hard to pin down exactly what we do because it's so different for every person. But the artists come through, they teach, they donate. We have very wealthy patrons."

"This seems... like you think I need to lose weight. Is that why I'm here?" I silently beg her to fight with me. I yearn to ruin this new fragile peace because I want nothing to do with this mad, false hope she's presenting.

"Do you think you need to lose weight?" Truth looks me straight in the eye.

"Of course, I know I do," I snap.

"Then let's get started." Truth smiles.

"Nothing works," I reply mutinously.

Truth throws back her head and laughs again. "Indi, you're killing me! I forgot how funny you are." As Truth leads the way to the Land Rover, she doesn't seem to realize I'm not laughing.

Chapter Thirteen

Salt and Citrus

The wellness clinic is so amazing it takes my breath away. Nestled into a valley, it's a vast rock, log, and glass building. Clearly, the same designer created this clinic to match my mom's house and storefront.

I can see various outdoor pools from the driveway.

"We have a Nordic spa that runs all year and eight massage therapists and four estheticians on staff for this Nordic spa alone. We're pre-booked for the next four months."

"Wow." I'm deeply impressed. I know this business because it's a close cousin to hairstyling.

The Nordic spa alone is worth a fortune. People sit quietly all over the beautiful grounds in white terry towel bath robes. They drink water infused with lemon and cucumber slices. Some lie reading in hammocks. One woman stands beneath a waterfall. As the water pounds down on her neck and shoulders, I yearn to stand beside her.

"That is a waterfall attached to an ice plunge."

"That sounds terrible," I whisper honestly. All that ice water pounding down on her neck? What could be worse?

"It's great for inflammation." Truth pulls open a big, gleaming glass door. "In here is our lobby, where we greet guests."

We enter the lobby that looks like a lodge. Light pours in through a skylight and illuminates a big desk. Two people work there; one on the phone while the other person comes around the desk to greet me.

"Is this Indi?" The young, gorgeous woman smiles from ear to ear.

"Hi!" I put on my hairdresser smile and hold my hand out to shake hers.

"I'm so glad to meet you. Your mom saved me... then gave me this job. I'm Hailey. I'm so thrilled you are going to keep everything going! Without this place—sorry." Hailey's eyes filled with tears of appreciation.

My heart kicks in concern.

"I'm really thrilled to meet you." Hailey throws her arms around me.

I hug her back. "It's great to meet you, too." My stomach twists with anticipation. I don't have the heart to tell her I am not staying. I'm not my mother. I can't carry on with this.

Detangling herself from me, Hailey pulls a picture from the desk and hands it to me. "This is where I started."

I can't believe the transformation in the picture.

"Tansy saved my life, Indi. Really, I am so glad this clinic is going to continue."

Gulp. "Thank you for sharing your story with me." I hand back the picture. I'm not sure what to say. My thoughts about my mother have been so negative, and I have nurtured such

CHAPTER THIRTEEN

terrible emotions surrounding her. Ford challenged me and now this young woman.

Suddenly, a dog comes bounding up to me.

My allergies kick right in. "Hello, Jasper." I try to stay out of his way and cringe as he puts his nose under my hand.

"Jasper," Ford calls.

Jasper immediately returns to Ford's side.

As I turn to look at Ford and say hi, I am distracted by a man on the other side of the glass.

His movements are jerky as he paces, muttering. "Hailey!"

My face must have creased in concern because, immediately, Ford tenses.

"Hailey, go to the staff room," Ford instructs. "Truth, call the police."

My heart pounds as Ford stands in front of the clinic doors with Jasper right beside him. He looks formidable, and the man on the other side of the glass takes a step back. Ford says nothing. He just stands there and keeps his eye on the man. The phone at the front desk rings, and I pounce on it. The tension in the room is palpable. I ask for a phone number so I can call the client back.

Fear makes me gasp when the man makes a move to the door, and Ford simply takes a step forward. I'm scared to death.

What if this man has a gun? What if he's high on something and does serious damage to Ford or the clinic?

The man on the other side of the glass doors puts his hand on one handle.

"You're high, and you aren't coming near her. Take your hand off that door and take a step back, Garrett."

"The police are fifteen minutes away," Truth whispers to Ford.

"Truth, send Carter out."

Truth goes to the boardroom, and within minutes, an older gentleman—in his sixties by the look of him—with white hair comes to the door and takes his stand with Ford.

Where are the police?

Garrett mutters threats. Ford and this older man, Carter, stand their ground. Finally, when we can all hear the sirens, Garrett runs for the bushes.

Ford pulls open the door to go after him, but Carter places a hand on his shoulder. "Let him go. We don't know if he's armed. You getting shot will not help Hailey."

The police show up, and Ford takes charge.

"We're pressing charges," Ford says to the police officer. "I'm representing Hailey as her lawyer. He's violated his restraining order."

Lawyer! I thought he owned a restaurant?

Carter and Truth turn to me.

"Ford's got it all under control. Come along." Truth leads the way to the boardroom.

"Does this happen often?"

"No. We hired that man to work on the grounds, and it turns out he's with a gang called X66. We fired him."

"What does that have to do with Hailey?"

"It's a long story. We'll talk about it later. For now, that's under control, and we don't have a lot of time."

As Truth opens another glass door, we stop talking about the altercation in the lobby. I have a panel of people to meet and take a deep breath before letting it out slowly. In front of me is my process. Whether I want it or not.

Chapter Fourteen

Silver-Haired Shark

I'm still shaken as I sit at the table. Inhaling deeply, I try to forget that police officers and a drug addict are on the grounds of the Salt and Citrus Wellness Clinic. I am worried about Hailey and wonder what will be done to keep her safe.

Carter, Truth, and I sit at a vast table. Carter is clearly the shark lawyer I expected. I steel myself and prepare for battle, aware that I am trade school educated. He has a university degree. I refuse to be intimidated. I can talk my way out of anything.

White-silver hair, clean-shaven, a very expensive suit, and a gold pen in hand as he checks things off on a paper in front of him, this guy is old school. No digital gadgets for him as he double-checks a paper copy of something. The ring on his finger indicates a very expensive university. His eyes are bright and clear, his hands broad yet manicured. I can't help but contrast them with Ford's.

I force Ford from my mind.

"I'm sorry your introduction to the Salt and Citrus clinic was so volatile. Ford is handling this legally, but I hope our heart rates can all return to normal. It's a pleasure to meet you, Indi." Carter holds out his hand, and I place my hand in his. He gives it a gentle squeeze.

I am not sure, but it seems like he finds it hard to look away, not in a creepy way, in a I've-been-waiting-a-long-time-to-see-you way. I can't place it.

"Indi this is Carter Thorne. He is the chief financial advisor and the head of legal counsel for Salt and Citrus Wellness Clinic." Truth smiles at Carter, and an inside understanding seems to transfer between them.

"Mr. Thorne, what do I sign so I can walk out of here today?" I hold his gaze—tough, strong right out of the gate. Exactly how to handle a mother-in-law with an insistence of vegan dog treats at a wedding. Take the matter in hand quick. Show no weakness. Never drop the gaze. Be fearless.

Carter says in a deep voice that has practice commanding attention, "Tansy told us of your childhood with her, and its completely understandable that you have cut her from your life. That was absolutely the right path to take at the time. However, I hope you will reserve judgment regarding what she built here."

"I'm not interested in any of this. Whatever paperwork I need to sign—"

"You're not here for a business alone," Truth spoke up. "You're here to connect with your family."

"There is no easy way to address this, so I'm just going to come out with it," Carter says. "I'm your father, Indi. I'm here to tell you how sorry I am that you went through such a difficult time and to make amends."

CHAPTER FOURTEEN

I gasp at the statement. "Father?" I ask in shock.

The room spins. I can't catch my breath. This man was who I longed for my whole life, to pick me up, to save me from my mother. Here he is... how is this possible? I'm equal parts furious, fascinated, frustrated, scared, and overjoyed. I can't process it.

"Yes. Your father." His eyes are gentle. "I'm so happy to meet you finally. If you are going home, I hope we can just talk for a bit. I would really appreciate it."

Tears fill my eyes—tears of disbelief, of tragedy, of so many emotions I can't corral them all or make sense of them. "Don't you dare." Anger surfaces first, my constant friend whenever my parents come to mind, and I rise from my chair. "Don't you dare, for a second, think you can come in here and be my father!" I am incensed.

"Please sit down, Indi," Truth says. "And hear him out."

I sit.

"I want to say that I'm so sorry, from the bottom of my heart." My father's eyes fill with tears. "I don't expect any forgiveness."

His apology takes me off guard. Tears sting my eyes. I lean back in my chair and wait for him to continue.

"I just want to explain, then you can decide from there. My parents are very wealthy, and when I started dating your mother, they disapproved."

"They were smart," I said, as vicious as a viper.

"I am really so sorry." Carter twists the end of his pen to move the nib inside the shaft. He placed the pen down gently, as if taking a moment to think. "They certainly saw warnings and concerns that I didn't see. I will admit that. After a year of dating Tansy, we got very serious. My parents wanted me to go to school, Tansy wanted me to stay. I went to my parents and told them we were engaged. I was only seventeen. They packed me up that night, and they sent me to a boarding school in Switzerland. I tried to get a hold of Tansy and ask her to wait. I sent letters, and they were intercepted. After Switzerland, they sent me to a university in the United States. My letters were returned as undeliverable. At that time, the internet did not exist of course. We only had letters and phone calls. They sent me away so abruptly that I did not know what was going on. I didn't know Tansy was pregnant, and I am certain she wrote, but I didn't receive her letters. I did not know about you until—well—so help me, long after you left Tansy."

My eyes fill with tears as he mentions the worst night of my life so casually.

"This is true?" I ask Truth. I can barely get the words past my tight throat. Quickly, I swipe at the tears.

"All true," Truth confirms softly.

"I can't speak of that night," I whisper. I look him fully in the face and hold up my hand.

Carter's eyes soften with sympathy as he nods from across the table. "Of course not. I just need you to know that I am sorry and my heart breaks at the years we have lost. I want to—"

Suddenly, I'm sobbing. I can't seem to stop. He is crying and so is Truth.

Carter comes around the table to stand by my side. He puts his hand on my shoulder, and I am so conflicted. I don't know what to do. I want to hold on to all this anger, but it's not helping. He didn't know. He couldn't know. How can I hold him responsible for all this pain in my life if he didn't know? It's not reasonable.

CHAPTER FOURTEEN

I place my hand on his, and suddenly, that isn't enough. I stand and turn into my father's arms. For the first time in my life, I feel like I'm home. It's a long, weepy, snotty hug. When we finally break apart, Truth is there with a box of tissues for both of us.

"It's biodegradable," she says, and somehow this breaks the tension.

"Indi, I am so glad you are here. I'm so proud of you." Carter smiles as he wipes tears from his eyes.

"How did you find out about me?" I ask as we all sit down again.

"When my father died, I was putting his affairs in order, and I noticed he paid a bill for a hairdressing course in 1994."

"Really?" I shook my head.

"Yes, really. I looked at the bill, and I wondered who on earth in our family was a hairdresser. Absolutely no offence, but everyone in my family has been through university, whether or not they were good at it."

A zip of yearning races through me. I wanted to go to university to take an English creative writing course. I never dared ask because it would cost too much. I think about the laptop and—No. I'm going home.

How can I go home and leave my father?

I am reeling. Nothing is secure now, and yet, everything feels a little more stable because of this man at the table. He's clearly a good man.

"Wow." I shake my head as I concentrate on what he said.

"There was a letter from Phyllis."

"Ah. Phyllis. That makes sense."

"She sent petitions for my parents to pay for your schooling and threatened to go to me if they didn't."

"Phyllis did that?"

"Finally, the internet was invented," Truth says. "And Phyllis took a night class on computers. She got on the internet and started searching for Carter, and she found him and his parents. She's a tiger when it comes to you." Truth hands me a glass of water. "We wanted to have this reconciliation a few years ago, when Tansy was alive. We asked, but you said no. When we contacted Phyllis, she said you weren't ready."

My heart beats hard.

"Why would Phyllis think you're ready now?" Carter asks so kindly that my heart trips.

I clear my throat and take a sip of water. "I don't know."

"I do." Truth holds up an old-fashioned letter. "I'll read the part that applies."

"Oh, please." I groan as I realize all the adults in my life are conspiring against me.

"'Indi and Estee have built a beautiful business. But her strength has become her weakness. Indi has quit reaching for the next goal. She has let her fear of poverty stop her from reaching out for other dreams, such as writing. I waited to see what would happen with her and her boyfriend, Ben. He is destroying her life with his dysfunction. She is standing on the sidelines and staying so busy that she is clearly afraid to take steps to build her own life. I see her use her chair like a shield. She has lied to herself and told herself that because her life is full of clients, it's whole, but it isn't. No real man, not even a cat.'"

"I'm allergic to cats." I hear the defensiveness in my tone.

Ugh! This is not new. Phyllis has been trying to reason with me for years, telling me to take risks, let a man into my heart, and I thought I was putting her off. Who knew she was cooking up this master scheme?

CHAPTER FOURTEEN

Truth ignores my allergy defense and carries on with Phyllis's assessment of me. "'She equates love with chaos. Indi needs you, Truth. She needs her father too.'"

"This is what Phyllis says, but what do you say? Do you need to heal, Indi?" Carter's tone is kind.

"I'm fine," I say as my nose betrays me and I sneeze. My nose runs so badly that I scramble to pull out a raft of tissues. The roof of my mouth is so itchy I can't stand it. Sure enough, my ears itch, too. I'm miserable here in this wilderness.

"This is all very touching." My voice is muffled behind my wad of facial tissue. "However, I'm here to sign the papers, giving up my share and to plan the funeral to bury to my mother. Where do I sign to give up my shares? You have everything well in hand."

"There are no papers to sign today." Carter sighs as he hands me another box of biodegradable tissues, which are thinner than normal ones, meaning I need twice as much.

My nose will not stop. Now, my eyes are running so badly that I can't see him. Carter and Truth don't mention it, of course. They are professionals. The state of my health is as plain as the nose on my face. I feel my resolve crumbling.

"We think the best approach is for you to take six months and submit to the process. You are free to go back if your business needs you. That's no problem, but we would love to have you here full time for six whole months. This clinic approaches health physically and emotionally, but we won't know what path to put you on until your blood work comes back. On October 18, we will walk your mother's ashes to the Cliffs of Consolation, where they are to be scattered."

"The cliffs of what?" My jaw drops.

"Consolation."

"It's only ten miles into the wilderness. It will take you about two or three—"

"Surely we have a helicopter?" I whisper.

"Tansy wanted her ashes walked in, but it's entirely up to you. You don't owe her anything. We'll walk her ashes in if you prefer not to. After the funeral, you are to inherit her shares of this entire wellness clinic on October 18. Or you can sign the papers to give up your shares and get nothing. You have six months to decide," he says softly.

My anger toward his parents is blinding. They stole him from me, his strength I needed all my life, but especially at fifteen.

"The Cliffs of Consolation." They've all completely lost it. "How is me having a heart attack in the wilderness going to accomplish anything? Are you sure we can't get this done at the Tranquil Meadow? I hear it's nice."

Carter frowns at me and looks to Truth to take over. It's eery. My mom's twin, the only human who looks exactly like my mom but with all her marbles lined up, and my actual father tag teaming to deal with a—what? Not a teenager. I'm too old. A rebel? No—a broken thirty-eight-year-old who just wants to live in her condo and work as a hairstylist in peace.

I roll my eyes at myself as I reach for another thin and almost-useless biodegradable facial tissue. "What if it doesn't work? Your process?"

"My darling girl, what do you have to lose?" Carter asked.

"I know it won't work for me." I wipe at my streaming eyes.

"The process works. It always works. You'll be ready for the Cliffs of Consolation way before October 18. Besides, the Tranquil Meadow is for new life. The Cliffs of Consolation is where we say goodbye to the dead. You aren't ready for the journey, so we have a lot of work to do. We also have a decision

CHAPTER FOURTEEN

to make. Your mother wanted to take this clinic to the next level, and we'll need a director of that operation."

"What operation is that?" I can't deny my curiosity.

We all look up at the same time as lawyers stop by the door, waiting to come in.

"Ah, perfect timing." My father waves them in.

Chapter Fifteen

Proof

Their eyes flick over me, and I immediately feel like I'm not good enough to be at the same table.

"Indi Blyss," I introduce myself.

"Tansy's daughter." The lead lawyer, Marcus, sits down and places a file on the table in front of him.

"Yes." I sit up straighter.

"From a legal standpoint, I think it would be prudent to have a paternity test. Surely you have no objections." Marcus holds a pen, ready to jot down my reply.

"That's a good idea. I'm not here for money. I am here to bury my mother." *My past.*

"Great." Marcus opens a file and hands me a photograph. "This is the next phase of Salt and Citrus."

I'm shocked as I look at a photo of an island, like a white-and-green sliver in the middle of the jewel-blue Caribbean.

CHAPTER FIFTEEN

"What is this?"

"Salt and Citrus Cay, the island. We are expanding, and we need someone on sight to run it. With your business experience—"

I take the photograph in my hands and can't believe how beautiful the island is.

"If you would consider running this island, you are our first choice. We hope Ford can handle the arrangements, if you agree."

"Ford?"

"He said he would give us a decision this week."

I pick up the photo of the island, and my heart longs to go there. The desire is so strong that I can hardly breathe. "This is a lot to process." I can't let go of the photo. "I have to be home tonight. I think it would be nice for us to have a bit of time to get to know each other. Once I can clear my schedule, maybe I could come back for a vacation." I reach for another handkerchief.

At a subtle signal from Carter, a nurse slips into the conference room. I look up at her in alarm.

"She's her to take your blood. We want to see where your A1C stands."

"You finished *Codependent No More*?" Truth gets down to brass tacks.

We are losing time. I have to fly in three hours.

"Yes. Except for one chapter." I press my lips together. "I'll remind you I haven't decided to come back—"

Truth ignores my comment. "This week, we want you to read these two books; *The Obesity Code and The Complete Guide to Fasting*. Both books are by nephrologist Doctor Jason Fung. We built our program using the science in these pages." Truth hands me the books. "You need to read them both before you meet with your nutritionist."

I push them aside, still reeling from the effects of *Codependent No More*. "I have tried." My chin wobbles, and I refuse to weep in front of these lawyers. "I've done every diet. I've joined countless programs. I've had a million apps count every calorie. I have dragged baggies of eleven almonds and one-ounce portions of cheese to the salon with me. None of it works. This won't work. Whatever you think you can do, it won't."

Truth lays out photos on the table in front of me. Men and women who have lost staggering amounts of weight. "We know what we're doing, Indi. This isn't a weight-loss program. This is a life renovation."

"That sounds terrifying," I whisper.

"It isn't." Carter smiles. "We're with you every step of the way."

I push the books a little farther from me. "I need a car to get to the airport."

"I'll have my driver take you. You are taking my private jet. We need you back here on Monday. By then, all your blood work will be done, and we'll have a process ready for you to start."

"But I could take a week." My eyes widen.

"We really need a decision about this island. So, I'm sorry. I need you back here Monday. I'll have an alternate plan if you decide to walk away from all this. You've got three days." Carter checks his watch. "My pilot is standing by."

"Oh, and I'm coming with you in case you get any funny ideas about bolting." Truth smiles sweetly.

"Fantastic," I say, utterly defeated.

Chapter Sixteen

Hot Rollers and Sheer Shape

As the miles between me and Salt and Citrus widen, I think about how scary it would be to change gears. If I give up my clients, I would have to start from scratch at the end of six months. I've watched hairstylists come back after maternity leave to barely a quarter of their clientele. It's devastating.

It feels good to be back in my salon. At the end of the day, I intend to tell Truth that the wellness clinic is beautiful and everything is lovely but it's not for me. I'm afraid to fail. I'm terrified to take on something this big. It's all way too much.

Essential oils and acupuncture? No. I'm a hairdresser, and I believe in the stability of chemicals. I love bleach and 40 volume developer because I know exactly what it will do. I do not and will not believe acupuncture and smelly oils help overcome anything. When it is necessary, I believe in prescription medication. My heart does a little dip when I think of

Sunshine in a Bottle but that is just nostalgia. Antihistamines and ibuprofen have gotten me this far. Those crazies will probably want to rub me down with a weed and make me eat roots. I won't have any of it.

I don't believe in the sheer magnitude of headbands and the serious lack of grooming happening in the entire town of Snow. It's appalling and distracting. The headband wrapped around Ford's head showing all that raggedy neck hair flashes in my mind.

Truth is in the back room folding towels and chatting with the staff of Blyss and Bloom. I put her and the upcoming conversation from my mind. She will take that private jet back to British Columbia alone. I'm ready to do what I love, really ready.

I want to get to know Carter better, of course. What I know of him, I already like. I don't need to take over the clinic to make that happen. I can spend time with Carter when I have time to book a proper vacation.

I plugged the hot rollers in. My irons are hot. I arrange all the equipment for Ariana as Elle breezes by with a fresh coffee for me.

"Happy wedding day!" she chimes as she places the coffee on my station.

"Elle! So happy to see you." I hug her hard. "I have some paperwork to finalize on Monday, but I'll be back at the end of next week. We'll leave the clients booked in your column, but you'll take yours, and I'll take mine."

"You're coming back?" Her bright-blue eyes blink.

"Of course. Sorry, Elle. I should've texted you earlier."

"I heard an amazing opportunity landed in your lap." Elle leans her slim hip on my station. Her face lights up in anticipation at the thought of taking over my life—I mean business.

It bugs me that it's basically the same thing.

Truth is safely in the back, so I can roll my eyes. "It's not my scene."

Elle's face falls. "Oh." Her eyes narrow just slightly, or maybe I imagine that, as I tend to be paranoid.

"But I appreciate your hard work on my clients in the meantime." I open the box of bobby pins and carefully crease the flap back so it isn't in my way. I check the nozzle on my Sheer Shape hairspray to be sure it's clean. It is.

"Good old Sheer Shape." Elle changes the subject as she picks up the canister I just placed on my station. "It's older than I am." Elle smirks.

"Yes, it is." I laugh. I'm pretty sure the smile on my face doesn't quite reach my eyes. Older than me indeed! "Tried and true," I say tightly as I adjust the dial on my straightening iron to make sure it's as hot as it can go. Ariana's hair is coarse. "Weird that Estee isn't here yet."

"She's getting out of Saturdays. Starting in July, she wants summer weekends with her kids. She's working longer on Thursday, and any clients that won't work for are transitioning to me."

"Wow. All my clients and now her Saturday lineup. You'll be glad I'm coming back."

Elle shrugs. "I work long hours. It fits my five-year plan."

"What is that?" My mouth suddenly goes dry, but I'm loathe to drink the coffee she brought me. I don't need help. Never have, never will.

"I will be married in five years, then I want a year of maternity. I want double the clients, so I come back to a comfortable clientele. Not all clients return, as you know."

"Right." I'm stunned by her strategic planning. "Not all hairstylists take an entire year." I hear the judgment in my voice and force myself to be professional.

"I will." Elle tosses her hair over her shoulder. "I want a year of baby snuggles and love."

"I see." I flash her my brightest-voltage smile that I don't feel at all.

"So, I'll build it then have the life I want." Elle's blue eyes blink at me, and I expect whatever Elle wants, she gets. That's the way the world goes for beautiful blondes with blue eyes and perfect figures.

I release a sigh that starts at my toes and runs straight through me. Elle is clever. Double her clients now. Have them all committed to her in the next five years, then she can walk away, have a baby, and not worry for a minute.

"Marriage and a baby? You are going to be busy."

"I can't wait." Elle smiles. "The bride is here!"

I turn to see Ariana with her crazy mother-in-law carrying the small dog in her purse. They wear matching neck scarfs, and I pray to the hair gods for patience. Elle has a vegan treat for the dog, and the mother-in-law softens. Elle is smart—very clever. I know Elle would run that dog over if it stood between her and her five-year plan, but the mother-in-law buys into Elle's attention and approval hook, line, and sinker. I roll my eyes.

Ariana sees me and squeals with delight. "You're here!"

As I walk across the salon to give her a hug, we hang onto each other.

"They tried to kidnap me and force me to sign up for a wellness weight-loss journey... wait. They called it a life renovation... I escaped."

CHAPTER SIXTEEN

Ariana hugs me hard one more time. "We have so much to talk about!"

I get her settled in my chair, and as I lean down to pick up my first set of hot rollers for the day, something gives out in my lower back. I hear a crick and immediately fall to my knees, gasping in pain.

"Indi!" Ariana leaps out of her chair and comes to my side.

"Oh, oh my goodness." I groan as I lay on the floor. My back spasms, and I can't breathe properly. The only way to stop the searing pain is to lie flat with my knees up. I can't even imagine the visual of my body splayed out on the salon floor. Mortified, I pray to slip into a coma.

Ariana's eyes are enormous and filled with tears as she looks down at me, terrified. Elle and Truth are by my side in a moment. Elle pulls out her phone and rapidly texts someone.

"Estee is on her way. She'll take my day. I'll do Ariana." Elle tells her assistant to call every client on her schedule and rebook her two-o'clock appointment, make sure all the clients know they are to come in half an hour later, then explain. Elle fires orders like she owns the place.

She likely will if I can't get off this floor!

Immediately, hairstylists and the receptionist jump into action.

"Oh, thank goodness!" Ariana collapses into Elle's capable arms.

Then the bride-to-be steps over me and settles back in my chair. My chair!

Elle goes around my prone form and stands behind her. "Let's put in these rollers. There's no time to lose—"

Just like that, I'm replaced. Tears sting my eyes, tears that have nothing to do with the pain in my lower back.

Elle picks up my beloved Sheer Shape and moves it aside to put her fancy new product Forge on my station. Out with the old Sheer Shape from the nineties, and in with the new Forge. Out with the old, fat, worn-out Indi, and in with the new, slim, laser-focused, five-year-plan Elle.

That thought subsides as I focus on breathing and trying to stop the outrageous pain in my back. Ariana talks about her florist and moans about a problem that has to be solved. She hasn't once looked at me on the floor beside her. Not. Even. Once.

Truth crouches down beside me. "Who is your chiropractor?"

"I don't believe in that new age..."

Truth rolls her eyes. "Ladies, who has a chiropractor? I need a number."

Ellis calls from the shampoo bowl, "I have one coming here in half an hour for a haircut."

"How perfect." Truth beams at Ellis.

During the half hour that I wait for the chiropractor to show up, I lay on the floor of my salon, and the stylists don't miss a beat. The owner collapsing doesn't cause a hiccup in any schedule but mine and Elle's and will ruin Estee's photo session with her boys. The stylists step around me. They sweep around me, and they work. They work hard. All of them are professionals and there is no complaining. I'm grudgingly proud of them.

Truth rolls a towel under my neck, and fresh mortification comes over me.

"Can I get you anything?" she asks.

"Can you help me crawl to the back room?"

"I'm not sure," Truth admits, and I burn red-hot with shame. "I think we'll wait for the chiropractor."

CHAPTER SIXTEEN

I can hear it in her voice, she hopes the chiropractor is a man who has the strength to drag my heavy, old carcass up off the floor. I pray again that the ground will open up and swallow me.

"Truth," I say as she leans forward and brushes pieces of hair off my forehead. "I'm thinking I may have been hasty. I think it's possible that I do, in fact, need that life renovation you talked about."

Truth grins at me. "I knew you'd come around."

"Every single person in my life has conspired against me, including my spine. What choice do I have?" The pain in my back takes the fight right out of me.

"Hey there, I hear someone needs a chiropractor?" A tall man with a big smile stands over me.

"Please fix my back without touching me," I beg from the floor.

He chuckles. "I'm Barrett. You're in expert hands."

I notice Ariana doesn't even look over. Elle is placing her pin curls.

"We have a massage table in here." Estee, in fishing gear, stands over me. "Hey, Indi."

"Hey, Estee." I give her a slight wave.

When I see her, I almost burst into tears. I want to talk to her about meeting my father, about the opportunity I was going to turn down. I want to run it all by her, and I can't because I can't even walk.

It takes two of them to help me crawl on hands and knees across my salon floor. I promise right there that I will change. I'm not sure how or what it will entail, but the photos Truth showed me when I met with her and Carter are fresh in my mind. If anyone needs a renovation, it's me. The searing pain in my lower back is so bad that it cuts through all my nonsense. I need Salt and Citrus Wellness Clinic. I hope six months is enough.

As Dr. Barrett adjusts the six vertebrae in my lower back, the horrific pain leaves me, and I can breathe. I would still be sore, but I'm able to sit partly upright.

"Right then, you're fixed. Take it easy. It's sprained, and it will be sore. You'll need another treatment in a couple of days."

"How much do I owe you?"

"Nothing. It's on me. Take care of that back." Dr. Barrett pats my shoulder and turns to leave the room.

"We've got a full staff ready to fix her right up," Truth says from the doorway.

"She should get some acupuncture," he suggests.

I would have rolled my eyes at one time, but I didn't dare.

"Indi, I called the pilot, and we're ready to go."

Dr. Barrett nods. "Ice. Not heat."

I sit on the side of the massage table, tentatively putting weight on my feet. They hurt. They always hurt. I'm weary of pain—not just physical, emotional, too. Anger is exhausting.

"Ready?" Truth asks me.

Tears fill my eyes as I put my hand in hers. "Yes. I'm ready."

"For six months and a hike into the Cliffs of Consolation?" Truth is taking advantage of my weakened condition to really lock me into her clutches.

"How long is that hike?"

"Around sixteen kilometers," Truth says.

"There's no Valley of Grief, say, two kilometers away that would do the trick? With a Pasta Paradise nearby so we can carbo-load after the hike?" I groan as I lean on Truth to help me out of the salon.

CHAPTER SIXTEEN

"No. It has to be the Cliffs of Consolation." Truth squeezes my hand and drags me forward.

"I'm in." Just like that, I lose my will to fight. Nothing like a sprained back from picking up a tray of hot rollers to snap me past my delusions and straight into reality. I can't hide from my health anymore. This needs to be fixed. I need to renovate, and I don't know where to start.

But when Truth takes my hand in hers, I feel a confidence there. I don't know the way, but she does. I trust Truth—for the first time since the day I perceived she had left me. Now that I know the whole story, I trust Truth with all my heart.

Chapter Seventeen

Process and Pain

Back in Salt and Citrus, I hobble into the boardroom to a team of specialists.

"You are borderline type 2 diabetic," Dr. Hall says as I lie on the floor, putting my feet on a chair to help my lower back relax. I am still in too much pain to sit on a chair.

The team of specialists have moved their chairs to make a circle around me. They have clipboards and plans. My nose streams because I'm allergic to Jasper, which means Ford is somewhere nearby looking at this spectacle!

Jasper lies right beside me with his head on my hand. I don't have the strength to nudge him away. After a few moments, I get used to his presence and find it actually comforting. I must be losing my mind. I don't like dogs, but something in me has shifted, and I'm so out of my depth that I am taking comfort from whatever I can. Tears form in my eyes.

"Are you in pain?" Dr. Hall's eyes are sympathetic.

"Yes." It's getting better, but it still twinges occasionally. Ugh.

"Your blood work indicates that we got to you just in time." Dr. Hall's face is professional, no judgment. "I will monitor your progress, but hand you off to Prairie, your nutrition coach. Lark will do double duty on massage and physio."

"Once you've read the books, we'll talk." Prairie flashes me a bright smile as she sets Dr. Fung's books beside me on the floor. "Can you cook?"

"No. I don't cook. I order takeout."

Prairie nods. "Ford, does your Friday night primal cooking group have room?"

"Yes. Lark needs a partner."

"Indi, Ford teaches cooking and nutrition on Friday nights, so we'll sign you up for that."

"She'll be fine. Between Tao and me, we'll get her in ship-shape by Friday." Lark smiles, then hums. "Once you're up, we're starting you with P. Volve."

"What is that?"

"It's low-impact strength and cardio. You'll love it." Lark's small face hovers over mine. "You all right, honey?"

"Nope. Sure not." I grit my teeth from the pain as I shift my feet on the chair.

Ford takes a seat beside Summer, who looks exactly like a summer day with her pretty sundress and shiny blond hair. Summer looks impossibly delicate beside Ford. I feel more and more like a hippopotamus.

"So, Friday, I have to walk right by your place to get to the clinic," Ford says. "I could be there around four to show you how to prep the vegetables."

Friday nights with Ford. My heart leaps with anticipation.

I remember I couldn't break up with Ben because they whisked me back to B.C. basically on a stretcher. I need to break up with him immediately.

"Let me know the night you make your Tuscan chicken. I'm coming." Summer places her slim hand on his heavy, hairy forearm, a forearm that looks like it belongs to a lumberjack. The contrast between her ultra-feminine hand and his ultra-masculine arm makes me feel a little faint with longing that it was my hand touching him.

My dream of private tutoring with Ford, possibly candles, for sure wine—a box—crumple as they joke together. Good grief, with stunning women like Summer around him, he won't give me a second look! I'm used to being invisible. That's my comfort zone. But that zone has started to hurt. I'm no longer behind a chair. Here I am, in front of a man—on the floor with my knees at a ninety-degree angle.

Ugh.

He's here to deal with the legalities and grill meat. That's it. This team has a plan to fix me. It doesn't involve a future with Ford. He's clearly besotted with Summer. She must be his wife, even though he's wearing a ring and she isn't. Curious.

I desperately want to hip check Summer out of the room then drown out this terrible feeling of loss, making my throat ache with unshed tears. What does it feel like to have a slender hand rest on a beefy forearm? I will never know.

This process sounds way too simple. They talk of detox and healing. I was expecting a million supplements and a zillion rules. They only give me a few simple ones.

Because of my traitorous blood sugar levels, I have to practice intermittent fasting to get my insulin levels down. Wine and alcohol are off the list until further notice. I will instead eat very nutrient-rich primal foods and walk at least five kilo-

CHAPTER SEVENTEEN

meters a day. I will be subjected to P. Volve—whatever that is—with Lark. Every week, acupuncture with Tao, and they want me to commit to at least eight hours of sleep a night. Also, I'm instructed to meet with Summer, my therapist, every week at least and more if I need it. She's cleared part of her schedule for me.

Deep down, I know this won't work. It's too loosey-goosey. Besides, I've failed every other eating plan in my life. This one will be no different. At the end of six months, they will politely ask me to leave. My body won't be their ideal. I would scare away their new clients. They'll eventually pick a supermodel to run the Belize clinic. That thought alone stiffens my spine, which immediately aches when I move.

I will give it my best shot.

Dragging my eyes away from Summer and Ford, I look at the list of things they encourage me to eat. In the first phase of this program, they're treating my insulin resistance first.

I eye The Obesity Code, by Dr. Jason Fung, with derision. I've been in too much pain to read it yet, but it's second on my list. How could a book about insulin make any difference? It won't.

I will fail. That's the only thought in my head as Truth slips back into the room. I'm shocked as tears sting my eyes. Truth gets on the floor beside me and pets Jasper's head. My allergies rear up again.

"You can do this, Indi. You're certainly not the worst case we've seen," Truth says.

"Do your clients often need to have their initial meeting lying on a floor with their knees up?"

"It's not the first time." Truth smiles encouragingly.

"It seems overwhelming, but we've all been there, and we are committed to helping. Why don't you go back to your cabin? After Tao does your acupuncture, I'll come by to talk," Summer suggests.

It's actually not a suggestion, it's more of a command. The team gets to their feet. Ford and Summer leave me with Tao and Truth. As they walk by my prone body, their eyes hold sympathy.

"Don't forget your salt and citrus," Ford reminds me as Jasper leaps up and goes to his side.

Tao works on me right on the floor. The pins in my lower back work almost immediately, which shocks me.

Once he's done, he takes out the pins and says he'll see me tomorrow.

Truth smiles at me. "This will all seem more doable once you really get started."

Chapter Eighteen

Weep and Purge

The next day, I can walk without gasping in pain. My father and Truth brew coffee in my kitchen. It seems strange to see them there.

"How are you, Indi?"

I lower myself onto the couch and put my feet up on the coffee table. "You've got me for six months."

"Really?"

"Yup. Elle took over all my clients. They settled everything at home. I saw the light and never want to be on my back on the floor again."

"I'm sorry it happened like this, but I'm glad we've got you." My father hands me a coffee with cream and some ibuprofen.

"Is this a trick? I thought medication was contraband." I watch him warily.

"This is not a prison." Truth laughs.

I sip the coffee and gratefully take the ibuprofen.

My father has a paper in hand. "The results of the paternity test came back."

"Already?"

"Marcus sent it to a private clinic." He doesn't have to say that this test likely cost a fortune, and that's why it was back so fast.

My eyes lock with his.

"Whatever this says, my will won't change. Tansy said you're my daughter, and I believe her."

I'm not made of stone, and his kind statement makes my heart soar with happiness. I can hardly breathe, waiting to hear what that paper says. Finally, he opens the envelope and pulls out the paternity test results. I hold my breath.

"You are officially my daughter." Carter smiles at me.

My eyes fill with tears at the statement.

Carter reaches forward and holds my hand. "I'm so happy you are here to stay."

"Me too." And I mean it.

After coffee, Truth pounces on me and has a plan to outfit me. "We'll head to the city and get you everything you need."

"Here's my credit card." My father hands me a platinum-coloured card.

"Oh. You don't have to—"

"I absolutely want to." His eyes warm. "I'll make supper here for you both tonight. Does that work for you?"

I try to hand the card back and notice it's in my name. "You're giving me a credit card?"

"Yes."

"I don't know what to—"

"Would you like chicken or beef or a different meat?"

CHAPTER EIGHTEEN 115

"Let's do shrimp," Truth suggests. "I haven't had that in a while."

"Sure. I'll cook that up. See you later!"

My father stands, and I struggle to my feet.

"I'm glad you're my father, and I'm so happy we have the test to prove it, and it has nothing to do with money."

Carter smiles at me, and my heart glows happily.

"I'm glad you're my daughter. Have fun with Truth."

After three hours in the Walton change room, I am trying to squeeze into clothes that should be my size. I'm mortified at the sizes that fit. I sweat with the effort to take off the bras. Grateful to the universe for the invention of the zip-front workout bra, I pounce on it. Cramming my breasts in, I pray I can get it zipped. Barely. I refuse to go up a size!

"You might want to invest in better-quality bras—"

"Truth, I've done it all before—every kind of eating program. I'm not wasting a lot of money on workout clothes. I'll end up boxing them up in a few months when this fails—because it will fail."

Truth opens the door to my change room. I yelp, as I'm only half-dressed. Truth ignores my discomfort. I am learning she doesn't care about discomfort—ever.

"Indi, this is tried, tested, and true. Please give it a chance."

"I'll try." And fail. I step back and close the door on her searching gaze.

Mutinously, I place the cheaper bras on the pile of sale-priced clothes.

Once we get back home, I toss all my new workout clothes onto the couch in my room. I have enough clothes that I can change up to three times a day if I need to. I'm a little concerned about how much exercising they expect. The only thing I know for sure is that I'll be walking everywhere, as I'm forbidden to use a vehicle unless it's an emergency or I need supplies from the city. I eye the dress-like bathing suit. I could go to the hot spring, but who knows who might be there?

Even though it fits, I don't want to be seen in the light of day. The thought catches me. How much of my life do I hide from because of my weight? This emboldens me.

Throwing caution to the wind, I pull on the tarp-like swim dress and head out to the hot spring. The water flows over rocks, creating a small beautiful waterfall that I can stand under and let it act like a natural shower. I'm surprised when Jet shows up at the trailhead by my cabin. She waves and joins me in the hot spring.

"So glad to see you're back." Jet dips under the water and comes up, wiping the water from her face.

"Not much choice. My back went out, and I returned here on my hands and knees. You have me for six months."

"I'm one of your team members for the first seven days of your detox. I'll be working on your neck, doing reflexology and cooking. We expect these first seven days to be very difficult, so between me, Summer, and Truth, we'll be here every step of the way."

"Difficult?" I tilt my head.

"Yes. Quite." Jet smiles. "This is more of a healing program, and healing sometimes causes a healing crisis. With your food and life histories, we expect to encounter some difficulty in the days ahead."

"I once broke my ankle and worked in a boot for six weeks. I can take a lot of pain."

"Ah, yes." Jet swims closer to me.

Uncomfortable with people touching me, I back up a little.

"But that is physical pain. The removal of alcohol and processed foods will cause your unmet emotional needs, the

CHAPTER EIGHTEEN

pain you mask with those foods, to surface, and they have to be managed."

Oh, gracious, that sounds terrible.

"You'll learn new coping skills," Jet says brightly. "This process will break you right down, but rock bottom is solid ground to build on, and we will rebuild you." Jet smiles. She has no makeup on, and she's stunning in the moonlight. The spark in her eyes is almost hypnotizing. Jet, a woman whom I would have dismissed as unprofessional a few weeks ago, captivates me.

"Everyone thinks this clinic is about food. It isn't. It's about what needs to be fixed in your life. It's about really looking at life and re-evaluating your work-life balance, your goals, and what dreams you gave up along the way. We support what your body naturally wants to do. Be healthy. It just needs the right food and exercise."

"That sounds very dramatic." I smile tightly. "Honestly, I assure you, I'll be fine."

Jet smiles knowingly. "Great."

I am not fine. Oh. Sweet. Heavens. I am really, really not fine. I understand the need for salt and citrus. The first day on whole foods and no alcohol, no processed foods, I have a raging headache by seven o'clock in the evening. Blinding and vicious, it doesn't relent.

Jet hands me water with the salt-and-citrus solution.

"How much do I drink?"

"Enough to take the headache away."

I guzzle salt and citrus, hanging on like it's a life raft.

"I'll draw you a bath before I go. I'm going to put in the new life-support bath salts."

"What's in them?"

"Epsom salt, of course, and minerals to support you as you detox. Your body can absorb magnesium, which is an essential electrolyte. The salt and citrus drink is our own blend."

"It's terrible." I gag it down anyway.

"Yes, because there are no additives. It's pure salt with the complete mineral profile and a hint of citrus."

"I hate it."

"Ah, but your body needs it." Jet smiles. "Cheer up. After the first three days, you should be in better shape."

"I thought you were supposed to make small, lasting changes." I grumble as Jet pours the contents of the mineral soak called Tansy's Wellness Soak into the bath.

The scent of Sunshine in a Bottle makes my eyes fill with tears as I think of my mother. I'm losing it—on the verge of tears constantly. I desperately wish for icy-cold Sauvignon Blanc, which typically accompanied a hot bath in my previous life. Instead, I have two gallons of water and as much salt and citrus as I can choke down.

Ugh.

"You are borderline type 2 diabetic." Jet doesn't soften the blow. "We have no time to lose. We need to lower your blood sugar and insulin levels. It's time for tough love. You need to quit alcohol so your liver can do what it needs to do."

"I was expecting supplements, lovely drink mixes that taste good," I reply mutinously.

"Nope. We don't do any of that. Fresh water is all your liver needs to clean itself. Your body, as it copes with this detox, only needs fresh spring water, salt, citrus, and primal food.

We'll add some vitamins and supplements once we monitor what your body wants to eat—"

"My body craves ice cream, enormous tubs of it."

"Yeah. Sugar addiction is stronger than heroin." Jet turns off the water in the tub. "Right then. The tub is ready. Enjoy. I'll be back tomorrow. We have a meeting for your first twenty-four hours."

My headache is blinding, so when Jet leaves, I turn out the lights in the bathroom and sink into the mineral bath. It is a delight I can't enjoy because my head feels like someone has sawed through it.

As the smell of Sunshine in a Bottle wafts around me, I transport to a different time, a time with my mother that was lovely. I give up the dainty sips of salt and citrus and gulp as much as I can. My headache improves a little.

After an hour, I take as much ibuprofen as I'm allowed and quietly apologize to my liver as I swallow the pills for the pain. I am in bed and sleeping by eight thirty.

───

After that first, worst rough night, I sit by my fire the next morning as Summer, Truth, and Jet let themselves into my cabin. They look happy and well rested. I look like I crawled out from under a car. The contrast between them and me is mind-blowing.

"Your first day and night is over. How are you making out?" Truth smiles in sympathy.

"Headache?" Jet joins us by the fire with a face cloth and coffee with cream.

"Constant." I press the hot cloth into my eyes with a grateful sigh.

"Do you need to stay close to the toilet?" Truth sips steaming coffee with cream that smells divine.

I pull down the cloth and look at her. "How did you know?"

"It's not our first picnic in this park." Truth grins.

"I thought health nuts didn't drink coffee," I growl from under the cloth.

"I'd rather die than give up coffee," Truth says so sincerely I actually laugh. Laughing hurts my head, so I press the cloth into my eyes a little deeper. "Yes, I need to stay close to the toilet." I don't detail to my support team that I was up four times in the night, weeping and—well, the only word is purging. Gross.

I'm tired. I feel emotionally raw. I've never gone this long without wine and hot, cheesy carbohydrates. I'm off balance and hurting. "I don't see how I'm going to heal when I'm up all night in my bathroom."

"That'll slow down, eventually." Truth sips more coffee.

"What about the weeping?" The cloth has cooled, so I place it on the glass coffee table. I sip the coffee gratefully and wish they had laced it with sugar. I want sugar so badly I can hardly see straight.

"For the first seven days and maybe longer, you'll go through a weep and purge," she continues. "So yes, stay close to the toilet. Your liver is cleaning itself. Lots of theories exist, but no one really knows why—when the liver cleans, many people weep through the process. You won't feel like yourself. There are no restrictions on food. What are you craving? As long as it's whole and not processed, you can eat it. Did the weeping start at one in the morning?"

"Yes." My eyes open wide with surprise. "How did you know?"

"Your liver really goes to work cleaning itself at one a.m. We have some tea that helps. It's not really necessary. Your liver is fine on its own, but some people like it because they tire of plain water. It's nettle, dandelion root, and burdock, of course."

"Oh, of course." I'm joking, but they all nod sagely as if everyone knew burdock was going to fix the whole world if everyone would just start drinking it. I sip more coffee, and my headache eases a bit.

"Hang in there, Indi. You'll be through this detox in about seven days or so, then we can start addressing the next phase. Have a healing mineral bath every night and morning. Your body will deplete sodium first, magnesium second, and potassium next. The salt-and-citrus water helps with your sodium levels, and the bath will adjust your magnesium. Drink your salt and citrus, and stay close to the toilet. You can do it."

"Here is your first meal of the day." Jet places a steaming bowl on the coffee table.

"What is it?"

"Maple walnut super seeds."

"Not oatmeal?"

"You are borderline type 2 diabetic. Once you become sensitive to insulin again, you can add in grain. This will keep your blood sugar low and nourish you with plant proteins."

I'm not sure about plant protein. Isn't all protein from meat? But they clearly know what they're doing, and since I'm hungry, I take a spoonful of the hot breakfast and am stunned at how good it tastes.

"What's in this?" I ask Jet.

"I call it Jet Fuel!" Jet smiles at the play on her name. "Hemp hearts, chia, flax, and a few other things. I make mine with coconut milk. It's the best."

The bowl of bird seed that is affectionately called Jet Fuel is so good I finish and carefully scrape the last bit from the bottom of the bowl. "I can eat this on my diet?"

"You aren't on a diet, my darling niece." Truth places her empty coffee cup on the glass table. She leans forward, and the sunlight sparkles on her silver ring. "You are on a life renovation, which you support with nutrient-dense foods. We're feeding you primal food so your body re-sensitizes to insulin. We'll be through every day until you can safely leave the toilet, then we'll add some walks. Feel free to swim in the salt pool. Sleep when you need. Your body is healing. The program really starts next week. This week, just detox." Truth smiles broadly and gets up to leave.

"And there are no supplements to help with the detox?"

"No. With no chemicals or sugar in your system, your body knows exactly what to do, as long as we don't interfere with processed foods."

I'm glad to see them go because I race to the toilet as soon as they're gone, and I start the whole process of weeping and purging again. I don't know why I cry.

Originally, I scoffed at the thought of meeting with a therapist when I made this change, but as I crawl into my bed with the blinds down, I reach for a journal and start writing the stuff that's bugging me. I document the thoughts in my head I would typically drown out with wine and sugar. It's a long list, and I wonder if shiny Summer is up for the task.

She looks so pretty and fresh, like nothing bad has ever touched her. My gaze slides over the list, and at the top is Ben. I decide I'll talk to her first, then I'll know how to deal with

CHAPTER EIGHTEEN

Ben. It's weird to break up unless we are in person, but that won't happen. I don't know when I'll be home. I frown at that.

Codependent No More has shifted my focus completely, and I have one more chapter to read, the one about learning to live and love. The Salt and Citrus crew are going to whip my life into shape, but what about love? I look over at the book and realize I'm not ready for that chapter yet.

This cabin has nothing processed, and the need for sugar screams and tortures me. My body begs for ice cream, and I don't even really like it. I have never craved ice cream in my life until now. I think about peanut butter and chocolate cups crumbled on a hot fudge Sunday. Tears well in my eyes as I crave pure sugar.

I groan and take more ibuprofen. I can't ignore how my body is cleansing from the loss of sugar, processed foods, and wine. I grudgingly acknowledge that I have needed this kind of cleanse for a long time. I marvel at the thought that I can do this without anything but salt and citrus. The tea is optional, but I decide to have a cup.

After my tea, I notice how beautiful the sun is as it filters down through the leaves and sparkles across the salt pool. I pull on my swim dress and decide to lounge. It's close enough to my bathroom that I risk it.

But as bad as the first twenty-four hours is, nothing prepares me for day three. Day three takes me to my knees. My father wants to stop by and have tea, but I request no visitors. My teeth feel slimy, which I am told is ketosis.

Jet slides through with her bowl of seeds and settles herself at my feet. "Let's do some reflexology and see how things are going."

She warms oil in her hands. I gulp down my super seeds. I am starving in the mornings. Her fingertips move over my right foot, and she works on a particularly tender spot.

"I haven't told a lot of people, but I'm pregnant," Jet whispers, as if someone might overhear.

"Oh! I am so happy for you!" I say through a mouthful of seeds.

"Leif is thrilled. We're going to get a crib next weekend. They're on sale."

"That is so great, Jet. Congratulations."

"Do you ever think about having kids?"

"I don't want children, no."

Jet works on very sensitive parts of my feet. She nods and works on a section of my feet that connects to my neck and shoulders. "So much old pain here."

"I think that's from my first year of hairdressing." I laugh. My emotions are all over the place.

Jet's determined to get to the bottom of things. "Maybe," she murmurs. "I'm curious. If you don't want kids, what do you want?"

It's on the tip of my tongue to say "go back to my hair salon and work," but I catch myself. Lately, I haven't been thinking of my hair salon. After ending up on the floor and Ariana stepping over me to get her hair done, I realized how replaceable I am. It hurt at the time, but now it's strangely freeing. Elle could buy me out, and I could—

"This is going to sound loony, but I started writing a book when I went to the Caribbean at age sixteen. It's called Castaway. I haven't looked at it since. I would love to go back and finish it."

I yelp as she works on my sinus points, and I forget all about writing a novel.

CHAPTER EIGHTEEN 125

Jet's phone lights up as she works on my feet. She glances at it and frowns. "Do you mind if I get this?"

"Not at all."

Jet answers the phone. I can hear Ford's deep voice.

"She's right here." Jet hands me her phone.

"Hi," I say.

"Hey, how are you?"

"Terrible, listen, I want to apologize for our conversation in the hot spring. I'm really sorry I came across so ungrateful and—"

"No problem. I know you're going through a lot. I get it."

"Thanks."

"So, I'm calling to assign some people to bring certain ingredients on Friday, and Tansy has a batch of asparagus that's ready for harvest. Can you bring enough for six people?"

"I was going to contact you about Friday. I can't come this week. Hopefully, I can next week."

"Oh, I'm sorry to hear that. Your back is still really bad?"

"My back and—" I don't want to tell him I can't leave my toilet! "My head is splitting."

"Still?" His deep voice actually sounds concerned.

My heart flips in my chest. "Yeah. I need a few more days, it seems. You can take the asparagus if you need it."

"Thanks. If you need anything, let me know. Do you want to borrow Jasper? He's a great emotional support dog."

"Not really a dog person." I laugh, and the laugh hurts my head.

"Okay. Well, let me know if you need anything. I'll be by to grab that asparagus. I hope you're up to the class next week."

"Me too."

Ford hangs up, and I realize I mean it. I was really looking forward to the class, and instead, I'll be weeping and purging, then in bed by eight p.m. *Ugh!*

Chapter Nineteen

Blindsided

It takes the entire ten days before I can safely leave my toilet. I'm stunned as I step off the scale in the boardroom where my team has assembled.

"I hate scales. This is the last time you'll see one for months, but you need to know what ten days of no sugar and no processed food can do for you," Truth says, as I am completely blindsided by the number.

"I lost ten pounds." I can barely breathe. "How can a person lose ten pounds in such a short time?"

"You lost ten pounds of fluid and inflammation," Truth says. "Maybe a pound of fat, but not likely. This is all water."

"How?" I gasp. I have noticed that my fingers move easier. I can flex them with no pain. My face is less puffy. But ten pounds!

"When you cut your processed carbohydrates and sugar and eat higher fats and protein, your body lets go of water, which is why your salt and citrus solution and the mineral bath are so important."

"My allergies are better, too. It's weird. I don't have to take my nighttime sinus pills."

"Not weird at all." Truth smiles. "I'm leading a three-kilometer hike with our beginners. Let's go."

"I'm not much of a hiker..." I feel weird in these new shoes, like an imposter. No one seems to care that my shoes are three different colours. If anyone looked closely, the shoes would blind them.

"Try it," Truth says a little tightly.

She's probably weary of my negative Nelly comments.

I plaster a smile on my face as I join the group of seniors. It stings a little that I'm with seniors, but then I remember the last time I walked was in high school—to the corner store for a chocolate bar. Suddenly, as the ladies pull walking sticks out of their car trunks, they look like they mean business, and I hope I can keep up.

The ladies smile back. Everyone is wearing headbands except me. Hair held back; they are ready to walk. It took me half an hour to fix my hair and makeup this morning because I thought Ford might be at the meeting, but it was only Summer and Truth. I put him from my mind. I refuse to entertain the obsession all these people have with headbands. My hair is an example of what proper maintenance can look like. Determined to hold the line, I absolutely refuse to wear a headband and fit in.

I take a deep breath of fresh mountain air and feel a happiness settle over me as I look at the sun shining on the lake water.

"Here is your water bottle." Truth hands me a woven bag.

CHAPTER NINETEEN

I sling it across my shoulder, and off into the wilderness we go. As I walk, my shoulders and lower back have a weird ache. It doesn't hurt, it just aches.

As we finish the walk, Truth gives some of the women hugs as they get into their cars.

"How are you?" she asks me.

"This is a beautiful property, Truth. I loved the hike."

"Great."

"But I feel this weird ache."

Truth nods. "As you walk, your body pushes blood through every muscle. It'll go away."

I hold up my swollen hands. I can barely move my fingers. "And this?"

"It's all part of the process, Indi. You're right on track."

Truth pats me on the shoulder, and I realize I have four kilometers to walk to get back to my cabin. Clever Truth. She smiles at me as I head for home. I'm starving.

"Don't forget, Friday is your cooking class. Ford said he would walk with you."

A zing of excitement slides through my heart.

"With his wife?" I try to sound casual. I turn around from the trailhead to ask Truth.

"He's divorced, Indi." Truth adjusts her headband.

"Oh." My moment of excitement is short-lived. Why is he still wearing that wedding ring then?

"Recently?" I don't even pretend to be nonchalant.

A smile plays at Truth's lips. "Three years."

"Ah."

"Interested? Because if you are, that's a good sign."

Who wouldn't be interested in a man who looks like a lithe linebacker, is a lawyer who would stand between a receptionist and a drug addict ex-employee, and cooks? It's impossible not to respect him.

"Well, I just wondered," I stammer as I turn to walk home.

"I'm glad, Indi. It's called living," Truth calls after me.

"I've been living a long time," I contradict her.

Truth shrugs because we both know that's a lie. I've been watching life pass me by, standing behind a chair, and this Friday, I will be in a kitchen with Ford. Divorced. Three years. I wonder how to get my hands on wine and sneak it in. Not just a bottle, a box—we'll need it.

―――

I wait nervously for Ford. We plan on walking together to the clinic, and my heart pounds with expectation. I've had boyfriends—of course—but none like him.

Oh, for heaven's sake, he's your cooking instructor and part of your process! He is not your boyfriend! Quit with all that nonsense.

I wait on the front deck, my eyes drifting to my mother's house. It's been two weeks of intense detox. I have a counseling appointment next week, and no one has asked me to go into Tansy's house since the first night. Everyone has given me lots of space while I detox and purge. My father has drifted in and out of my house to check on me. It's nice, strange, but nice.

I shake those thoughts from my mind as Ford's dog, Jasper, comes up to me. I have never really enjoyed dogs, and this one is especially ragged. Like his owner, ragged and scruffy, in need of clippers.

I itch for a comb. From the first day I learned to cut hair, I loved the orderliness of sectioning, the precision of lining

CHAPTER NINETEEN

up the sections with the teeth of a comb. Cutting involves no chaos. It's clean and precise—nothing at all like the bohemian coming toward me.

My stomach flutters in a way that has nothing to do with his neck hair. He's everything that should terrify me. I don't know enough about him. I want to know what caused his divorce. I don't know how much chaos he could bring to my life if he were interested, which he's not. Rolling my eyes at myself, I adjust my shirt for the millionth time so it doesn't cling to my stomach.

I'm actually nervous. I tell myself not to be a ninny, but I'm drawn to him like a moth to a flame. His smile is broad as he adjusts the backpack on his shoulders—shoulders that make my mouth completely dry.

"What's in the backpack?" I try to be casual as we set off down the trail to the clinic.

"Garden produce."

"That's a lot of food."

Is he assuming I eat a lot because I have a weight problem? I tell myself I'm being paranoid and to quit being a lunatic. My face burns in shame. Thankfully, he can't tell if I'm turning red because the sun is setting. I step over a fallen log, and Ford takes his time to actually pick it up and move it out of the way. I hope I can climb the incline by the lake without huffing. I can't.

Ford says nothing as I pant up the hill and have to rest at the top. I want to weep in mortification. I never walk in my normal life. Certainly not through breathtaking pine forests with carpets of moss and ferns. Yellow flowers dance along the side of the trail, and the whole thing is so perfect I feel like my panting is out of place. I can't help but breathe deep the scent of lake water and pine cones.

"There is no better smell, is there?" I gasp as I catch my breath. I wish my statement were breathlessly poetic instead of a hissing wheeze.

"There really isn't. But when it rains, I love walking in here because it smells even earthier. It's a beautiful place. Your mom had an amazing vision."

I shoot him a look as he pets Jasper and carries on down the trail. I want to disagree, but I can't. My mom had clearly changed into a person with an amazing vision.

Ford isn't avoiding the subject of my mother. We've disagreed, but he doesn't shy away from it. I grudgingly respect that he has retained his opinion despite what I think.

When I moved in with Phyllis and Al, that was a final decision. Giving Tansy credit for anything feels disloyal to Phyllis, who helped me completely recreate my life. I shake my head, put those thoughts aside, and mentally add them to the list I will hash out with Summer. I turn my attention back to Ford as he talks.

"All this food is for the clinic kitchens. They needed a salad blend that I have bales of, so I thought I would leave it for the morning crew."

"I love how everyone here seems more like friends than colleagues."

"I only work here in the off-season. When I started my journey, I had eighty pounds to lose, so I had to teach myself to cook. I do this as my way of giving back. I'm not on the payroll for this Friday night cooking lesson. It keeps me on track. Watching people start this journey and teaching them how to make healthy food is really rewarding for me. I'm on the payroll for legal assistance. I take over for hassles Carter doesn't want to manage besides running the restaurant."

"Really!" I gasp. "Eighty pounds?"

CHAPTER NINETEEN 133

"Really." Ford grins as he picks up the pace.

"You volunteer to teach people how to cook?"

"I eat primal, so I had to learn from scratch." Ford slows so I can keep up.

"Is wine in the primal diet?" I step around a patch of mud on the trail.

"I drink alcohol about once a week on some weeks, no alcohol other weeks, but never more than once a week—one or two beers. I quit because I love my five-kilometer hikes with Jasper at around seven in the morning, and if I drink, I find it harder to wake up."

A blush of shame crawls up me when I think of how much and how often I drank before coming to this place. "You've already done five K this morning?"

Ford shrugs his big shoulders. "Yeah."

"How many kilometers do you have to do in a week?" I'm scared to ask.

"Have to?" Ford laughs as we near the end of the trail. He looks back for a moment and lets his gaze rest on the lake, reflecting the setting sun. "I look forward to and crave that five K in the morning. It's a treat. In the winter I put on my snowshoes and can't believe how lucky I am that I get to live here. It's so far from my other life."

I stand still, breathing heavy from the walk, and wait for him to elaborate. Curiosity pulses through me. What was his other life like as a lawyer? He looks like he was a Sherpa on mount Everest. A traveler climbing Machu Picchu. I could envision him wandering down sand streets with a beer in his hand. Relaxing in a hammock. He was an incredibly chill presence and I am not. I am a complete control freak and I couldn't relax in a hammock with a fist full of tranquilizers.

I notice he absently rubs the string of beads on his left wrist. He pressed his thumb and forefinger on the two little strands of leather that are held together by a metal clip. I can see clearly that the clip clearly looks permanent. The wrist band would have to be cut off if he ever wanted to remove it. His face changes as his fingertips move over the beads. I think I see a glimmer of tears in his eyes, but he presses his fingertips over the beads one last time, then pulls a mask of professionalism over his face.

"Time to cook."

Chapter Twenty

Weeds and Wisdom

M y hairdresser brain recognizes the shift in him. I read him clearly. No talking about the beads, no talking about the tears. Change of subject required.

"What's on the menu? If it's weeds, I'm tapping out right now." I can't quite take the criticism out of my tone.

"We're learning to cook the perfect rib eye, Hollandaise sauce from scratch, and a vegetable medley of asparagus and red peppers—with a side of weeds." Ford laughs.

"Don't tease. No diet in the world allows Hollandaise sauce unless its fat free and calorie wise. I'm in for a plateful of weeds, I can tell. I'm sure I'll have to massage a head of kale, or whatever you do with it."

Ford throws back his head and laughs even harder. "First, this is not a diet."

"Ugh. I keep hearing that, but it's not clear. There has to be a list."

"You haven't read The Obesity Code by Dr. Jason Fung?"

"I read it twice," I grumble. It made perfect sense and seemed too simple to work, all at the same time.

"You need to lower your insulin, and the best way to do that is by upping your fats and lowering your carbs. Once you try Prairie's Hollandaise sauce, you'll be buying it from my restaurant by the tub."

"I'm here to lose about sixty pounds."

"Yeah. So, you'll need this sauce. It's a miracle."

"Teach me your ways, wise one. I can't wait to try it." I say it jokingly, but part of me is so skeptical I can't even fake believing any of this.

I'm excited to have a steak supper with this man, even if I'm certain Truth will pull me off the Hollandaise sauce and reprove me, flog me in front of the other patients as a warning to all. I'll risk it. I've been living on seeds and detox tea. I'm ready to eat. Also, full disclosure; I can't wait to watch him cook.

Once we get to the kitchen, my heart zips in disappointment as I realize the women are going to do the vegetables and the men are going to grill. A few women brought really nice bottles of red wine. My mouth salivates at the sight of them.

"I didn't think we could bring wine," I stammer as I watch them share wine so the other women can try a taste.

"We're in maintenance and know how to cook all this, but we went through our process together, and now we love our Friday cooking nights. I take over for Ford when he's too busy during tourist season," says Prairie, my nutrition consultant, a woman with straight black hair and a fine fringe.

"Grill is ready," Ford announces. "Men—let's grill."

The men take their platters of rib eye rubbed with a blend of spices and file out of the kitchen.

CHAPTER TWENTY

I look at the three women as they grab their cutting boards.

The women get right down to work so everything will be ready and hot at the same time. Placing the asparagus in their frying pans, they sauté mushrooms and peppers in a separate pan.

Women I know. Women are my business, and these ladies are all my age. "I'm Indi."

They introduce themselves as Tamsin, Prairie, and Lark, and everything stops as they all welcome Hailey from the front desk. She looks nervous when she sees me.

"I'm not part of this group. Ford told me to come." Hailey's eyes are red rimmed.

My heart goes out to her. She had such a terrible scare. My heart warms to Ford even more. He didn't want her alone on a Friday night.

"You're welcome in this group anytime, honey." Lark gives her a side hug. "We're so proud of you."

"We should have a mother-daughter night," Tamsin suggests.

"We should!" Prairie agrees as she peels the foil off a pound of butter.

I catch the look on Hailey's face. Something about the emotion in her eyes reminds me of my own. I yearn to ease the hurt I see there. "Maybe you could be my daughter at the mother-daughter night," I offer. "I am warning you, I only know how to order takeout, so the cooking would be all on you. I don't know what to do with weeds."

"I'm very good with weeds," Hailey says slyly.

"We're a team, then." I hug her.

"I would love that!" Hailey's eyes light up with excitement. "I thought you would be mad at me after what happened when we met," Hailey whispers as she hugs me back.

"Not at all. Everything in the world is fixable," I whisper. What is happening to me? If they drag their drama to work, we fire them. Where did my hard edge go? I must have lost it in the weep and purge.

"You don't have any wine," I point out to Lark.

"I'm in the second phase. No wine for me yet. I had some extensive liver damage, so I'm letting that heal." Lark has curly black hair and a tiny face. She slides her slim arm around me and gives me a squeeze. "I'm so glad you're here, honey. We have a WhatsApp group chat. Can we add you? You'll likely be at Friday nights."

My heart warms to her immediately. "I would love that."

I feel at home with this group of women immediately. Tamsin makes slicing peppers somehow glamourous. Prairie smiles at me and gets right down to work. I can tell she loves to cook.

"I'll do the Hollandaise sauce." Prairie grabs a heavy-bottomed saucepan.

I don't have an assignment. "Should I learn to grill meat?"

"Yeah, no. Ford likes the men out there because he privately asks them if they're facing any obstacles to staying on their protocols." Tamsin hands Prairie another pound of butter. "He says they don't open up in front of us. So, we pretend they're grilling steak when they're actually bonding."

Out comes a whisk, and I can tell Prairie is most at home in a kitchen. The women watch her deftly work her magic.

Lark sips a wineglass full of something I have never seen before.

"It's the only time they actually interact about what they're facing." Tamsin grins and sips merlot. "We all went through this process together. We're a family and so happy to have a new face—two new faces."

CHAPTER TWENTY

Tamsin winks at Hailey, and Hailey warms to her.

"Why am I in this advanced course?" I ask.

Lark hands me a wineglass that matches her own, full of ice and lemon wedges.

"We're tired of watching Ford eat alone. We really hope you can help him move forward," Lark says.

"Forward to what?" I look at each of the women.

"He's stuck. He's come a long way, but he's stuck." Tamsin keeps her eye on the men outside.

I don't ask about Ford and his "glue" or his beads. I can tell the friendship between these men and women is deep. It's like the salon, where we are more family than coworkers.

I remember Estee caring for me when I cut the top of my knuckle off. I couldn't even look at it as she carefully rearranged the skin over the exposed knuckle bone, then glued it with crazy glue and Steri-Stripped it together. My heart still warms at the thought of her placing a glove over my hand and taping it to my wrist to keep the water out because I had six hours of work ahead of me. She worked so hard to stay ahead of me so she could wash all my clients' hair—to save my hand from flexing any more than it had to.

The hair salon is a place of transcending joy and deepest sorrow and despair. It often requires tough talks and hard hugs. I didn't know that sort of interaction exists outside a hair salon, but it does. I'm living it, watching it in action. The only difference is I'm not standing behind a chair this time. I was actually invited into and am part of a group coming together out of love and support for each other. I've never taken time to cultivate my own friendships. I'm always paralyzed at the thought of getting hurt by people.

Now, I have no time to be nervous. These women took me in like I have always been with them. This supper feels like a group hug for me. I'm in a new place, facing a life-changing diet—I mean process—and exercise, counseling, and even a newly discovered father. These women are so healthy and happy. For the first time since I got here, I feel like I'm with my people.

Prairie looks up from her saucepan and shoots me a smile. "It's ready, and it's perfect."

I peek into the pan. "It looks too good to eat."

Prairie has a homegrown sort of goodness that I loved straight off. Like, if I were sick, she would drop off soup. She doesn't have a mean bone in her body. She's just good—all the way through. I see it in all of them, an inner goodness that shines through as they talk and encourage each other.

"Oh, you'll eat it." Prairie laughs. "You'll eat a lot."

The men return to the kitchen, clapping each other on the back, and the room shifts from calm to high energy.

"I've never had Hollandaise sauce as part of a—process," I say.

"You'll be pleasantly surprised." Tamsin slides in beside her husband.

He dishes her a steak, and she puts the vegetables on his plate.

"You asked about this drink. It's called a Clemon," Lark announces as she points to the drink in my hand.

"What on earth is a Clemon?"

"Club soda and lemon juice with lemon wedges and ice. Try it."

I take a sip, and it is fantastic. Tart and refreshing. "I like that." My eyes widen with excitement. Who knew sparkling water could transform my life?

CHAPTER TWENTY

"Your cabin has a Soda Stream. We drink gallons of it. It's so good, and when it's in a wineglass, it feels like you aren't missing out." Tamsin slides into the chair beside her husband.

When we're all seated, Prairie comes to each table and pours her precious Hollandaise sauce on our vegetables. Ford sat beside me, and he picks up my plate first to get sauced by Prairie, then his own. It's oddly chivalrous and thrilling. My heart flutters with excitement. On some level, it tells me he puts a woman's needs first, and that strikes a chord inside me. I realize acutely that I've never had that. This is a man I would be safe with.

I catch a glimpse of myself in a mirror by the kitchen door, and I'm disappointed at my reflection. I want to weep. No one will ever look at me with desire. This won't work.

"Try it," Ford says cheerfully, oblivious to my turmoil.

I take a dainty bite of rib eye with a spear of asparagus and sauce, and I nearly swoon with delight. "This is—" I reach for my Clemon and take a sip. "This is incredible."

"When Prairie does the sauce, it can't get any better."

Ford compliments Prairie, but she is so intent on serving everyone she doesn't even look up. She's across the room, and I realize she hasn't heard him.

"You all eat like this? Like all the time?"

"Yes." Ford takes a sip of beer and attacks his meal with such joy it's fun to watch.

"I ate an entire field of asparagus when I started my protocol," Lark admits. She closes her eyes with delight as she eats her steak. "Asparagus is a liver cleanser, so I craved it and ate as much as I wanted."

"It's all so good." I'm surprised that I can barely finish my meal. I love it.

I have lived my entire life with a list of what I couldn't eat. This is a weird new approach—finding joy in healthy cuisine and letting go of unhealthy food because it interferes with living my best life. Not once have I heard about a goal weight. Everyone is talking about what has healed and what needs to heal next.

It's quiet as everyone savours their food.

As empty plates get piled, Prairie pulls out a Tupperware container. "My cherry cheesecake."

"There is no way—" I'm stunned that this is acceptable.

Prairie shoots me a smile. "No sugar. You can have one."

I ignore myself in the mirror and hold out both hands. "I want."

Ford grins as he takes my plate, and Prairie hands me a little plate with a fork. The cheesecake is covered in cherry sauce, then a dallop of whipped coconut cream. Hot herbal tea is served, and I can't believe how good this meal was.

I could live like this. The thought catches me by surprise, and I see how their clever plan has worked. Suddenly, I'm not nervous about this process. All at once, with this group helping me, I'm invested. Right up to my eyeballs invested.

"What do I bring next week?"

Ford smiles at me, and I smile back, fervently hoping I don't have asparagus in my teeth. "Next week is Tuscan chicken. And Prairie will surprise us with a masterpiece for dessert."

"Yes, I will." Prairie sips her hot tea.

Tamsin finds some upbeat music, and the men wash dishes while the women dry. The kitchen is back to normal in half an hour. Everyone hugs everyone before they leave for home.

I give Hailey an extra hug. "Don't forget. You're on my team."

"I won't." Hailey grins.

CHAPTER TWENTY

It's ten p.m., and I can't believe how much fun I had at my cooking class. Ford flicks on a flashlight, and together we start for "home."

Chapter Twenty-One

Cheap Bras and a Snap Hook Carabiner Clip

My heart pounds, and not just because of the walk. "I love every single person in that group." I take a deep breath and let it out slowly.

Suddenly, there are fireflies surrounding us. I stop and hold my breath. The moment is so perfect that I am struck silent.

"Indi." Ford turns to look at me, concern in his voice.

I hold up my hands. I don't want to scare off the fireflies. They dance and weave around us. I am so touched by their beauty that my eyes fill with tears. It's all so perfect. Ford smiles as he clicks off his flashlight. We stand on the trail in between the towering pine trees and watch as fireflies dance.

"Are you crying?" Ford whispers.

"I am."

"Are you alright?" He sounds alarmed.

CHAPTER TWENTY-ONE

"Have you ever just been perfectly happy?" I whisper as a firefly hovers between us. "A moment where you are so happy you can't stand it?"

"Yes, but typically, I'm not weeping. I am usually laughing," Ford says softly.

I'm grateful he turned his flashlight off. "Since I quit drinking, things have changed." I gulp down tears at the confession I'm compelled to give him. The shift in me since I got here is profound, and I need to talk about it. "The detox was so brutal that I thought I would never feel better, but now that the alcohol, sugar, and processed food is out of me, I feel lighter. I feel like I want to hug nature. I feel a spark inside me from seeing these fireflies. They are so perfect. This sounds like madness, but I feel like I want to enjoy life. I feel clear. My head is clear. For the first time, I am in balance. I mean, this sounds crazy, I know. I feel more. Like I was numb before, but now I'm—"

Ford moves closer to me, and I wish I were thin enough for him to love me. I wish I were someone he would look at with desire.

"This is normal, and it will level out," he says gently. "The real reason you're so happy, though, is as I told you. Prairie's Hollandaise sauce is magic. I knew it would transform your life," Ford whispers.

"You were right."

"It's normal to have a lot of emotional release as you shift your life and eating. That's why your mom wanted you here for six months," Ford says quietly, as if he doesn't want to disturb the perfection of this night, either.

Our eyes meet in the dim light of the moon. At that moment, I feel my bra give out. The zipper is breaks, letting go from the bottom up. Truth's words to buy an expensive bra come back to me. The zipper of my bra comes apart, right to the top.

"What was that?" Ford's face creases with concern.

I want to die a thousand deaths. "It's—"

"Are you okay?"

Why did I buy a cheap bra? My father gave me a platinum card!

The moment is lost. I'm grateful it's dark as my face reddens with embarrassment. "Ford, I am having a technical difficulty."

"What is that?"

"Well. My bra zips in the front, and the zipper just broke under the intense pressure... I couldn't bear the thought of buying my actual size, and the zipper is no match for my—"

Why am I confessing everything?

Ford throws back his head and laughs.

"I'll just hold it together. It'll be fine." I wish the ground would open up and swallow me.

"I can fix it."

"I don't think it's fixable. The zipper is broken." I turn from him to confirm that it has completely come apart. It's hanging on by a thread, a very precarious thread.

"Take it off and give it to me."

I break into a sweat. I would rather die than hand him this bra that looks like it could winch a four-wheel-drive truck out of a ditch.

"Come on, we're adults here. Hand it over. It's a long hike back, holding everything in place."

Mortified, I turn around and wrestle the bra off, then slide it out of my sleeve and hand it to him.

He unhooks his backpack and takes out a knife and a snap hook carabiner. A sort of clip I've never used in daily life

CHAPTER TWENTY-ONE

before. Sitting on a log, he holds out his flashlight. "Here, shine this so I can see what I'm doing."

My hands shake as I hold the flashlight. He takes the knife and makes a slit alongside each zipper, then threads the snap-hook carabiner through to hold it together.

"There you go. Not as good as new, but it should work to get you home." He hands back my bra, then takes the flashlight from me. He walks down the trail a few feet and turns his back, clicking off the flashlight so I will have privacy.

Quickly, I pull off my shirt, drag the bra down over my head, and wrestle it into place. I sweat from the effort as I drag my shirt back down. Why did this have to happen to me? Why can't I get one decent, almost-romantic moment? Ugh.

"All set?" Ford asks politely as I catch up to him.

"Yes. All set."

"Don't worry. We all have a wardrobe malfunction at one time or another."

"You've had a bra break before?" The question is so suggestive I want to bite the question back.

"Not my bra, no." Ford laughs as he moves the flashlight from the hand nearest me to the other.

Is he going to hold my hand?

No. He isn't. He simply keeps walking, and I keep trying not to pant from the exertion of keeping up.

Finally, my cabin comes into sight. "Thanks so much for the cooking course. Please make sure you send me a list of things to purchase for next Friday."

"Check the WhatsApp group. The women decide the menu, and we do what we're told." Ford whistles to Jasper to leave the front deck of my cabin.

"I don't believe that for a moment."

"It's true." Ford grins in the dark. "Prairie will lead the way, and we will listen. I don't know what she'll bring in her Tupperware next week, but I guarantee you'll want it."

The thought overwhelms me with joy. It's such a new feeling that I can't stop myself from expressing how I feel. "They're a great group of people, and I want you to know that I feel so thankful to be part of this class."

"I'm happy you're happy."

"Thanks."

"One last thing; thank you for being so kind to Hailey. I should have asked before I invited her, but I didn't want her to be alone on a Friday night. She was nervous about the altercation that took place, and you really put her at ease. You're a kind person, Indi."

"Oh, she's a sweetheart. I'm so glad she could come. Is she going to be all right?"

"I thought we could meet with her and help her plot her next step. Would you be able to make time for that?"

"Of course. Just shoot me a text."

"Great, I appreciate that. Good night, Indi." Ford beams a big smile and then calls Jasper.

"Good night, Ford." I stay on my front porch and watch him disappear down the trail to his home.

Worry for young and vulnerable Hailey slides through my heart. I'm glad Ford is determined to find a solution for her, and I'm flattered to be part of the process.

Now that I'm not thinking through a fog of alcohol and sugar, it's time to ask a few questions about how my mom got from a run-down trailer to here. I just hope my heart can handle the answers.

Chapter Twenty-Two

Drama at Work

The next morning, Ford and I sit in the boardroom waiting for Hailey. She looks anxious as she lets herself into the room.

"Thank you for meeting with me." Hailey takes a deep breath and lets it out slowly. "I really appreciate your kindness last night. I felt welcome."

"The most important thing is that you are safe." I reach across the table and take her hand, squeezing it.

Tears fill her eyes.

"How are you?" Ford asks gently.

"I'm scared." Hailey tries not to blink so the tears don't stream down her face.

Jasper places his head on Hailey's lap, and she pets him. His tail thumps on the floor, the only sound in the room while we waiting for her to continue. I look at Ford and hope he has a solution.

"They arrested Garrett." Ford's deep voice is comfortingly authoritative.

Hailey presses tissues to her eyes. "I'm not just afraid of him."

Ford stiffens beside me—automatic male protection mode activated by her words. Hailey hands Ford a white envelope.

Taking the contents out, he swiftly reads it. "You're being subpoenaed to court." Ford folds the letter and places it back in the envelope.

"How do I get out of it?" Hailey presses her hand to her heart.

"Who is Slay?"

"The head of X66." Hailey's face is white with fear.

Ford's jaw tightens. "We'll ask for protection."

"Would it help to stay at my mother's house? No one needs to know you're there."

Hailey sobs harder. "I'm so sorry. I feel so stupid."

"Aw, sweetheart, people make mistakes. Look at you! You're doing so amazing. We can figure this out." I get up and go around the table to sit beside her and give her a hug.

They bring their drama to work, and we fire them. I am not sure where that version of me went, but I don't miss my hard edge.

Ford's eyes lock with mine, and I can see he's happy about my offer.

It's not a show. I really mean it. Somehow, this clinic and the people in it are doing different work than I expected. I thought it was about weight. It's about life.

Watching Hailey blink up at me with new hope in her eyes melts my heart. My mom had given her what she wasn't well enough to give me, and I want to continue to help her on my mother's behalf.

CHAPTER TWENTY-TWO

"Please, Ford, you have to get me out of this. I can't be in court with those men." Panic laces Hailey's voice. "I can't be anywhere near them. I know what they're capable of."

"Witness protection will be available for you." Ford's eyes are sympathetic. "Do you have any other family?"

"It's complicated."

I know what that feels like.

Ford nods. "Right." He comes around the table.

Hailey stands and presses her face into his shoulder like a little girl. She is. Hailey's barely twenty-five. "Thank you," Hailey whispers as she hugs him hard.

"Did you finish your acupuncture course?" Ford asks quietly.

"Almost. I'm supposed to start this week with Tao. I have one hundred hours left of the four hundred to be fully licensed, but there is no sense building a clientele if—"

I step in. "Are you able to work?"

"Yes." Hailey lets go of Ford and kneels to hold on to Jasper. The poor thing is a nervous wreck.

"I think she should get her last hundred hours done as soon as possible. Is that all right with you, Indi?"

Hailey blinks up at him.

"Absolutely." I nod.

"Thank you," Hailey says.

When Hailey leaves, we sit back down at the table.

"That was very kind of you, Ford. To offer to help her."

"You too. She's done so well. I hope this doesn't derail her."

"So, you're helping her legally?" I lean forward.

"Yes, unless she's moved to another place in Canada. I'm not sure what they'll do for her."

"I'm really concerned about something." I bite my lip and fidget with Jasper's ear.

"What?" Ford frowns.

"That gang sounds very dangerous." My eyes widen.

"Hey, I'm used to this." Ford's tone is gentle. "I've dealt with all manner of bad guys in my career. Nothing to worry about. Yes, it's a terrible gang, but I'm—"

I lean forward and put my hand on his arm. "Please hear me."

"I'm listening." Ford takes my hand in his.

His hand is big, hard. He holds mine tight enough to lend support, but not so tight as to hurt me.

I lower my voice, and he leans in closer. "Don't take this the wrong way, but I just can't see that neck hair in a legal environment."

Ford throws back his head and laughs.

"I mean it, Ford. You really need a haircut."

Ford laughs harder. "Indi, your mom said you had a sense of humour."

"A sense of humour and a very sharp razor!" I plead with him to see reason. "In two minutes, I can have all that hair shaved off, and you'll look professional."

"Professional. I honestly can't think of anything worse." Ford gets up, grins at me unrepentantly, and calls Jasper to follow him.

Chapter Twenty-Three

Healing Crisis

Hailey moves into my mom's house and apprentices every hour she can to finish her course. I barely see her. She works and sleeps, and I wonder how long it's been since she felt safe enough to really sleep.

While she works at her apprenticeship, I spend the time rising early and writing a thousand words before the world wakes. I don't know what I'm doing, and I don't let that dampen my enthusiasm. The more I write, the more scenes appear in my head. I'm delighted as the word count builds on the left hand of my computer screen.

When Hailey finishes her apprenticeship, it feels natural and right that Ford and I stand together to say goodbye to her as she leaves for witness protection. I have a bad feeling about it.

As I press my hand to my heart, watching the police drive off with her, Ford slides his arm around me. "She's going to be okay."

"She's so young." My heart breaks for her.

"So were you."

"I didn't have the same challenges. I'm worried."

Ford tightens his arm around my shoulders. "I told her when she accepted protection—she can always come to us."

I nod my approval. "No matter what."

"Always."

My life revolves around the clinic, but I'm finding a healthy balance between writing, walking, and working. I notice that when I walk my five K in the early morning, I often run into Ford on the trail. I start to think that this isn't a coincidence. He and I bump into each other often now.

Every afternoon I dedicate to my P. Volve exercise and meal planning, as well as attending meetings to decide about the clinic.

I love Friday night cooking class. Ford and I walk together to the kitchen to meet up with our friends. At other times, we handle legal issues surrounding the Salt and Citrus clinic like a well-oiled machine. Sometimes, I notice him looking at me at the same time I look at him. I like it.

Two months of perfect summer slide by as I explore new trails with Truth, my father, and my beloved senior citizens and their flashy walking sticks. The wild and beautiful Canadian Rockies nourish my soul in a way that astounds me.

Nature has always been something I drove past to get to work. It was there, but I never actually engaged in it. Now, I crave the smell of pine cones crunching under my feet. Ferns dripping with rain drops causes a calm inside me. At first, I thought it was totally mental to have trails to all the properties my mother owns, but now I see the genius in it.

Built-in cardio in the most perfect setting. The hills challenge me, but I find I can jog up them now. I marvel at how fast my body has changed and adapted to this new way of life. My hands and neck no longer ache. I get up in the morning, and my feet don't hurt. My appetite decreases because my carb consumption is less. I love my Jet Fuel super seeds that I eat hot every morning. I relish my meal salads and power bowls. Slowly, my appetite has shifted, and my hunger is so low it seems strange. What sounded completely impossible now seems doable and natural.

Jet does my reflexology, and the woman I so nearly dismissed as a complete cuckoo when she picked me up in the airport has become my biggest cheerleader. She listens to all my craziness with no judgment, and she cheers on anything I dream of doing.

Three times a week, I lift heavy weights with my new friends, and we plan our Friday meals. Prairie gives us our assignments. I'm thrilled with this group. As we open up to each other, I love checking in our WhatsApp group to find out what their fasting and eating protocols are for the week.

But my pulse quickens as Truth breezes into my cabin and hands me a manila envelope. "This came for you from Estee."

I don't call myself a writer, of course, but seeing my old manuscript—written before anyone owned computers—fills my heart with a little leap of excitement. It's heavy. I haven't looked at this for almost twenty-two years, and I'm filled with the anticipation of checking it against what I've already written. I itch to see if I can integrate scenes.

Truth doesn't ask what it is. She pours herself a coffee and adds heavy whipping cream.

The old Indi wouldn't have told her, but I feel like, as I purged and wept, I didn't just process toxins. Somehow, I purged the anger that was holding me back, too. My Chinese doctor says it's because a congested liver makes you angry. I disagree. A disaster of an upbringing probably has something to do with it. Whatever it is, I feel like that anger was a weight holding me down, pulling me back. Somewhere in the purge and weep, my liver healed and my emotions settled. I feel free.

"This is a book I started writing when I was on vacation with Estee. I was seventeen. I can't even imagine how terrible it is. It's about a girl who runs away from her tragic past and ends up in the Caribbean. It's a silly beach read. However, I find myself with all this time. I might as well write."

Truth smiles so brightly, I have to smile back. "That's wonderful!"

"I don't know if I would actually make anything on it."

"That's what hobbies are for. It doesn't matter if you make money."

Immediately, her comment gets my back up. I guess I haven't lost as much anger as I thought. "I had my first job at thirteen. No one would hire me when I tried to get work earlier. The anger is right there. It bubbles up out of me as I try to sound at peace, but I'm not. I want Truth to feel bad for leaving me with my incompetent mother. As she hears the truth about what I went through, I want to see her face change. "I bought my own food for school lunches. I worked every Saturday at a restaurant busing tables."

Truth's face pales as I knew it would.

I can't stop myself from continuing angrily. "Sometimes, my mother found the money and spent it on booze." That

CHAPTER TWENTY-THREE

statement hangs between us. The air crackles with hurt. "So, I didn't eat that week."

Tears fill Truth's eyes. "I am so sorry."

It doesn't feel good to see her cry. I know now that she was battling cancer. Truth was trying to keep her family together while she fought for her life. Could I do that and take in another child? No, I likely couldn't. Watching her face crumple hurts me.

"I'm sorry." I put the envelope down.

Truth covers her face with her hands.

"Truth. This was not your fault." My eyes fill with tears, too.

"I didn't know things got that bad. I didn't know about the drinking until Phyllis told me." Truth sobs, and I feel like actual garbage. "You were already safe by that point. But I was an adult in your life, and I failed—"

I slide my arms around Truth, and she trembles with deep emotional hurt. Until this moment in my kitchen, hanging on to each other for dear life, I did not know Truth felt this deeply about me.

"I love you. I wanted the best for you." Truth sobs, and I join her.

A knock at the door interrupts us. I ignore it.

"You should get the door."

"I should stay right here with my aunt," I say. "My aunt who dragged me up off the floor when my back went out and put up with all my moaning and sarcasm while I was detoxing. I will stay right here until we're healed."

"Indi, I love you."

Truth squeezes me so hard I am not sure how I survived this long without her in my life. I should have listened to her side of the story years ago. I've lost all these years with this amazing woman.

"Auntie Truth, I love you too." I hug her like she's a life raft.

"If I could go back, I would change everything for you."

"Me too. I would take your cancer away."

"I would build you a guesthouse." Truth holds me so tight I feel all my unglued parts fuse. "That's the thing about illness, Indi. It takes our power away and shifts our lives onto a trajectory that we can't control. Unfortunately, we are all along for the ride. It's chaos."

"But I'm finding today that love is the constant in the chaos. All this time, I thought you didn't care. I didn't know."

"That's why you're here." Truth pulls back and wipes her face with tissues. "Feelings start as thoughts." She gazes at me steadily. "We treat the thoughts to correct the feelings."

"I just thought feelings were feelings."

"No, they are rooted in thoughts. You think, then you feel. It's important to base what you feel on truth and logic. That is the cornerstone of good mental health."

"And here, all this time, I thought I was the picture of mental health."

At that ridiculous statement, Truth stops crying, and a smile tugs at her lip. I can't stop a half sob, half laugh from bubbling up through me. Suddenly, we are laughing and crying and clinging to each other. We don't even notice my front door open.

"Is everything all right?" my father asks from the doorway.

Truth and I wipe our eyes and turn to face him.

"Healing crisis." Truth drops her soaked tissues into the garbage.

"You're doing all right?" My father asks me.

It feels good to hear him ask.

CHAPTER TWENTY-THREE

"She'll be fine once she eats these weeds." Ford comes in with a Ziplock bag of mixed lettuce. He puts it in the crisper in my fridge as if he lives here.

My heart tingles with happiness to see him so at ease in my home.

"I have to run. I have a meeting with a lawyer. See you Friday, Indi." He's out the door in a flash.

I'm pretty sure weeping women unnerve him.

My father waits patiently for us to pull ourselves together.

"Indi, I wanted to stop in and say hi."

I was furious with this man for leaving me with Tansy. All my life, I wanted to shred him if I ever met him. Now, I am reminded that he did not know I existed. His parents protected him from a consequence and gave the punishment to me. They are dead now. I go to him and slide my arms around him.

"Good morning," I whisper as his big arms close around me.

My father is overcome with emotion.

Hearing his voice catch on a sob breaks the dam of emotion choking me. As we hold each other, weeping, Truth hovers near us. Finally, my father reaches for her, and the three of us—the ones living with the fallout from my childhood—unite in one embrace, weeping, apologizing, re-establishing our love for one another.

We don't speak as we weep. As the storm calms, I lay my head on his left shoulder and Truth lays her head on his right. I close my eyes and commit this perfect moment to memory.

The arms of a father have a safety I have never felt before, and at this moment, I don't know how I lived without it. Phyllis's husband, Al, was lovely to me, but he was always a little awkward. He was careful to keep any touch with me very formal. A hug from Al was almost professional. If I needed real hugs, I always got them from Phyllis.

But I marvel at the difference between the hug of a mother and a father. Phyllis made me feel loved and understood. This hug, this gift from my father, makes me feel not just loved and understood, but safe. I feel the power in his arms and know he would use his strength for my protection. If I told him I bussed tables to pay for bread and lunch meat, he would lose it.

It's time I see the counselor. I have been putting it off, but letting go of the anger surrounding Truth and my father frees me in a way I didn't know existed. I wonder what my mother's story truly is. Maybe the truth about her will heal me.

I don't know, but for the first time since I was fifteen, I feel ready to find out. Besides, if I can't handle it, I'll finish out my six months here and give my shares to Truth. I can't sell this place, because it's too important for too many people. Carter and Truth are on the cusp of doing even more amazing things. I don't think I can reconcile with my mother, but I won't stand in the way of this clinic and its people. I see them for what they are. I look beyond the quirks, and I love what I see.

Chapter Twenty-Four

Summer

I put off speaking to Summer about the night I left my mother for two more weeks. I don't want to talk about it. I want to bury it. Who wants to hear about that night?

As I sit on a couch in Summer's office, I wonder if I am supposed to lie down. Ugh. I don't know what the proper protocol is when baring my entire soul.

Blond and blue-eyed, Summer enters the room. I immediately approve of her mane of highlights that look like they cost a mortgage payment. Her smile is bright as I sit down. She looks over the paperwork in front of her in such a way that I am certain she has all the information well in mind.

"So, you're the one challenging everyone." Her smile is bright as she holds my gaze. Summer is confident in the way that all beautiful people are.

"Am I?" I smile at her tightly.

"Ah. Yes. Hairstylist." Summer beams as if she's excited about the challenge of getting into my brain and shrinking it, or whatever they do. "How long have you been behind a chair?"

"Forever."

She chipped away my icy exterior with that one question. I can talk about my work all day. Immediately, I'm at ease.

"Your file says since you were seventeen when you started hairstyling and you are thirty-seven now."

"Yes."

"Twenty years of listening to women." Summer adjusts the file on her lap.

I nod. "In every aspect of their lives—the triumphs and the tragedies. I've heard it all."

"I can imagine. I bet you could take over my clients today and not miss a beat."

I can't help but smile because she's so engaging. "It would be easier. I wouldn't have to raise my voice over the blow-dryer. It's so much easier to sit and talk than stand and work and talk. Although I've been a hairstylist for so long, my work is completely subconscious. My hands just do it. I don't know how to explain it, but there is no actual conscious thought when I work. It frees up my mind to give lots of advice."

"I love my hairstylist and can't imagine life without her."

"Your hair looks incredible. You're the only person here who isn't in a headband. It's a sight for sore eyes. Your stylist is very good. Those highlights and lowlights are perfect."

Summer beams at me. "You're a delight!"

"Thanks! I think you get me. I can go."

Summer laughs and shakes her head no. "They have tipped your life upside down. You have decisions to make about your mother's clinic—a mother who you left to protect yourself at the very young age of fifteen. However, I can imagine you feel like this is a lot to process. When did you find out about your mother's diagnosis?"

"Her cancer?" I bristle and don't like it.

"No. Her bipolar diagnosis."

"Her excuse, you mean. The reason she gave everyone for destroying my life?"

"Do you typically think of illness as an excuse?" Summer holds my gaze.

"I broke my ankle ten years ago, the month before the Christmas rush. I spent six weeks in a boot, working. Yes. I think many people use illness as an excuse."

"As you went to work in your boot, was it work ethic or fear?" Summer asks as stealthily as a ninja.

I shift uncomfortably. "Fear."

"Fear of—"

"Poverty—I never want to come home to darkness because the electricity isn't paid. I still remember the red sticker on the door and having to go to bed cold."

Fear of a coat across the window of the back door and being terrified of what I will walk in on. I think it; but I don't say it.

Summer's eyes soften with sympathy.

"Fear of hunger." I gesture at myself. "Although that hasn't been a problem."

I get up and walk over to the huge windows looking out over the Rockies. The mountains are breathtakingly beautiful. Coming from flat Manitoba, they are a feast for the eyes.

But unfortunately, all I can see in my mind is my mother's broken-down old trailer with the screen door hanging off the hinge. I can almost feel the icy cold as I remember standing there. It brings back memories of finding that she took my money out of the sock in my dresser. My mom stole my lunch money from me to buy alcohol. Anger burns in my heart at the memories. It's fear, but it's anger, too. Tansy was a burden, and I refuse to be a burden to anyone. Ever. No one will have to look after me because I got hurt, sick, whatever.

"I will never be a burden." Why is my tone so harsh? "I live within my means. I work hard, and I keep my footprint in other people's lives very small. It would be great if more people were like that."

"I'm curious. Do you resent having looked after all the business decisions when Estee had children?"

That sentence challenges me further. I bristle. "No." That's not quite true. "A little maybe. I was kind of envious that she chose something so dangerous with such enthusiasm."

Where did that come from? I never fully formed that thought until this minute. I have this secret resentment toward Estee. Here I thought Summer was too sweet to get to the bottom of anything.

"It's dangerous to have children?" Summer tilts her head to the side.

"Very. I'll never do it."

"What does Ben say about that?"

"Ben can't keep a job. Ben doesn't get a say in this." I shut my mouth on such a terrible, cold statement.

"Are you still with Ben?"

"I haven't broken up with him."

"Hmm," Summer says.

"I will. I just feel like I can't do that over text, and I can't leave."

"What is holding you back?"

"I don't think I've held back, actually. I think I've just had a lot of change, and it was one more change."

Summer leans forward. "Is that all?"

CHAPTER TWENTY-FOUR

I take a deep breath and let it out slowly. Until she asked why I'm hesitating, I hadn't really thought of it, and the answer is shocking. "This is completely insane."

"It's okay. Just say it." Summer smiles brightly.

"I think..."

"Yes?"

"I think I can tell myself that no one is interested in me because I have a boyfriend and not because of my size." A hot fist of tears closes my throat. My eyes water—and not from allergies for the first time in my life.

"Is there anyone in particular?" Summer asks softly.

"It's madness, but when I saw Ford protect Hailey, I think I had a moment of clarity. Like that is the sort of person I want in my life. It sounds ridiculous, but the way he handled her and is continuing to protect her. It's..."

"It's what?"

"Scary."

"Explore that."

"I have never had an equal partner for a man in my life, which meant I could call the shots, but if I were with Ford—which is completely impossible—he would call his own shots. I wouldn't have control over him."

Where is this coming from? Stunned at the revelation, I can't believe I just said it out loud.

"And you need complete control over your domestic life because not having control was terrifying." Summer's tone is soft.

Tears spill down my cheeks. "Right."

"By hanging onto that control, what are you losing?" It's like Summer has a skewer and she's twisting it into me.

I gasp as the thought roars through my mind. Her questioning links with my knowledge from the book about codependency, clicking together. "I'm crippling my life with dysfunction because it's comfortable. It's what I knew for so long with my mom."

"So, what should you do now? What steps do you need to take?"

"I need to break up with Ben immediately and read the last chapter of Codependent No More."

"Great, let's meet after that happens."

"I'll do that tonight." I stiffen my spine, stunned I waited this long.

"Now, moving on. Did you resent Estee when she got married?"

"Of course, I don't resent Estee. I was happy for her, and if I resent her, I'm off base. I have to re-evaluate that."

"Does she resent you for taking this time to make your health a priority?"

"She forced it. Had everything organized so I could go."

"How do you feel about that?"

"At first, I felt betrayed, but I've lost about twenty pounds in a few weeks short of five months, and I have to say, I never could have done this without help. I could go back, but I haven't after my back went out. I think I started to see what everyone else saw."

"So, acknowledging that you need help and receiving help has been what for you? How is that now?"

My spirit lightens as I think of all the changes I've made here. I sleep better. My feet no longer hurt. I can walk the trails without losing my breath. I sprint when I'm behind on time and actually enjoy it. Truth told me other things would change now that my body can achieve autophagy. The process where your body cleanses itself on a cellular level when in a fasted state.

CHAPTER TWENTY-FOUR

Truth was totally right. This process isn't about weight loss. It's about an entire system reset that allows the body to heal itself. It's about taking time to reassess and heal, drinking salt and citrus to keep the electrolytes on point and give the rest of my organs the chance to heal themselves. Weight loss is a side effect of a healthy body, which includes the mind.

I understand what Ford has been saying.

Now, instead of panting and trying to stay alive as I walk to the clinic and the storefront, I take pictures with the camera my mom left me. I no longer crave wine and carbohydrates. I crave Prairie's Hollandaise sauce and her stuffed mushrooms. The thought of a rib eye on a barbeque makes me swoon with delight. Goat cheese on a salad is a thrill. A Clemon shared with Lark has replaced wine.

My new friends want a meeting with me in the healing pools tonight to debrief after my therapy session today. I smile at the thought. Carving a new life means new friends, and I am learning so much from them.

"What are you thinking about?"

"You're clever. Here I am twenty pounds down and feeling amazing after just two months here. I had to accept help. There was a problem, and I had to admit it. I was sick and had to stop to heal." I turn back to the windows. I don't see the trailer I fled from anymore. The sweeping majesty of the Rocky Mountains fills my eyes. I turn and fix my gaze on Summer. "So, I should acknowledge that my mom needed help and was sick. Is that what you are doing? Drawing a parallel?"

As that puzzle piece slides into place, I'm shocked that it changes my perception.

"I'm just here to see how you are doing and help you reach mentally healthy conclusions." Summer smiles.

"I don't know what her diagnosis was. I don't know why she died."

"That was a secondary diagnosis," Summer murmurs.

"I don't want to hear about alcoholism as an illness. It's a choice. She made choices that destroyed my life."

"I wasn't talking about alcoholism," Summer says so softly I strain to hear.

"You want me to forgive her? You'll say that's the only way to move forward."

"It depends on how you interpret forgiveness." Summer tilts her head, and I see a calm in her that intrigues me. "You have post-traumatic stress from the events of your childhood."

I reel from the truth of that statement. I didn't know that could be an actual thing. PTSD is something soldiers get. To hear that diagnosis validates my feelings in a way I have never experienced before.

"We can't change the past, but we can change our perspective. That's my job. To help shift your perspective, find out what's holding you back, recreate your mindset with the tools you find here so you live your best life. In the words of your mother, 'I stole her first fifteen years, but I want to give her the next forty living the best life she can live.'"

"She said that?" The truth and humility of that statement stops me in my tracks.

"She said much more than that." Summer smoothes her hands over an envelope with Tansy's handwriting on it.

I take a deep breath and let it out slowly. "I'm not ready."

"That's totally fine. I am curious. What has been the hardest thing to give up? Alcohol or sugar?"

"Sugar." My shoulders loosen as the subject changes to food instead of the past with my mom. "Within about three

CHAPTER TWENTY-FOUR

days, I didn't miss alcohol much. But the sugar withdrawal headaches nearly killed me."

"How are you now?"

"I sleep through the night for the first time..." My voice trails off as a memory of my mother blindsides me.

"Are you alright?"

"It's weird saying those words. I just had this memory of my mom."

"Oh?" Summer leans slightly forward, pen poised to write my thoughts.

"I remember being around twelve and my mom woke me up because she was painting our kitchen yellow at like two in the morning." I shake my head as I remember her standing on the countertop with a roller dripping on the cabinets. "She was singing and painting, music blaring."

"Manic," Summer says softly.

I cross my arms over my chest, take a deep breath, and let it out slowly. "I suppose that makes it all okay. You want me to say she was sick and didn't know better—she did her best and I should get over it."

"Has someone said that to you?"

I'm silent as I remember the paint dripping on the cabinets and without her noticing. The weary feeling of having to clean up her mess had nearly taken me to my knees that night.

"She made my life a living hell."

"You were raised by a mother who had undiagnosed and untreated bipolar disorder. She self-medicated with alcohol, and she absolutely made your life unbearable. She was very sick. It took her years to heal."

Tears sting my eyes and close my throat.

"They committed her against her will the night you left. According to her notes to you, she tried to get you back from Phyllis's house, and Phyllis called the police. Tansy told anyone who would listen that your leaving was the best gift you could have given her. She spent her life helping other people facing similar diagnoses and addictions. Food was just one of them."

Hailey.

Summer's statement sends a jolt of shock straight to my heart. I did not know my mom came after me. I can hardly breathe. In the back of my mind, I have felt so much guilt about the night I left. I numbed the guilt with anger.

"As she was dying, she wrote you this letter. It details her diagnosis. Not just mental health, everything. A complete work up so you know your medical history from her. I don't expect you to read this. You aren't required to do anything. Your mother was confident that you could never forgive her. She's dead, so your refusal to reconcile won't hurt her, only you. She just wanted you to know the whole story."

Truth's words came back to me. The fact that she had cancer and was battling to stay alive and couldn't take me. Knowing that made sense. It didn't change the past, but it changed my perspective. It drew me closer to Truth.

My father didn't know about me at all. They shunted him across the world the minute his parents found out about Tansy and their plan to elope. He had no contact with her until much later. He couldn't save me because he didn't know about me. It didn't change the past, but I could understand his absence. I no longer feel abandoned by him. My angry thoughts that he knew about me and left me no longer oppress me.

Anger isn't protecting me now. It's oppressing me. The heavy, drowning weight of it is holding me back, holding me

CHAPTER TWENTY-FOUR

down, dragging me under. The thought blares through my mind like a bolt of lightning.

"Feelings start as thoughts, Indi. We treat the thinking—we change the feelings. I want to read this." Summer pulls out a note and clears her throat. "My hope is that Indi will know that losing her was my worst nightmare. But without her strength to say what happened wasn't right—I never would have gotten treatment. She saved my life, and now I want to save hers."

"I'm not dying."

"Do you feel like you are truly living?" Summer levels that question at me like a bomb.

Tears sting my eyes. I think of sending food and money to Ben, how he holds me back, keeps chaos in my life. I think of my notebooks full of scenes that I have hidden in a closet for years. The thought of writing and publishing a book. A dream I don't allow myself to think of. I remember lonely nights in my very clean and tidy, sterile condo. My mind races to the island on my screen saver. That last thought hurts, a physical hurt that almost flattens me. "No," I whisper.

"Do you want marriage and children?"

"No." I meet her gaze. "Family is all obligation, and I'm not interested."

"Did you find that at Phyllis and Al's?" Summer's scalpel-sharp questions slice right to the core.

The question challenges my thinking. "No. I didn't. That was warm and lovely."

"So, not all family is chaos and obligation," Summer suggests.

I cross my arms over my chest. "I guess not."

Summer's eyes bore into me. "Do you want anything you don't have?"

"I want to write a book."

Where on earth did that come from? How does Summer get right into my deepest dark thoughts and drag out all this truth I haven't even acknowledged to myself? Ugh!

"What about personal relationships?"

I sigh from the depth of my soul. "I don't want children, and what man doesn't want children?"

"Many. You might be surprised. But that is enough for today. You have lots to process."

I'm not ready to quit talking, actually. I need to think. These new thoughts need to be written.

Summer hands me a wellness wheel and a beautiful leather-bound journal. "You mom left this for you. You don't have to take it, but it's yours if you want it."

It's so gorgeous that even though it's from my mom, I reach for the journal. I love that a leather string wraps around a beautiful stone on the front—as if she knew I would have secrets and it would be the best place to write them out, but that string would keep them safely inside.

Summer nods. "Children of parents with addictions often end up in similar relationships. I want you to look at the wellness wheel and figure out if you have filled all five spokes in your life."

I take the paper wheel from her. A few months ago, I would have dismissed this as silly, but I'm learning that I've been wrong. In a lot of ways, this entire process is actually healing me. I stop being so critical. Gathering the journal and the wheel, I open my backpack and tuck them inside.

Summer has the envelope from my mother. "It's yours if you want it."

I hesitate to hold out my hand.

CHAPTER TWENTY-FOUR

"Please remember that all of us here at Salt and Citrus are cheering for you to live the most fulfilling life you can. You are driven to work because you refuse to be vulnerable, and you're reacting like many people who have post-traumatic stress. You can't handle another trauma, so you have to protect yourself at all costs. For you, that means standing behind a chair and being terrified of engaging on anything but a professional level. You keep a distance from anything that could be messy. Family relationships are scary. You want a functional man in your life, but then you would have to trust him. Trusting a man in a domestic situation is the most terrifying thing of all. This was a good first session."

I blink at how concisely she has summed up my life and my thoughts. She detailed everything I thought I was carefully concealing, managing.

"We'll get to the bottom of it. I think your mom's house has another one of these journals. If you run out of pages."

"I will not enter her house." The statement iced with fear hangs between us.

Summer sits still, as if willing me to say more. "Any reason why?"

"I think our time's up."

"That's my line." Summer grins.

"Not today."

Summer nods. "Thanks for coming in. Text me when you break up with Ben. We'll talk after that. But let's rebook for the same time next week?"

"Yes."

"You want to stay with me or shop around? We have amazing therapists here."

"I'll stay with you." I give Summer a tentative smile. "If you want to put up with my insanity."

"I think you mean post-traumatic stress disorder, and I'm happy to help." Summer looks me straight in the eye.

I see there that she won't allow me to put myself down. She won't allow me to hang onto anything oppressing me. For the first time I can remember, a part of me is excited by the change I can feel coming. My thinking is shifting in a way I can't ignore. It's like a truth has been exposed, and once I know it, I can't unknow it.

I know—down to the ground—when this woman is done with me, I won't be the same person I was when I got here. I also know that I won't miss the Indi I was. I can see clearly that the anger I needed to propel me forward is oppressing me, holding me back, keeping me down. Now, it's time to let it go—and live.

―――

That night in the Hot Pools of Healing, all of us from the Friday night supper class file into the pool with their Clemons on ice. The mood is different as the women settle into the hot water.

"Something happened," I observe and sip my Clemon.

"You didn't hear?" Lark leans forward.

"No. What happened?" A trickle of fear races down my back. "Is it Hailey?"

"No. Jet has suffered a miscarriage," Lark says quietly. "We are here to plan the walk with her to the Valley of Loss."

"Ford cancelled Friday because he offered to hike in supplies so Leif could give Jet the attention she needs. Would you like to come? We leave on Thursday. It's about ten kilometers. We're going to do it over two nights."

CHAPTER TWENTY-FOUR

I think about five kilometers a day and know that ten would be absolutely no problem. Then I pause. The Indi of a few months ago would have moaned for a helicopter. "Of course. I want to walk with you all. I've never camped before."

"You'll need gear, which means shopping... and you might need a guide. I volunteer." Tamsin's face breaks into a smile of anticipation.

I make a mental note to invest in a bra that's guaranteed to be up to the challenge.

"I have a spreadsheet of what foods to prep and bring." Prairie sips her Clemon. "We leave at first light on Thursday. The Free Fall Trailhead."

My first camping trip. "I'll be there."

Chapter Twenty-Five

The Valley of Loss

While shopping for camp equipment, I look for something I can give Jet when we make it to the Valley of Loss. It's really kind of Ford to carry the gear they need and go with them.

The women remind me to take half of what I think I need. It costs a tiny fortune for the bra alone. I grin as I try on the most expensive bra I can find that zips up the front. I keep reaching for the wrong size.

After the first few pieces of clothing, slowly, I realize I'm more than one size down. Unfortunately, this bra still has a big job to do. I take a long look at myself in the mirror. At first, all I see is that I have a way to go yet, but I can see definition where there was none before. I have a waist for the first time in years. I'm a little over halfway to where I want to be. But it really isn't just about looks. I feel amazing.

CHAPTER TWENTY-FIVE

My feet don't hurt every morning when I wake up. I no longer swell with inflammation. My allergies are under control without drugs. Truth said, "Don't get fixated on a goal weight. Get fixated on a goal life." All at once, as I try on new walking pants a full size smaller than when I started, I'm excited by these new tools.

Walking every day, eating properly, and putting my health first makes my entire being better.

I look in the mirror and carefully move my head to my left shoulder. The pain is almost gone. I straighten my head and move it to the right. No pain at all.

How will I keep up with the progress if I go back?

If I go back. That thought hits me hard. I frown at myself in the mirror.

Of course, I'm going back...

But the thought of leaving Salt and Citrus makes me overwhelmingly sad. I love my new life here so much, I can't bear the thought of the long work hours in my old life. How can I go back and lose out on my precious trails with breathtaking scenery of lakes and forests? The thought of losing the Friday night suppers, especially Prairie's desserts, makes me really sad.

Alone. Never peeking at Ford as he grills red meat on a barbeque. I'm not sure I'm ready to give that up. Ever.

Plus, I started reading a book about how to structure a novel, and I had planned to work on Castaway tomorrow. Instead, I'll walk into the Valley of Loss. Even with that necessary interruption, I'm excited about working on a novel.

Jet, whom I had written off as a complete lunatic, is my reflexologist. She pushes me so gently and yet so firmly. I love my weekly sessions with her. We often have lunch, and she tells me about her plans for the nursery and the baby names they're deciding on. My heart aches for Jet. This isn't fair. She deserves to be a mother.

The word mother makes me think of my own, but I table that.

I adjust my new pack on my shoulders and think about the changes I've made in the last week that have nothing to do with weight but make me feel light all the same.

Summer dropped in just as I connected with Ben on FaceTime. She placed her homemade trail mix on the table then made a move, as if asking if I wanted her to stay or go. I waved at her to stay. It wouldn't hurt for her to be there, as it would save me explaining everything to her in the next therapy session.

Ben was as weepy and weak as I expected. He begged, then he tried to threaten. Summer raised her eyebrows as the tone of the conversation shifted. I told him it was over and not to contact me again.

He had a long list of requests. I firmly said that I was no longer available for a relationship, financial or emotional. This was a final goodbye. I wished him well.

"What can I do to change your mind?"

"Good bye, Ben." I hit the Leave button on the screen and Summer smiled.

"Good job. Very firm."

"I feel free." I closed my laptop. "Completely free." This shift made my steps lighter.

Summer checked her watch. "I have to run. I have an appointment, but I hope you have a great first camping trip."

As I pack my bags, I reflect on the following. Tansy, even though she's dead, dragged me here against my will, and it has absolutely changed my life for the better. That's the truth. As

CHAPTER TWENTY-FIVE

a hairdresser, I listen to enough rationalizing and excuses to realize when I'm giving myself a load of nonsense.

The hard facts are that Tansy saved me and gave me a father. That thought hits hard, too. He's been hovering until I'm ready to talk. I wonder what superpower Summer uses because I really feel ready to have a conversation with him about his life now.

The irony is the minute I became totally self-sufficient is the minute I needed this intervention the most. Strangely, I was doing it all and falling apart inside. I fixated on work and forgot about life. Until Ariana stepped over me to get to my chair so Elle could do her hair, I did not know I was nothing more than a hairstylist to her. I had blurred a line between client and stylist. I was watching life go by from behind my chair and somehow fooled myself I was living. I wasn't.

I hid myself in work, and I was completely terrified to actually live. All the out-of-my-control bits were so frightening that as I thought about a relationship with someone competent, it made my stomach flip with fear. What if I learned to depend on that man and he fell apart and I was back out on the front step? Screen door hanging by one hinge, in the dead of winter... wondering about—terrified about—

My throat tightens with tears. The night I stood outside my mother's door scarred me, hurt me, traumatized me to the point that I can't go through her vastly different door now. Post-traumatic stress—right—her home is stunning, and I'm still afraid. I have to face it, and I'm still not ready.

I think about the letter from Tansy and wonder what it says. Maybe I'll read it in the Valley of Loss. I did lose her. Maybe going to the valley isn't just about what we leave behind. Maybe it's about what we need to make peace with.

Suddenly, I want to feel light, not just physically light. I want my thoughts to be brighter. Negative thoughts, worst-case scenarios always plague me. I'm weary of it. It's stolen enough of my time.

What if the answer is in that letter?

I pick up the gold-coloured carabiner, the one that made me smile. I bought it for Ford as a reminder of the night he gave me one to hold my bra together.

Who knows what might need to be held together in the Valley of Loss? On that note, I clip it to my bag.

My backpack at my feet; I sit on my veranda and drink my hot coffee with heavy cream as I watch a bird have a bath in a puddle of water near the Hot Pools of Healing. Taking a deep breath, I let it out slowly. The morning sun waking the mountains is so perfect that it almost brings tears to my eyes. I take another deep breath of mountain air and realize it smells really sweet.

I savour every sip of hot coffee as my spirit settles with happiness just at the surroundings of fir trees and rocks and grass. I marvel at the fact that I can breathe through my nose for the first time since I was eighteen. Surprise thuds through me.

How can I go back to work with ammonia?

I can't. I know it with certainty. The colour we use is ammonia based, and I can't put my sinuses through it. Colours with no ammonia exist, but how could I change the entire salon to a different colour line just for one stylist? Could I create my own room somehow? No. Ammonia's a gas, and I can't use it now. It's done so much damage. I can't.

My thoughts race about work, and then I stop thinking as Ford's old truck pulls to a stop by my cabin.

CHAPTER TWENTY-FIVE

What happened to him? Why is a competent lawyer driving a rattle trap? Why is he opposed to grooming? Ugh. I can't figure him out, and it's like an itch I can't scratch. I take a final gulp of coffee and sling my backpack over my shoulder.

Jasper sits between us in the truck.

"Good morning." Ford's smile doesn't reach his eyes.

"Good morning." I can feel an alarming shift in him.

I'm quite certain he's been crying. His eyes are red rimmed, and he doesn't touch drugs or excessive amounts of alcohol, so it has to be tears. I'm not sure how to handle that. I have always lived in a world of women, and men in crisis are out of my depth.

"Thanks for the ride." I watch him out of the corner of my eye. I wonder if he'll break down here. What would I do?

"Of course." Ford puts his truck in reverse.

I watch the beads on his left wrist slide down a fraction as he moves the steering wheel. Jasper is weird too, quiet, as if reading the room. He puts his head on Ford's shoulder, and I wonder if this dog is actually part human.

"Is Hailey all right?"

"Yes. Hailey is in witness protection until she testifies and beyond."

"Oh, good."

"We moved her from your mother's, and it's better if no one knows where she is except me."

"Good idea. I'm glad she has you." I mean it.

My gaze sneaks over to him, and my heart pounds when I notice what's different about Ford. No wedding ring. My forehead creases in surprise. I want to comment on it, but I'm sure if I should. What do I have to lose?

"You aren't wearing your ring."

"Yeah."

Not the heart-to-heart I was hoping for.

"Are you all right?"

"I was at Leif and Jet's last night, and it was really hard. It brought back a lot of memories. I'm going through some—"

Ford hit the brakes, which mercifully work, as a moose wanders out of the wilderness, looks at us, then keeps walking.

"Wow. They are impressive," I breathe in awe.

"Not something you want to run into." Ford's voice is flat.

"No, of course." I shift in my seat to watch him. "You're going through some...?" I let the statement dangle between us, hoping he'll fill in the blank. He doesn't, and we don't speak as he drives again.

"We're here." Ford puts the truck in park and scratched Jasper's head.

He will not open up. Disappointment wings through me. I care, and I want to help.

Correction; I care about him, and I want to help. A warning bell in the back of my head sounds. I have always chosen broken men. I'm drawn to the broken because I know it. Or am I drawn to his amazing muscles and kindness regarding everyone around him? It's all too new. I can't decide. I don't trust myself at all. I'll run it by Summer.

Ford—if he is a train wreck, as I suspect—isn't for me. Therapy has made that very clear. My heart takes a dip of sadness at the thought. Not only is he rugged and incredibly attractive to the point it's hard to concentrate—he's a gentle but protective person. He stood between a threat and Hailey. I watched him manage that situation and put himself in harm's way—selflessly. In staff meetings, he listens to everyone with respect. It doesn't matter if they're a doctor or an

CHAPTER TWENTY-FIVE

esthetician or the cleaning staff. Everyone has an opinion, and he listens to them all. Patiently.

I wonder how he is with his own staff, and I bet it's the same. Leif works for him, and Ford's carrying Leif's wife's belongings to complete this walk to the Valley of Loss. Clearly, he cares. This isn't about money. This is about people.

From his actions, I can tell we have the same philosophy. Love the work, love the people, and the money takes care of itself.

I'm falling for him, and it's scary and exhilarating all at the same time.

Together, we get out of the truck and join the group at the trailhead. Everyone hugs each other, and when Jet and Leif show up, we shed lots of tears as the women of my cooking class, and me, surround her with love and hugs. Tears fill my eyes as Ford pulls her into a hug that lifts her right off her feet. He cries with her. Openly. I lose it.

Lark puts her arm around me. "It's okay, honey."

This love for his friend is pure. When he carefully puts Jet down, he gives Leif a bear hug. It's more awkward than the hug between Ford and Jet.

"So sorry, man," Ford says.

"Thanks for coming."

"I wouldn't be anywhere else." Ford clips a tent to his pack. Leif picks it up and puts it on Ford's back. Ford doesn't seem fazed by the weight of it. The women, not just me, I notice, watch him adjust the strap across his very broad chest. Lark and I sigh together at the sight of him and catch each other's eye. I feel like I have known Lark my entire life. We read each other like a book.

"Thank you for coming. It means a lot to me that you're all here." Jet wipes her tears with the edge of her shirt.

"Of course, we're here, darlin'." Lark gives her an extra hug. Jet has a tiny backpack that Leif takes from her and hangs off of his. Jet will carry nothing into the Valley of Loss except her pain. Leif will carry his pain, too, but also everything they need for the hike. But he doesn't carry it grudgingly. He carries it as if looking after her in this time of vulnerability is a gift, a blessing. My heart opens up at the thought of that. Was Al like this with Phyllis? I don't know. They hadn't dealt with a tragedy this deep. Seeing this gives me hope that true love exists. It's strong enough for the heartbreaking times.

I watch the group get organized and realize that it's as if this wild and difficult land makes men and women rise to the occasion, but in different ways. It doesn't bother me that we prepped all the food for the men, but they're doing the heavy lifting. We're a well-oiled machine and are happy to use our strengths on behalf of each other.

I take a deep breath and let it out slowly as we set off down the trail. They will have to wrestle the food spreadsheet from Prairie. She attached a special pan to her backpack, and I wonder what she plans to make on this trail with that pan. I eat primal food, but I no longer get hungry, nor do I crave anything.

Leif moves a piece of wood from the trail to make an easy path for Jet. At that moment, I'm struck like a bolt of lightning. What does that feel like? To have a partner who's prepared to handle the heavy parts when you need that?

I hold my breath, then look away as Leif kisses Jet and wipes her tears with his thumb.

The mountains and trees behind them are so beautiful, it all looks too intimate. The love between them is so pure, so bright, so perfect that my heart breaks at the thought of them not having a baby together.

CHAPTER TWENTY-FIVE

Leif and Jet continue down the trail. They can walk together at this point. The rest of us follow, with Ford behind us. We walk in silence for hours. I can't tear my eyes from the amazing scenery in front of me. We pass a mountain stream that trickles and sings to our left. The beauty of the Canadian Rockies is awe-inspiring. Stunning. As the sun climbs in the sky, we all find our rhythm. My backpack isn't too heavy, and I feel for Ford. He's carrying one of the tents.

As the day wears on and we all hit our stride, I seem to walk at the same pace as Lark, which makes me happy. Lark, with her darlin'- and honey-peppered speech, warms my heart.

"I've never actually been camping," I confess.

"Oh, I think you'll love it. The place we're staying tonight actually has a hot spring and fresh water."

"Oh, good. I wasn't sure how this worked." I was rationing my water, and now I guzzle it with zeal.

"Where we are going is beautiful," Lark says softly.

"You've been there before?"

"Yes, when your mother died." Lark doesn't beat around the bush. "Tansy helped me with a tough situation in my life, and when she died, I needed to come to the Valley of Loss to process it."

The old me of three months ago wouldn't have asked. I wanted to hear nothing positive about Tansy. However, being surrounded by her accomplishments, I realize I froze her in time. People change. I had already changed a lot since coming here. The night I left wasn't here anymore. It was over twenty years later.

"I don't want to pry, but how did she help? Only if you feel comfortable."

Lark stops walking, takes her water bottle, and drinks deeply. "I almost lost everything in the divorce. Everything.

My kids, my home, my pet. Everything. My ex had a shark lawyer. The month before the paperwork was to be filed, Tansy knew something was wrong. She had a meeting with me and when she heard I was going to lose my kids because of a really stupid mistake five years before the divorce, she lost it. She asked your father if he would represent me. For free. I was on the verge of being homeless, so she moved me into her house that day."

Lark's eyes fill with tears. "Your parents were a force to be reckoned with. She told me to stop working and focus on the trial. Your father was amazing. I was so scared, but your mom kept saying, 'You are not losing your kids. You are not. There is no greater pain.'"

A lump forms in my throat as Lark speaks not only her truth, but Tansy's. No matter how much I tried to deny it all these years, Tansy's truth is my own. That thought just about drops me to my knees.

I try to dispel the idea and can't. I can almost feel the letter in my backpack pressed against my back. I need the whole truth.

Tansy came after you, but I wouldn't let her in.

This letter is from your mom, to explain… she can't give you back your first fifteen years, but she wants to give you the rest of your life—we can't change the past, but we can change the thoughts because it's the thoughts that drive the feelings. We can change perspective.

You don't know the whole truth.

Phyllis's and Summer's words swirl in my mind.

My eyes fill with tears as I think of my mother's words to Lark.

You are not losing your kids. There is no greater pain.

CHAPTER TWENTY-FIVE

The woman I left on the couch in the north end of Winnipeg is no longer alive. The feelings she brought up in my heart are raw and painful, and I need to acknowledge them and heal. I thought she had brought me here for my weight. I was wrong. I'm here for my heart and soul.

Together, Lark and I walk again in silence. Lark's words caused a shift. Her perspective had shone a light into my past and revealed something new. I had focused so intently on my pain, my suffering that I had given no thought to my mother.

Shame burns in me as I remember refusing to be part of a reconciliation when Tansy reached out before; when Phyllis gently suggested I try to reconcile and I shut it down and worked harder. It is no coincidence that the year she reached out; I expanded my salon and buried myself in work.

As we round a bend, we find the entire group has stopped in a clearing. Just as Lark said, there's a massive hot spring and Prairie fills three canteens at a natural spring.

Ford drops his backpack beside mine. "I hear this is your first camping experience."

"It is." My heart flutters with excitement at his words, his nearness.

"Do you want to learn how to put up a tent?" He smiles, and my heart melts into a puddle.

I remind myself that only a few months ago; I was not a sap. I was a hard-edged businesswoman with a business plan. I don't know where that girl went. Honestly; I didn't miss her.

Chapter Twenty-Six

Hot Pools of Healing

"Sure." I try not to sound like a grade-six schoolgirl. I try to be casual and fail.

Together, we lay out one of the tents. It's huge. I can't imagine how heavy this was for him. He places the stakes in the loops and bangs them in with the blunt end of a hatchet. I thread the tent pole into the silver joint and create a long pole. Then I thread that through the flap to meet him on the other side of the tent.

"Sorry you had to carry the tents. I hope they aren't too heavy. Do you want me to carry it for a bit tomorrow?"

"We won't take tents tomorrow. It's no problem." Ford shrugs. "I often hike weighted to be able to do this."

"Ah. That's good." I have no idea what weighted hikes are, but he seems to enjoy them.

CHAPTER TWENTY-SIX

I thread another pole through the tent, then we bend it to slide into the flap at the ground. As we both stand up, our eyes meet across the tent.

"Are you alright?" I ask tentatively.

"I was supposed to come here a few months ago on the anniversary of the finalizing of my divorce. I couldn't come here yet. I wasn't ready to fully process that loss until now," Ford says simply as he comes around the side and unzips the tent.

We go inside and start making beds. When we finish making the last bed, Ford sits cross-legged. He takes out a picture and hands it to me. "This is what I'm leaving at the Valley of Loss tomorrow."

I take the picture in my hands and frown in confusion. The man and woman holding a baby in a hospital look foreign to me. The man looks like Ford, but he has a super-short haircut and wears a pressed shirt. Clean-shaven, he wears no beads on his wrist. How is that shirt pressed? I am convinced Ford has no idea what an iron is and, if he stumbled across one, he would use it to hold open a door.

The woman is supermodel gorgeous with a mane of three-coloured hair, perfectly placed balayage that screams wealth. The stylist threaded copper through the warm deep auburn and level-eight highlights that only a certain type of human can pull off. Her eyelashes are perfect. She has beautiful makeup on her perfect, radiant face and looks like she just stepped out of an expensive spa, not survived the rigours of childbirth. The baby is newborn, with a little band on the tiny wrist. This power couple looks like they have everything.

"Boy or girl?" I squint as if I can see a clue in the photo.

"Girl," Ford whispers. His hand shakes a little as he takes the picture back.

"Is she with your wife?" Lark's conversation about almost losing her kids in the divorce strikes fear in my heart.

"No." Ford wipes tears from his eyes. "Madison Mae died, Indi. She died at the age of four. Three years ago. Of cancer. I died that day, too."

"Oh, Ford." Tears fill my eyes. I reach for him and hold onto him as hard as I can. "I am so sorry."

He is like hanging onto a tree. He's so rigid with pain. As a sob bursts out of him, one bursts out of me—like a storm that has been brewing and needs to erupt. A bolt of sadness and hurt that is breaking us both. I know he can't bear this pain, but I hope sharing it helped lessen it.

Finally, we pull apart.

"Sorry, I haven't talked about this to anyone but a therapist and your mom. Tansy got it."

"I am so sorry." My throat closes again at the mention of Tansy.

Had she wept like this?

A curl of grief snakes around my heart and tightens. I know, suddenly, what the beads are. I've seen moms with children being treated for cancer. They have these beads on necklaces. Each colour represents a surgery, a needle, anything that hurts that child in treatment is recorded.

I reach out and press my fingertips to the bracelet Ford wears. "I am so sorry for your loss."

He takes a deep breath and lets it out slowly. "Melinda really didn't have a choice but to leave, you know. I lost my job. I was a mess. I couldn't get out of bed. Finally, I received treatment for depression, but by that time, I had neglected my wife so badly that she'd found another man. I have to take responsibility for the divorce. I fell apart and couldn't hold it together for her. When Melinda said she was leaving,

CHAPTER TWENTY-SIX

I didn't blame her. I was relieved when she left because I couldn't bear her pain and mine. We had everything—and I mean everything—and we lost it all. I couldn't face it."

My heart splinters with sympathy. I can't imagine what it would feel like to not only watch a child get sick but die. It was unimaginable. "I am so sorry."

"Yeah. Me too."

We sit in quiet silence for a while.

"So, I'm here to say goodbye to Melinda and to commit to living some form of life. I have a big decision to make, and I've been putting it off... I have to decide—"

"What decision?"

"Carter wants me to head the legal team that will purchase and set up Salt and Citrus in Belize."

"He told me about that."

"Yeah, I decided to sell the restaurant to Leif and Jet, so I am available to handle the transaction." Ford twists the beads on his wrist. "I originally turned it down because we buried Madison in Canada."

My heart dips to my toes at the thought of him leaving.

Prairie calls everyone for appetizers.

I wipe my tears on my shirt as quickly as I can.

Both lost in thought, we quickly make up a tent for Ford. He brought his own, likely so he can have privacy as he processes the feelings that will surface tomorrow. I fluff his pillow and adjust his sleeping bag. I feel a tingle of anticipation as I look up and he's watching me make his bed. It seems completely innocent and yet somehow intimate.

"Prairie gets irritated if you don't come when she calls."

"We can't ruffle Prairie's feathers. She'll cut us off the Hollandaise sauce."

Ford smiles a sad smile and holds the tent open for me.

Together we leave the tent, and Lark comes by to give Ford and me a hug.

Had she heard us weeping?

I'm not sure. Prairie hovers with a saucepan of appetizers. The rest of the women put peppers, onions, and mushrooms into a big frying pan. A bunch of steaks were ready to go on the fire.

"I think we need some wine." Tamsin breaks the tension as she grins and pulls out a bag of wine from her backpack.

I could kiss her.

"This is a perfect pairing with rib eye."

I swoon with delight. My favourite meal. Ford hands me a glass of wine, and we smile at each other as we clink our tin glasses together. All of us have a glass of wine on an empty stomach, and we replace weeping with laughing. We dry our eyes and fill our plates. Prairie passes through the group with a hearty helping of Hollandaise sauce for everyone. I can't believe I get to eat like this and lose weight. It's a miracle.

As I sit with this group of people, all here mourning different things, I feel a lightness of spirit because I'm not alone. We all have pain from our past, but together, we can bear it and carry on. Lark finishes her plate of food then slides her arm around me, and I put my arm around her. Ford refills my cup with merlot, and I think that this is absolutely the best night of my life—sweaty from the trail, physically exhausted from hiking, eating primal food with Hollandaise sauce custom made by Prairie. I suddenly understand the allure of camping. No one has phones out. There's no service here.

We sit around a fire like our ancestors did for thousands of years, drawing strength from each other, finding peace in the snap of the sparks. The stars are brighter in the sky over our

CHAPTER TWENTY-SIX

heads. They seem so close we could reach out and pluck them from the black velvet of the sky.

As my eyes travel over the faces in front of me, I make a conscious thought to store this memory in my heart.

It hits me that I'm here because my mom forced me out of my comfort zone. She knew from Phyllis and Estee that I was watching life from behind a chair. It's time to get in the chair myself—get ready for the big moments, even though, with the good comes the bad. Behind the chair, I had complete control. I knew exactly what my tools did—every chemical, every blade, every iron. There was no chaos behind the chair. It was ordered. Right to the minute, I had complete control of my life.

But I didn't have this. Nights of companionship with friends—friends that I cultivated myself. I remember Ariana stepping over me after I hurt my back, and the memory still stings.

At the end of the day, she was a client who needed a service. I had put all this other meaning into the relationship that didn't even exist. So, in reality, there was pain behind the chair, too. Living means the potential to get hurt, but standing back, staying behind the chair, is a certain kind of hurt. It was lonely. That truth slices into my heart.

I watch Ford add more wood to the fire, and I think about the letter in my backpack, my name written in Tansy's handwriting. Maybe I'll read it in the Valley of Loss because I know I'm here to grieve. Not just my mom. Everything. The actions of others had stolen my father from me until now.

I resolve to read that letter tomorrow.

After the men secure the food so no bears will be attracted to our campsite; we all make our way to the hot spring. I sink into the water with relief. We're going to the Valley of Loss tomorrow; but tonight, as my friends chatter in the hot spring around me, we find hope in our company, in our shared grief and pain. As the fireflies dance around us, my eyes meet Ford's across the water. Steam swirls between us, blocking out his face for a second. I don't look away, and he reappears.

He smiles at me, and I smile back. He takes a sip of merlot, and I do too. I'm not sure what the future holds for me. I knew that there was a big difference between being broken because of your own actions and being broken because of circumstances beyond your control. He was destroyed with grief because of circumstances out of his control. I understand that. The red flag I thought applied is permanently put down.

As he moves closer to me, my heart pounds with anticipation. He puts his wine down and reaches for mine. My heart nearly explodes out of my chest.

He places his hands on my shoulders and leans in. "Indi, just move with me over here."

"Alright." I hope with my entire heart that my teeth aren't purple. I want to say I'll go anywhere with him, but my mouth is completely dry with anticipation.

His hands are hard on my shoulders as he moves me to a different place in the hot spring. Quickly, making no sound at all, he goes back to where I was sitting and, lightning fast, he grabs a snake. I'm horrified as I realize the snake was lurking near the back of my head!

I feel a scream tearing up out of my soul, but I stifle it with every ounce of inner strength I can muster. The mood in the hot spring is calm, and me screaming over a snake is hardly welcome. Ford takes off into the darkness with the snake, and I don't know what he's going to do, but in that second, through a haze of terror, I fall head over heels, completely in

CHAPTER TWENTY-SIX

love with Ford. Like all the way, hopelessly in love, which is ridiculous. Sternly, I tell myself I'm being the sappiest sap of all time.

He comes back and gets into the hot spring as if nothing happened. He brings my wine and his over to me. "You alright?"

I open my mouth to speak, and I can't.

He puts the wine down and reaches for me. "It's fine. It's gone. Good for you for not screaming."

"I'm... terrified of—"

"Most people are." Ford shrugs, then wraps his arms around me. "Aw, you're trembling. It's okay. It's gone. It wouldn't have hurt you, anyway."

I shudder and can't stop, but his arms tighten, and I don't try to. This is heaven, and I want to stay right here forever.

"You're safe here. It's okay," Ford whispers into my ear.

"Stay close," I whisper back.

"I will."

Ford gives me another hard hug. I don't pull away, and to my delight, neither does he.

Chapter Twenty-Seven

Sulphur and Stone

The next morning, the smell of camp coffee and bacon wakes me out of a dead sleep. I have never slept in a tent, and I am stiff in places I never knew I had. My neck and shoulders ache from the hard ground under my mat that promised a better sleep. I look across the empty sleeping bags and see a tuft of curly black hair hanging over a pillow. Only Lark is still sleeping in the tent. Everyone else is gone.

I crawl out of the tent quietly and cautiously. Eyes on the ground for any slithery creatures, I notice the camp is in full swing. Sunshine breaks through the leaves on the trees. The dew sparkles on every green leaf and blade of grass. Leif and Jet sit by the fire, her back against his chest, and he cradles her as she sips coffee. Their grief is so intense and so personal, I leave them alone and instead move toward Prairie, who is cooking up a storm.

CHAPTER TWENTY-SEVEN

The smell of bacon makes my mouth water. The rest of the hikers are in the hot spring with tin cups of coffee in their hands.

"Good morning." Prairie smiles brightly as she hands me a cup of coffee.

"This smells amazing." I add cream and take a deep breath of mountain air.

"Nothing in the world is better than camp coffee." Prairie smiles. "Everyone is in the hot springs."

"When it's my turn to cook—"

"It's always my turn to cook," Prairie corrects me as she returns to her bacon masterpiece.

"But you must get a break. I really don't feel like I'm pulling my weight."

"This is how I show love." Prairie replies so openly and honestly that I have no response. "I never wash a dish. So, it's a good trade-off."

"I will wash up, I promise."

"Get in here," Tamsin calls from the steamy spring. "It's the only way to survive another day on the trail."

What I love about Tamsin is she can take a sulphur smelling hot spring and make it sound like a decadent spa experience. The way her head tilts back, you would think this is a five-star resort.

I sink into the water, take a sip of coffee, then after being sure no snake is lurking, I place my coffee cup on a rock so I can submerge my head.

In my entire life, I have never felt like this. Completely at peace in my own skin. I still have weight to lose, but the weight I'm carrying is less about my body and more about my mind. I am starting to think if I could come to terms with things, the rest might take care of itself. It's weird because Summer and therapy were part of the plan that I resisted the most. But she has made massive inroads into my thinking—why I reach for wine after work, why I date dysfunctional men, why I made work my focus in the first place. As she peels back the layers, I realize these responses were all failed coping mechanisms. But what is the right thing to replace them with?

Hiking miles with good friends is definitely not something I ever thought of as a certain form of therapy, yet it is.

My muscles are sore, but they are sore because they're getting stronger. My body is tired from the walk, but my mind is refreshed. I had some wine last night but not a lot, and I am clear and bright this morning. The people I'm with need nothing from me. That in itself makes me feel completely uplifted.

I never want to leave here. The thought shocks me right to my core. I never expected that.

The beauty and peace around me is all so perfect that my heart sings with happiness.

After a long soak and breakfast, the camp mobilizes. No big packs, only our lunches and, for me, the letter from my mom. We will be back to the camp and the hot spring that night. The valley is only five kilometers away.

Lighter physically yet heavier in heart, we start down the trail to the Valley of Loss. I walk with Lark. Ford is behind us again. We seem to have the same speed, and I'm happy about that.

"How is it today, honey?"

"I wish I could say I'm ready to read the letter from my mom. I think I will, but I'm not sure." I take a deep breath of clean mountain air and let it out slowly. "I just can't get past something inside me." My chest tightens with sadness.

CHAPTER TWENTY-SEVEN

"It'll come, honey. It all takes time. That's why the commitment is for six months." Lark stops to take a deep swig of water from her bottle.

"What about you?" I step over a root.

"I have a list to make peace with in this valley every year." Lark puts back her water bottle. "I make peace with my mistakes and forgive myself for them. I silently call it the Valley of Peace, not the Valley of Loss. Some losses you just can't heal from, but some you can make peace with. This trek is good because sometimes I need to remember how far I've come so I can keep moving forward."

"Wow."

Lark shrugs. "The biggest thing you need to learn here is how to prioritize self-care. How to slow down and examine what's wrong and what's right. Everything else sorts itself out. Your mind is powerful. You'll get there, and you'll cope differently, and you'll heal."

"I wish I had that confidence."

"That's why you're here. No one does at first." Lark lets out her wild laugh.

"That's why we bring you, Lark," Ford calls from the back of the group. "That manic laugh will scare every bear in a six-mile radius."

The group laughs.

"Or maybe it's your humming," I grumble in mock disapproval. "Honestly, I love you, but the humming makes me crazy."

Lark isn't affected in the least. "You'd miss it if it were gone, honey!"

I'm pretty sure I'll never know because Lark is like a sister I never had and never knew I needed until now. All of them are, but Lark is my P. Volve instructor, and she's seen me at my grunting, sweaty worst. Estee was in that role for years, but babies and responsibilities have made our paths diverge. Now, this singing, drawling girl is charting my path to recovery.

However, as I look back over all the years of being a workaholic, I am humble enough to admit I need help, and this crazy girl beside me is exactly what I never knew I needed. Even as that thought slips through my mind, I smile as I am temporarily blinded by the sun glinting off Tamsin's sparkly visor. I hear Prairie's sauce pan clank against her canteen, and I'm home, all-the-way-down-to-the-ground home in a way I never have been before.

Lark lets out that crazy laugh again at something Ford said, then she starts humming—again. I don't know if I would miss it if it were gone, but I don't want to find out.

Chapter Twenty-Eight

Truth and Peace

The Valley of Loss—or Peace, depending on what the person is processing—takes my breath away. I hear the waterfall before we get there. As I walk into the valley, I'm aware of the change in the people with me. A hush takes over the group as if this setting is a place of reverence. For them, it is.

We make our way around the side of the lake to a place with different trees planted in different stages of growth. In the back, closest to the waterfall, is a beautiful weeping willow that sways gently in the breeze. It warms my heart to see it.

Everyone stands back as Leif and Jet move to an empty space, and Leif brings out a spade and digs a hole. Jet has tears in her eyes as she holds a pair of baby shoes. My heart breaks as I look at the tiny shoes in her hands. As I cling to my friends, sobbing, I am so grateful I could be part of this. I love Jet. I am moved to tears again as she kneels beside a sapling that's ready to be planted.

Lark nudges me as my father and Truth step into the valley. Truth stands closest to Jet. My father stands closest to Leif.

It hits me that Jet and Leif don't have parents here, and silently, Truth and Carter stand in for them. The love I feel for Truth and Carter deepens and is rooted in respect. They are just tremendously good people, and I am overwhelmed with gratitude that they are finally in my life.

I am not sure what will happen next, but a silence settles on this knot of people I consider my own.

Leif speaks. "Today, we acknowledge our first-born child, whom we would have called Oaks. We didn't get to meet him, but we loved him with all our hearts. We are planting this oak tree in his memory."

Jet wipes tears from her eyes and places the baby shoes in the hole. Then together, they add a layer of dirt. Jet sobs, and we all move to her to form a circle.

When Jet picks up the tree, Leif puts his big hands on hers. Everyone places their hands on Leif and Jet in the most beautiful act of solidarity I've ever seen. My father's face is soft with sympathy. Ford's eyes are red rimmed as he places his hand—the hand with the bracelet—on Leif's heavy shoulder. A sob crawls up me as I realize that of all of us here, Ford knows this pain intimately. Looking at that bracelet, I can't pull my eyes away from him. He wipes his eyes with the tail of his shirt, and I can't help myself. I move toward him, and together we stand by Leif, holding hands. It feels right.

Truth, Lark, and all the women put a hand on Jet's back as she and Leif place the oak tree in the hole and settle the dirt around it.

CHAPTER TWENTY-EIGHT

"We will come here to remember you. We loved you so much, Oaks," Jet whispers as she pats the last bit of earth around the bottom of the tree.

Leif helps Jet to her feet.

Did my mother weep like this when I said no? I think she did. My heart breaks again.

Ford gives my hand a gentle squeeze before he lets it go. He goes to the lake, fills a big bottle with water, and hands it to Jet to water the tree. He is so kind and gentle with her that my eyes fill with tears again. Once the tree is watered, Ford hugs her hard. He hugs Leif in that awkward way that men show emotion.

As Truth comes to me to put her arm around me, I lay my head on her shoulder.

No one says anything as Leif and Jet's tears are wiped away by their closest friends. It hits me as I watch their grief that I have spent my whole life focused on what I lost that night I left my mom, but not once, not one time, did I think about her loss.

Every time she reached out and I said no, did she come here to grieve?

My father comes to me and stands by Truth. "Please come with us."

The three of us walk to a big weeping willow, the first tree I noticed when I got to the lake. It is so pretty. The sun shines on it, and the wind plays with the boughs as they sweep the forest floor.

"Your mother planted this tree eight years ago. For you," Truth says softly.

Eight years ago, when she was doing some step, I don't know which one.

I swallow a hot lump of tears at the memory of Phyllis's face as she tried to reason with me.

"She was on the verge of starting Salt and Citrus, but she had to come to terms with the idea that she had lost you permanently." My father doesn't hold back. "Her home belongs to you, no matter what you choose to do with her clinic. She said that she could finally provide the home you deserved. She also thought that since she was gone, you could enjoy it without worrying about her letting you down. She wanted you to know her diagnosis so you understand that she did her best with what she had." Carter's tone is soft.

I know he feels terrible about how things worked out. So do I. My heart hurts at my father's words. I curse myself for losing these past eight years. I take my necklace, hold the stone to my nose, and take a deep smell of Sunshine in a Bottle. The sweet mandarin and earthy oak scents immediately make tears come to my eyes as I think about that perfect day. I'm ready to read the letter.

"We'll leave you here for a moment to reflect," Truth says gently. "We're taking Jet back with us because Leif says she's too tired for the journey home."

"How?"

"You can drive here, but we always hike it."

"Ah."

"I suppose you want to hop in the Land Rover with us?" Truth asks.

"No. I don't, actually." I smile at Truth. "This is my first camping trip, and I love it."

I take off my day pack and pull out the letter from my mom. "Before we go, I think I'll read this."

Truth's eyes fill with tears as she takes a step back from me. Carter puts his arm around her. I settle under the beautiful

CHAPTER TWENTY-EIGHT

sweeping boughs of the tree and carefully slide my finger under the flap of the envelope.

Dear Indi,

Thank you for reading this note.

I want you to know that I love you and I am so sorry about the first fifteen years we had together.

The night you left, I followed you, and Phyllis took me to the emergency room.

That was the worst and best night of my life. They properly diagnosed me with bipolar disorder, and I thought I could get you back as soon as I got better. Unfortunately, because of my alcohol addiction, that took far longer than I expected.

Please know that if I could go back and fix it, I would have gotten treatment much sooner. I did not know I was sick. I just thought I was really happy and really sad and never knew when those times would hit.

I am so sorry that your first fifteen years were so tragic.

Your strength saved me.

As I read those words, I gasp. I thought I had been so weak, but she calls it strong. I can't believe it.

If you hadn't left, nothing would have changed.

Please take this time to fully heal. I hope you are here for the entire six months to create the beautiful, happy, full life you deserve.

I love you with all my heart.

Mom

PS. I made Sunshine in a Bottle for you. When I smell that tangerine oil, I remember you hate even a speck of white pith on your orange segment. Hopefully, you eat it now. It's good for you.

Oh, Indi. I miss you. I love you.

I love you with all my heart,

Mom

PSS. I know you've had tremendous success with your salon. I'm proud of you. But if you are ready for a change, please head the Salt and Citrus Cay development in Belize. Handpick the most honest-hearted and loving people. I know you can do it.

Mom

As the wind moves the weeping willow boughs around me, I come to terms with the fact that my mother wasn't a bad person. She was a very sick person. Untreated bipolar disorder with an addiction to alcohol is a difficult diagnosis to get over. Tansy Blyss was stronger than I ever knew. She did the best with what she had, and she had very little. She had less than nothing.

All the guilt I felt from that night lightens as I read, Your strength saved me. If you hadn't left, nothing would have changed. My heart both breaks and heals with those words.

"I love you too," I whisper into the heart of the weeping willow tree. "I love you too."

I read the letter again, and I can't stop the tears as they well up in my eyes. I take a deep breath of the oil Sunshine in a Bottle again and let that scent settle all through me. I smile at the smell of tangerine and can almost taste that naked orange segment she handed me under the leaves of an oak tree. I still don't eat the white pith. Instead, I carefully peel it off just like she used to. Maybe next time, I'll eat it.

The scent of Sunshine in a Bottle fills a hole in my heart that was torn the night I left.

Pressing my forehead to the trunk of the beautiful weeping willow, I think I should come back with an oak tree. That was our perfect day. I get why she planted the weeping willow. Tansy needed a tree to represent her loss. But I need to plant

CHAPTER TWENTY-EIGHT

an oak tree here to represent what I have lost and found. I lost my mom, but I gained my father and my aunt.

Carefully, I fold up the letter and place it back in the envelope, then tuck that envelope into my daypack and stand. I give the weeping willow tree a hug, which should feel ridiculous, but it doesn't.

As I part the branches, my father engulfs me in a hug so tight I can't breathe.

"We will get through this," he says.

Truth joins us, wrapping her arms around us both.

"Once I get home, I'll go into my mom's house, and if you come with me, I'll tell you what happened. Then I think I can let it go." My voice shakes.

Your strength saved me.

My father lets me go, but Truth pulls me into a tight hug.

"That's a great idea." Truth gives me a hard squeeze.

"Once I get back, maybe we can make a plan to do that."

"Of course." Carter pats my shoulder. "Whenever you are ready, I am here for you."

"Me too, sweet girl. But this is where we leave you. See you when you return."

"Thank you."

"I'm proud of you." Truth kisses my cheek.

"Me too." My father smiles at me, and together, they go to Leif and Jet.

Out of the corner of my eye, I see Ford sitting by a birch tree. He wipes his eyes, and my heart goes out to him. Gathering my courage, I make my way over to him. He looks up at me.

"I planted this tree for my daughter the day my divorce was finalized." Ford slides his fingertip over the peeling bark of the birch tree. "Every year, I write Madison a letter about what she missed and how much I love her. Every year, I place another bead on this bracelet to remind myself of her life."

"When did you start doing that?"

"Her first hospital visit." Ford points to a black bead then names off what each bead signifies. "Chemo, needles, surgery, every hurt documented."

I cry openly and can't stop. "I am so sorry."

"So am I." Ford wipes his eyes and gets to his feet. "How are you?"

"A mess."

Ford nods, and I can't stop myself. I put my arms around him, and he puts his arms around me, and we hold on to each other. I shake with emotion. He does too. I take a deep breath, and so does he.

"I don't know what to say except I'm so sorry," I repeat.

"Me too," Ford says.

Finally, we pull ourselves together and step apart.

Ford takes a gold ring from his pocket, digs a hole near the tree, and drops the ring inside. I'm certain it's his wedding ring. I gulp at the implication of that.

We stand silently by the tree, then Ford speaks. "Your father wants me to head the legal department of Salt and Citrus Cay, but how can I leave her? How can I go? It seems impossible."

"I wish I had words of advice, but I am such a train wreck, I'm certainly in no place to tell you how to move forward."

Ford nods. "Yes, we're supposed to move forward. I don't know how either. It comes back to this—why should I have an amazing life on Salt and Citrus Cay when my daughter can't?"

"Survivor's guilt?" I ask quietly.

"Crippling survivor's guilt," Ford agrees.

"You should talk to your therapist."

"I have."

"You should again."

Ford sighs.

"I know. I tried to refuse, but it was part of my terms and conditions."

Ford nods. "I think it's time to go."

"Is Leif going with Jet?"

"Yes, he won't leave her side. He's going back with Carter and Truth."

"They're in very good hands."

Chapter Twenty-Nine

Heavy Weight

On the last leg of the journey, Ford picks up my pack and places it gently on my shoulders. It's odd, but I kind of instinctively know where he is in the group at all times. I notice his gaze on me more than once.

"Are you sure this isn't too heavy?" he murmurs.

"I'm fine." I shift things so the pack rests against my back more comfortably.

"I'm glad Leif could go back with Jet. I was worried it was too soon for her." Ford picks up his pack and sets it on a log.

"I could lift that up for you," I offer.

"I doubt it." Ford grins as he tightens the strap across his chest.

I move to do the same thing, but my breasts are too big—not big in a good way. I would love them to shrink, but they stubbornly refuse.

CHAPTER TWENTY-NINE

Ford moves closer and adjusts the straps so they're higher on my pack. "I think they just shifted down. This is how women adjust these."

I blush like a schoolgirl in grade six. "Thanks."

Back at the trailhead, husbands wait to greet their wives, except for Lark, Ford, and me. Once Lark leaves, it's just Ford and me. Ford puts his pack in the back of his truck, then lifts mine in. We both hear honking.

"Who would be honking?" No sooner are the words out of my mouth when a pink sports car stops by us. A beautiful woman with hundreds of dollars' worth of highlights, lowlights, lip filler, and Botox slides out of the front seat. Her face crumples as she stands by the car.

"Are you alright?" I move toward her. I wonder if she's lost or hurt.

She smells amazing, like she just stepped out of a luxury spa. I feel like a sweaty beast in her presence.

Why am I comparing us?

"Ford." The woman brushes past me and puts her hands on Ford's shoulders.

Ford takes a step back. "Melinda, what's going on?"

"I—I think something's wrong."

The blood drains from Ford's face. "What?"

"I don't know if I lost the baby or if—"

"Where is Derek?"

Melinda breaks down sobbing. "In Europe. He had a deal to broker, and only he could do it."

"Your mom?" Ford keeps her at arm's length.

"In Bora Bora." Melinda weeps harder.

Ford's eyes meet mine as he holds her. "Are you in pain?"

"Yes." She presses her face into his shoulder. "I need help, and you're the only person I trust with Zoe. You know how I am with hospitals... I just need your help."

"Right." Ford helps her into the passenger side of her car, then turns to me. "This is a massive imposition."

I wipe sweat from my brow. "I'm happy to help."

"Really?" Ford frowns. "You don't even know what I'm about to ask."

"You saved me from a snake, and now I am in your debt."

Ford shakes his head, and worry etches his face. "Melinda and I parted on good terms. But her husband isn't so keen on our relationship. He doesn't get it. It would help if you stayed with us. When he gets back, if there is a chaperone—I know that sounds ancient and ridiculous—it would put his mind at ease, and I will need help with Zoe."

"You're concerned about your ex-wife's husband's mind being at ease?"

"Yes. Once we get Melinda sorted out, I'll tell you everything. Zoe is barely two, and I don't know if Melinda will need surgery. I need your help." Ford's eyes seem desperate.

"I'm in." I wouldn't walk away from him in this situation for anything. No fear there.

Together we stand by Melinda's car with a weeping almost-two-year-old in the back seat, a sobbing Melinda in the front seat. We're two bewildered, sweaty humans standing by the car.

Suddenly, I realize again that I'm not consumed with work and standing safely behind the chair anymore. This won't be a half hour appointment after which everyone will go their separate ways. This has the potential to get very messy. A jealous husband, a teething toddler—yikes. But it means being with Ford.

CHAPTER TWENTY-NINE

Ford shoots me a concerned look. "I can get Lark or someone else if you want to stay out of this."

"Why would I want to stay out of this?"

Relief replaces the worry on Ford's face. "Thanks, I'll take her straight to emergency. There's no time to lose."

I watch easygoing Ford shift into high gear.

"I'll follow." You anywhere, I want to add, but I don't.

Chapter Thirty

A Toddler and a Team

Watching Ford carry Melinda into the emergency room while I come behind him with a weeping Zoe in my arms is a completely foreign experience to me. He handles the staff with respect, but his concern is evident. I ask myself six million times why they aren't together. He's so gentle with her. It makes me jealous then mad at myself.

We aren't on a grade-six playground!

"She's just waiting to go into ultrasound now." Ford takes Zoe from me, and she calms right down.

"Hey, Zoe, sweetie!" Ford jiggles her in his arms. "There should be a bottle in her bag."

I search through the diaper bag and find it.

"If you could feed her, Mel wants me in the ultrasound with her. She's terrified it's ectopic."

I knew about the deadliness of an ectopic pregnancy. One of our stylists had one. She had tried for a year to get pregnant,

CHAPTER THIRTY

and it absolutely devastated her. She quit cutting hair after. After losing her baby, she couldn't bear to work on clients with healthy babies.

My heart goes out to Melinda, and my respect for Ford shoots up to a whole new level. "I hope not."

"I hope not too. Sometimes, in a healthy pregnancy, there can be some bleeding. We'll see what the doctors say. Do you know how to bottle-feed a two-year-old?"

"Yes." I actually do. I've bottle-fed Estee's kids.

Ford hands Zoe to me. I place the nipple of the bottle in her mouth, and she stops crying as she eats.

Ford places a blanket over Zoe and me. She snuggles into me and plays with her ear. As she drinks the bottle, her eyelids get heavy.

"Aw, she's going to go right to sleep. Good." Ford tucks us both in.

I rock her gently and find that I love the solid weight of her against me. Zoe sleeps in my arms, and I let out a sigh of relief.

The nurse opens a door and calls for Ford.

"I can't thank you enough. I'll be right back."

When Ford leaves us, Zoe's eyes blink open, and her gaze meets mine. She doesn't look away. She just watches me as she drinks her milk.

Her eyes are deep blue with a black ring. There's a wisdom there, as if she has everything figured out. I trace my fingertips over her fine, pale eyebrows. She closes her eyes, as if satisfied that she's safe with me.

I press my lips to her forehead, and my heart melts as she gives a little sigh of contentment.

Moments later, Ford returns, and his face is grim. He sits by me and scrubs his hands over his face. "They're prepping her for ultrasound. I want to stay with her until they know exactly what is going on. Would you go to your mom's house? The mudroom closet has a playpen."

My heart seizes in my chest. My mother's house! I want to say no, but my mouth won't form the words. How could I possibly do that? How could I possibly not? We were dealing with a life-or-death situation here. There was no time for ridiculous fears about entering the house of a woman who had clearly gotten her life together and flourished.

Maybe Lark could? No. Lark walked as much as I have and she'll be in a hot bath with her Tansy's Wellness Salts.

I need to tackle this, and the time is now.

"What about Zoe?"

"I'll take her. Mel wants to see her before the surgery. I hate to say this, but time is really—"

"Yes. I understand."

"We need some supplies for supper, too. We'll need milk and baby food. You and I don't have supplies for a baby, obviously. Can you pick up some wine and some steaks for us? Once we get Melinda and Zoe settled for the night, I'll come to your place and make supper. I'll explain everything."

Supper made by Ford sounds absolutely incredible and the best salve for what's coming next. Entering my mom's home. My stomach lurches at the thought.

"Do you think Zoe and Jasper could stay with you for the night? If Mel needs surgery, I might get called back here, and I don't want to disturb Zoe's sleep. It wouldn't help the situation."

"Of course." I take a deep breath and let it out slowly. "What kind of wine?"

"Red." Ford grins as he cuddles Zoe in his arms. He pulls his keys out of his pocket and hands them to me.

"Merlot, Cab Sauv, Malbec, Pinot Noir—"

CHAPTER THIRTY

"You choose. I used to be a wine snob and gave it up at the same time I quit shaving my neck. More on that later."

"No one gives up on being a wine snob. It's in the blood. Also, I have a pair of clippers—"

Ford shakes his head and opens the driver-side door of Melinda's car. My heart zings with jealousy, which is ridiculous.

I wonder what happened between him and Melinda. I decide she's completely insane to have left him under any circumstances.

"Jasper will need to be fed and watered, too. His nose will be out of joint from being stuck in that truck."

"He thinks he's human."

"I think he's more human than some. Thanks, Indi." Ford pulls out his wallet and takes out a credit card.

My eyebrows raise to my forehead. Memories of Ben needing rent money engulf me. I'm dealing with an entirely different man here—a confident leader who doesn't dither. My knees get weak at the thought. "I can pay for everything. You don't need to worry about that." I try to hand him back his credit card.

"No way." Ford shakes his head. "No. I want rib eye please, and I insist. I know women have all these rules about paying their way, but that's not how it is with me. I won't change, so if that's a deal breaker—"

Suddenly, my heart pounds and my knees get shaky.

Getting groceries with his credit card feels very intimate. It's such an unfamiliar experience I can't quite wrap my mind around it. I know now from therapy and books that I choose dysfunctional men on purpose, but nothing about Ford is dysfunctional. In a heartbeat, he can handle a toddler and a life-or-death potential surgery for a woman he was previously very in love with and not lose his stride.

In all honesty, it makes me nervous. When I dated the dysfunctional, I knew my needs would not be met.

Thank you, Summer, for dragging that painful truth out of me!

Knowing my needs wouldn't be met made it easy to cope. With no true trust, there's no nasty heartbreaking disappointment, no coming home to the electricity turned off. I went into relationships knowing I could only trust myself, and that was comfortable. That I knew. I couldn't even trust my mother. Not until now.

Fast forward to today. As I stand here with this man's credit card in hand and his dog that he loves more than most humans waiting in his truck, I realize this all comes with a heavy price. With no true trust, there is no true love. I can't have one without the other.

I also realize I've been missing out because I didn't respect the men—ugh, train wrecks—I've dated up to this point. I couldn't. That lack of respect hurt them, and it hurt me, too.

Since I've been here, I've watched Jet fall apart and Leif gather her up and make sure he did everything possible to ease her burden and pain. Ford stood between Hailey and a threat to her safety. That gave Hailey a safe space to unravel because he created it for her. I saw, for the first time, that men protect women far more than just physically. They protect them financially, like my father has for me since I got here. But they also protect a woman emotionally. I didn't know that.

Never in my life have I known that level of protection existed until I watched Leif carry Jet's pack and her. Or, until I heard my father's plans for me in the clinic or the cay, depending on what I chose. Watching Ford pick up all the pieces for

CHAPTER THIRTY

Melinda, including Melinda herself, as he didn't want her to walk into the hospital, caused me to respect him even more. No questions asked, no judgment. Just manfully making sure she had what she needs.

I knew, deep down, my mother conspired with Phyllis because she wanted me to see and experience different manifestations of healthy relationships between men and women. I had seen it with Phyllis and Al, Estee and Craig, but my mom wanted me to experience it for myself.

Jasper puts his head on my shoulder as I slide into Ford's truck. I can't believe only a few short months ago I didn't like dogs. The feelings are so intense that I hug Jasper. I need love.

"Jasper." My voice is shaking. "We need groceries, then I need to go into my mother's house to get a playpen." I burst into tears. "I'm really worried about what it will feel like to open the door. It's ridiculous."

Jasper looks up at me with dark eyes. He puts his head on my lap.

"You'll have to come with me because I can't go in alone." This is when I know I have completely, utterly unraveled. It's official. I completely lost it.

Talking to a dog and taking that dog into a home I had sworn never to enter.

As I gather our supplies, I look at the wine and buy a bottle of the most expensive merlot. Aside from camping, I haven't had wine in weeks, and I'm not about to waste my one glass with supper on anything cheap.

I hesitate to tap his credit card. I almost pull out my wallet. It feels too weird to let someone pay the bill, make the meal, take care of me. Ugh. I add that to my list of things to hash out with Summer, who will need her own therapist at the end of all this madness. When I can't put it off any longer, I tap the card. I wait for it to decline. That I understood. It says "Approved". Hmm.

I tuck his card safely in my wallet, pick up the bottle—not box—and leave the store.

I buy steak and salad and dressing, formula, milk, and a stuffy. Once I get over the sheer oddness of using his credit card, I find it gets easier. Maybe too easy. I add ice cream and chocolate sauce because we deserve it.

Finally, I can't put it off any longer. I stand outside my mother's house of rock, glass, and rough-hewn logs for a long five minutes. I pet Jasper's head and take a deep breath.

Chapter Thirty-One

Canine Therapy

The ferns and ivy on my mother's front verandah sway in the soft evening breeze. I'm running out of time. I have a text from Ford saying he'll be home in about an hour.

My heart pounds with anticipation. I have to get past this ridiculous fear of entering my mother's home. A two-year-old needs me to get it together. A very promising relationship needs me to be whole. This fear isn't rational, and it's time to face it, put it away, and move forward.

I place my hand on Jasper's head. "I've never told anyone but Phyllis."

Jasper moves closer. His tail pounds on the boards of the veranda.

"It was a really cold night." I take a deep breath and I let it out slowly. "Our trailer had a little porch that was always filled with garbage. I stood inside the porch, and I remember thinking that the only thing good about the cold is that I couldn't smell the garbage." Tears fill my eyes as I say the words that break my heart.

"I noticed a coat hanging across the window of the inside door. We never hung clothes there, never. I thought the coat was hanging there because my mother had killed herself and she didn't want me to see it." My throat closes on a sob. "I was absolutely certain that I would walk in to her—" My voice cracks with agony. I pet Jasper's head.

Jasper moves closer.

"I remember thinking that coat was there as a warning. Like she wanted to end her life in privacy." I hide my face in Jasper's neck.

Jasper moves closer.

"So, I stood outside in the cold until I couldn't feel my hands or feet." Tears pour down my face. "I tried to think of who I could call to help me, and I couldn't think of anyone. I didn't want anyone to know my shame, my deep shame, of how we lived." I lose it.

That truth is as hard to admit as anything else. I stood in that freezing cold with no one to call. My life with Mom was so dysfunctional I was convinced no one would understand.

"Finally, I couldn't stand outside anymore, so I forced myself to open the door. My mother was sitting on the couch, watching TV. She had garbage bags on all the windows to keep out the light because she was so depressed. It was winter in Manitoba. There's no light after four p.m.—"

I stop talking for a moment, and Jasper shuffles closer.

"This is my truth, Jasper. I had no idea what I would walk in on, and when I opened the door and she was alive, I felt heavy. Like the weirdest heaviness landed on my shoulders, a weight I could no longer lift." I weep. "It's the worst thing anyone has ever admitted, I'm sure. Now that she's gone and

CHAPTER THIRTY-ONE

I know her diagnosis, I wish we had reconciled when I had the chance. That night, even though I was completely frozen, I walked out of the trailer without saying goodbye. I just left and started running. The police picked me up. Phyllis took me in. I left my mom. I didn't reconcile with her and now I can't. I can't even believe I am saying this out loud. I am a terrible, awful person." I weep into Jasper's neck.

"No," someone says in a deep male voice from the other end of the veranda. Carter walks over to me and places his hand on my shoulder.

I look up in shock at my father.

His eyes burn into mine. "You were a child at the breaking point. Phyllis said you spent three days in bed once you got to her house."

"I did." I pull away from Jasper and turn to my father.

He hands me some biodegradable facial tissue, which means I need three times the amount.

"Your reaction was completely normal, Indi."

"It doesn't feel normal. It feels wrong. I have so much guilt."

"Indi, you were a child dealing with a parent who had untreated bipolar disorder and a raging addiction to alcohol." His deep voice cuts through my thoughts. "My darling girl, you are human, and humans have limits to what they can handle. That night was your breaking point. It's okay. Everyone breaks."

My father pulls me into his arms, and together, we weep on my mother's verandah. We cry together and hold each other with Jasper right between us.

"You need to forgive yourself for that night and the thoughts you had as a child when facing the greatest and most tragic of circumstances."

"I left her." I sob.

"You saved yourself, and you saved her." My father's voice is so deep and so firm that it cuts through all the painful memories.

I believe him, and the relief is intense.

"She came after you, and the police put her in a psych ward, where she was finally treated. She told me more than once that there are so many ways to die. Until she found the right medications, she was like a dead person. Because you had the strength to leave, she pieced her life together. She always regretted the hurt she caused you. She wept about the fact that she didn't get help sooner."

I lay my head on my father's shoulder and breathe in the fresh scent of pine that clings to his shirt.

I speak softly so as not to disturb the peace between us. "She did the best she could with the tools she had, and when she knew better, she did better."

"Where did you learn that?" My father hugs me harder.

"Mandatory therapy with Summer." I wipe the tears from my eyes.

We let go of each other so we could clean our faces.

"I'm so glad to have you here," he says.

"I'm glad to be here."

"Do you mean that?" Truth peeks around my father's shoulder.

"Truth! What are you doing here?"

"I'm an auntie, and aunties interfere."

I nod. "I see. Yes. I mean it. I'm really glad to be here."

Truth's eyes fill with tears, and that makes me burst into tears again.

CHAPTER THIRTY-ONE

She hugs me. If either of them thinks it's odd for three grown people to awkwardly hug around a dog, no one mentions it. Jasper doesn't budge an inch as we weep together.

Finally, we pulled back, and more tissues are produced.

"It's biodegradable," Carter explains to Truth.

A grin tugs at Truth's mouth. I giggle. An actual honest giggle. Suddenly, we're laughing. Really laughing. We all had this heart-baring and healing conversation, and Carter's worried about biodegradable facial tissue. Just the thought makes me shake even harder with laughter. When we finally come to grips with our emotions—all of them—we all take a deep breath and let it out slowly.

"We'll cancel our supper plans." Truth tucks a piece of hair behind my ear. "We can have supper with you."

"That would be lovely, but I have plans tonight."

"Oh?" Carter shoots Truth a look.

I give them the rundown about the playpen for Zoe and the groceries in Ford's truck.

"Let's get that playpen then."

My father and aunt step back and let me open the door to my mother's house.

I do it. I step inside to a light-filled, beautiful room. The sun is starting to set, so the inside of my mother's house glows pink and orange. She left the darkness in our Winnipeg trailer. She embraced the light. Now it's my turn.

Chapter Thirty-Two

Terms and Conditions

"Just breathe," Truth says as I look around. Instead of those horrible garbage bags on the windows, I look through the shiny window panes at pine trees, a lake, and snow-topped mountains in the distance.

I stand in my mother's house, full of light and love, Carter on one side of me, and Truth on the other. Jasper's head leans against my thigh.

We hold hands, and I close my eyes. I take a deep breath in and let it out slowly.

The only words in my heart are "thank you." I am letting go of that cold, dark night, that night of overwhelming despair, and I am moving forward into this pink light of the sunset—it feels like the colour of hope. Like maybe since my mom could heal, I can too.

We're silent as we let the rose-and-coral glow of the sunset settle over us.

CHAPTER THIRTY-TWO

Finally, I open my eyes. Duty calls. "I have a toddler and a supper to sort out, so I better get a move on."

My father goes to the mudroom of my mom's house and returns with a box. "Here you go. A playpen for a special little toddler."

"Thanks." I can't help but smile at him. This is what families do, they rally.

"There's some bedding for that. Let me grab it." Truth goes to find sheets and a blanket.

It's heartwarming to see my father and Truth scramble to get supplies for Zoe.

"I could send some food—"

"Ford gave me a credit card and a list. I don't think Zoe is up for your kale concoctions." I grin at my aunt.

Truth laughs.

My phone dings.

Is everything okay? The text from Ford reads.

I quickly text back that I'm almost home. "I have to go." I tuck my phone back in my pocket.

"Have fun." Carter hugs me hard.

"We love you." Truth hugs me, then lets me go.

"I love you too." I gather up the playpen and the bedding; then I step out of my mother's house with a lighter heart.

Lights are on in my house when I arrive. Everything's chaotic. Zoe's upset and hungry. I feel bad about making them wait.

"Everything all right?" Ford's eyes darken with concern.

"Yes." I hand him his credit card and immediately put the bag of baby food on the counter. "I have some lovely carrots and peas, as well as macaroni and cheese."

"Perfect. I'll hold her. You feed her."

As a team, we feed Zoe, then give her a bottle.

"How is Melinda?"

"She's good. The baby is safe. She lost a lot of blood and will need to stay in bed for the time being. But they think the baby will be fine. I told her I'll check on her later tonight."

"Good to hear."

"I also heard from Derek, and he's getting on a flight tonight, so we have Zoe until he gets here. I hope that's all right."

"Perfect."

"Really?" Ford asks.

"Yeah. Really." I meet his gaze. "I'm all in for this adventure."

I honestly feel like I've slayed a dragon. Entering my mother's house was a deep fear that's over. Hearing my father's account of the night I left was a healing. Somehow, it meant more coming from him. I didn't know why, but I feel a peace inside me from his words.

"I'll put her down if you want to start supper?" Ford suggests.

"Sure. I just need a quick shower."

After my shower, I look at all the rigmarole to do my hair and decide against it. I'm hungry. He's hungry. We have a baby that might sleep through the night and might not. It would take half an hour to dry and style my hair. I don't want to waste that time. I pin it up.

We'll have a proper date at some point. I'll wow him then.

I wish for a pretty dress that fits, but I haven't had time to shop since losing the first bunch of weight. I'm not stick thin, and it doesn't matter. I really don't care.

CHAPTER THIRTY-TWO

Losing what I lost so far means my feet no longer hurt, my lower back doesn't even ache, and somehow, my allergies are way better. Truth told me about autophagy, and I looked it up. Apparently, the body heals itself when in a fasted state. It goes after something to eat, and it cleans up damaged cells and all sorts of yucky issues when given the chance. I have no intentions of dwelling on my sinuses when a gorgeous man is ready to grill meat. I throw on a tunic and leave the bathroom.

Ford is also scrubbed and changed and starting on supper. "It's not Prairie's sauce, but it will have to do." Ford hands me a glass of wine.

I take a tiny sip. "I better wait on this."

"I'll put the steak on the grill if you want to do the asparagus?"

"Sure."

Like a well-oiled machine, we work on supper and finally sit on my front deck with the door open so we could hear Zoe. He serves my supper first; I notice and waits until I sit to follow suit. It's so strange. The entire night is him putting me and my needs first. It feels unusual and amazing, as if I'm precious to him.

"In normal life, I would have done my hair and worn clothes that fit properly." I take a sip of wine.

"In normal life, we would not be babysitting my ex-wife's toddler, and this table would have a tablecloth, flowers, and candles. I would not be on call to return to a hospital to deal with a potential miscarriage."

I shake my head. "It's a crazy life."

"We will have a fancy supper. I promise. But sadly, not today." Ford grins as he cuts into his steak. "Perfect."

"You're good in a crisis." I eat a spear of asparagus and nearly swoon with pleasure. I love it so much. I crave it. Since

I arrived in B.C., I have eaten bales of asparagus. Truth said it wasn't uncommon. The body craves what it needs as it detoxes.

I think back to the first week with no processed food and shake my head. I had no idea until I came here how sick I really was—not just physically, emotionally, too.

"I am really glad to hear Derek is coming back so soon."

"Yes. He is worried sick."

"About Melinda or you in Melinda's life?"

Ford stops chewing, takes a sip of wine, and nods. "Both."

"I am curious. Is it like you're best friends?"

"Well, I take full responsibility for our divorce. We came to terms long after it was irreparable."

"You don't have to tell me."

"I do. You're in this now, so you need to know. When my daughter was dying, I was working. Like really working. Fifteen hours a day, six days a week. Some people drink, some do drugs. I work. It was my default. I guess I could blame my parents. My dad worked and provided materially, but all the emotional stuff was up to my mom. Anyway, no excuse. I worked, and Melinda handled all the health needs for our daughter. I went some days when she insisted, but I couldn't handle it." Ford leans back in his chair. "I was there at the end, and it broke me."

Absently, he rubs the bracelet on his wrist. "When Maddie died, I fell completely apart. I was so depressed and such a wreck. I lost my job. I went to bed and didn't get out. Melinda was really patient, but I was a mess. She wanted more kids, and I said no. I would never have more kids. Slowly, she gave up and found Derek. She left me, got remarried, and got pregnant right away. I pushed her to it, and I take full responsibility."

CHAPTER THIRTY-TWO

"Wow."

"Yeah. That's the whole truth. I fell apart, and she did what she needed to do to heal."

"Do you think you've healed from it?"

"I think neither of us will ever heal from it. I think you learn to go on with a broken heart. That is the best you can hope for, I think.

"I'm so sorry."

"Me too."

"So, children are still off the table for you?"

"Yes." Ford sips his wine and finishes his steak. "I can't go through all that pain again. I can barely deal with it even now."

"I see."

"What about you?"

"I swore off kids because I was worried I would turn into my mother. Although, here I am living my best, healthiest life because of a clause in her will."

"It's a crazy life," Ford repeats what I just said. "You've changed since you came here. Gone is the girl who was allergic to everything, hated dogs, had perfect hair."

I laugh. "I have an arsenal of tools and products to give me perfect hair, but I was too hungry. Next time, you'll be blindsided by perfect hairdresser hair."

"There will be a next time?" Ford holds the wineglass to his lips.

My eyes are immediately drawn to his lips. Butterflies flip in my stomach. "Yeah. I hope so." I take a big drink of wine and hoped it will calm me down.

Ford's eyes meet mine in the dim light of the sunset. "Usually, the no-children thing is the deal breaker. Most women want children."

I shrug. "Before I came here, I divided my life into fifteen-minute increments. That's how tight I booked myself because I wanted to make as much money as possible because I was terrified of being in a trailer with a broken door."

Ford frowns.

"Long story."

"We've got until Zoe wakes up." Ford pours more wine into my glass.

I take a deep breath. "It's funny. I told Jasper the whole thing, and my father and Truth overheard."

"What did they overhear?" Ford pushes his empty plate aside, and his eyes lock with mine.

I repeat the story I told Jasper. I don't hold back. I tell Ford all the gory details, but I add my father's comments about people having a breaking point and that I had found mine. That was all. I stop when the emotional pain makes my throat hurt.

I cover my face in my hands at the end of the long, sad tale and am really surprised when Ford suddenly gathers me into his arms. Gently, he pulls me to my feet and holds me while I weep.

"I am so sorry," he whispers as his arms lock hard around me.

I cry harder.

"Fifteen years old. I can't believe you survived it."

"I didn't." I pull back so I can blow my nose.

Ford hands me a box of tissues. "They are biodegradable," he says, as if I would refuse to use them unless they were.

I laugh through my tears. "Funny. My father said the same thing."

"Truth is a zealot about the environment. We're all afraid of her." Ford whispered.

CHAPTER THIRTY-TWO

I laugh through my tears.

Ford gently wipes tears from my eyes with the pads of his thumb. "I knew you were a strong woman, but I didn't know why."

"I'm not a strong woman. I'm a lunatic. I am a workaholic. I spent my life behind a chair watching brides get ready for weddings, then baby showers, then their kids' graduations."

"You flew back for a bride. I am certain she was thrilled to see you." Ford brushes a piece of hair from my eyes.

"Yeah. About that." I clear my throat and rest my hands on his shoulders.

He tugs me closer.

"You may as well know everything." I bite my lip as I look up at him.

"What?" Ford laughs. "I'm afraid to ask."

"I flew back and was at my salon an hour early to make sure everything was hot, really hot. I'm old school and damaged hair is of no concern to me."

"Okay. Damaged hair is okay, but neck hair is out."

"Oh. Completely unacceptable."

"Noted."

"You won't care."

"Unless I start working as a corporate lawyer again."

"Are you planning that?"

"We're talking about you."

I sigh. "I was ready. Ariana walked in and to my chair. I went to pick up my hot rollers."

"Very hot."

"Yeah, like surface-of-the-sun hot, and I felt this terrible click in my back as if the vertebrae came apart."

"Ouch." Ford winces on my behalf. "I remember you in your first meeting with your team, flat on your back, knees up."

"Yeah. So, I go down to my knees, and the only way to survive the pain is if I'm flat on my back with my knees up at a ninety-degree angle, as you saw."

Ford's eyes soften with sympathy.

"While I was on the ground, three things happened that completely changed my life." I stop talking for a moment and think about that—how when we hit rock bottom, it forces a change, and we can decide to change for better or worse. I chose for the better because my mom made that possible. A glow of gratefulness lights my heart.

"What was that?"

"Ariana stepped over my prone body to get her hair done. Elle, a shark, didn't even look at me. She was so busy with Ariana; she didn't look at me once. Then I got a text from my boyfriend that he couldn't afford his rent. He asked if I would e-transfer him money right then."

"What?" Shock whips across Ford's face.

"Yeah. According to Summer, I was codependent."

"Completely understandable, considering where you came from."

"Right."

"The third thing?"

"Truth wanted to help me up, but she wasn't strong enough to get me off the floor. One stylist had a chiropractor coming in for a haircut, and he helped me crawl into the spa room and fixed me up, but that's when I knew, as the stylists were sweeping around me, that I had to change. Everything. I had to do this without grumbling."

"There was a fair bit of grumbling, if I remember correctly."

CHAPTER THIRTY-TWO

I laugh at that. "Anyway, here I am." I take a step back.

"Here you are." Ford smiles.

"I'm too old and crotchety to deal with drawn-out dating and schemes. I'm a train wreck trying to come to terms with things and move forward, and I might blow it."

Ford grins. "I'm dealing with a few hang-ups myself, so let's put our cards on the table. I'm not having children. We're way too old to waste our time if you're yearning for babies."

"I am not way too old!" I bristle with indignation.

"Sorry, that came out harsh. I will not have children, and if you want them, we should part ways as soon as this crisis is over. If no kids works for you, I want to see you when we aren't dealing with my ex-wife and a toddler."

"I would like that very much."

"Are you going back to Brandon and your salon, or what's your next move? Maybe we should get that out of the way first?"

"Is there a contract I should sign?" I shake my head.

"Sorry—corporate lawyer." Ford holds up his hands in surrender.

"I find that more difficult than the no-children clause."

"Oh, but you'll use my skills shamelessly to secure a cay off the coast of Belize."

"That was my father's doing," I correct him.

"Right. He's buying it for you. Out of guilt."

"Good. I deserve it." I smile slyly.

Ford throws back his head and laughs. "You're a terrible brat."

"Yes. I am."

"Brandon or here or Belize?" Ford asks again.

"I'm still deliberating."

"Hmm. I like clear-cut parameters."

"Me too." I agree.

"I guess this time we have to—what is the word?"

"Be flexible and easygoing?" I suggest and shudder.

"I think I can manage that." Ford grins.

"Yes. Corporate lawyers are the hippies of the corporate world." I laugh so hard I can hardly stand up.

"What about you with your fifteen-minute increments? How will you manage?"

"I won't. I like my parameters clearly defined, too."

"What do you think?" Ford tugs me back into his arms.

I looked up at him. "I'm willing to risk it if you are."

He tenderly cradles my face in his hands. "I am."

My stomach explodes with butterflies, and my knees go weak as he leans down to kiss me. As my eyelids slide closed in expectation, Zoe lets out a wail that could wake the dead. Ford stops. My heart withers with longing.

"That's our cue to go."

"Right."

Instead of a passionate kiss that would stop the world, I get a kiss on the forehead like an old grandmother. Disappointment wings through me as I follow Ford into the spare room, where Zoe stands crying in the playpen.

Everything changes inside me as I watch, my heart in my throat, as he leans down to pick her up. He kisses her and soothes her so sweetly that I can't help myself. I fall even more completely in love with him. His gentleness with a two-year-old undoes me. He's the kindest person I have ever met. There's not a mean bone in his body. A man like Ford I could trust and respect.

"Oh, sweetie, Mommy is sick. We will see her tomorrow," Ford whispers in Zoe's ear as he jiggles her up and down. "I think we need another bottle."

CHAPTER THIRTY-TWO

"Coming right up."

Once she eats, Ford settles Zoe, and I clean off the table and load the dishwasher. When Zoe's back asleep, he comes to help.

"You should get some rest. That was a big day," he says.

"Yeah."

"I don't know if she'll wake up again, so sleep while you can."

"Right." I place a plate in the rack and turn, bumping into Ford.

He kisses me, gently at first, but then he deepens the kiss. The world falls away, and my knees buckle. His arms lock around me so I wouldn't fall to the floor.

Finally, he pulls back. "I've been waiting to do that for a very long time."

"Me too." I'm breathless with anticipation of kissing him again.

His phone lights up. I want to grab it and throw it in the lake.

"It's Melinda. She needs me to come now. They are taking her in for another ultrasound, and she's scared."

"Right."

"You're all right here? Is there anything you need?"

"No. I'm fine," I whisper.

Ford leaps into action. "Really, get some sleep. This was a very long day, and tomorrow will be even longer."

I think about asking a question, then don't. It would leave me too vulnerable. Is it desperate? I open my mouth, then shut it.

"What were you going to say?" Ford asks softly.

"You promise a proper date, like with a tablecloth and everything?" I hold my breath. "Did you mean that?"

"I promise." Ford smiles and kisses me again. Then he's gone into the night.

Chapter Thirty-Three

Morning Breath

The next morning, I wake to a heavy body on mine. The morning breath is so bad I have to pull a pillow over my face or I'm sure I'll die from the smell.

Jasper.

Jasper is in my bed, his head right next to mine, on my pillow. I adjust the pillow so I don't smell his breath, then snuggle against him.

Finally, covered in dog hair and not minding in the least, I slowly get out of bed and go to the ensuite bathroom. I'm stiff, and the skin of my feet is sore from where my shoes rubbed.

My heart stops when I see a bouquet of flowers in my ensuite bathroom along with a collection of high-end girly products from a drugstore. Made with natural ingredients, of course, but I know these products are really expensive. I take a deep breath of the roses' scent. I'm touched as I pick up the shower gel—real soap, not something made of hemp. I flick open the lid and take a deep breath. The soap smells like a meadow where people only know happiness. Taking the products with me, I slip into a very hot shower and happily use the new supplies. Feeling human, I pull on a loose sundress.

It's quiet in the house.

Ford stands on my back deck with a big, steaming coffee in his hand. His stubble looks rough. He looks a bit tired. I can tell he had a long night. The dark blue flannel shirt stretches across the breadth of his shoulders. His pants are the same colour as tree bark; he blends perfectly with the rugged scenery behind him.

Honestly, he takes my breath away.

I pour a big cup of coffee and add cream, then bring the coffeepot with me.

"Good morning," I whisper as I step out onto the deck.

The sun filtering down through the trees makes my heart sing with delight. The prettiest orange-and-black bird chirps at the bird feeder. I wish I knew what kind of bird it is. Dew sparkles on the leaves and grass. I take a deep breath and let it out slowly.

"Good morning." Ford takes the coffee pot from me.

Together we settle into the wicker love seat. I tuck my feet under his thigh as if I've done that all my life.

"Cold feet?"

"Always."

Ford adjusts the way he sits to keep my feet warm but still can talk to me face-to-face.

"When did you get here?" I sip the creamy coffee and nearly swoon with delight.

CHAPTER THIRTY-THREE

"Half an hour ago. I thought I would make coffee and leave you a thank-you gift, but then I saw Jasper made himself right at home. I thought I would just stay until you got up and make sure your night went well."

I giggle. "Yes, Jasper loves to snuggle. The night was fine. Zoe slept the whole time."

"I've never been so jealous of Jasper in my life." Ford leans forward and presses his lips to mine, softly, just once.

I can't stop the blush from creeping up my neck. "He's great with emotional support, but his morning breath leaves a little to be desired."

Ford chuckles. "I noticed. Indi, why are we whispering?"

"It's too perfect." I sip my coffee, close my eyes, and lean my head back for a moment to commit this perfect moment to my memory. I shift my feet under his thigh and then open my eyes as I address him. "Do you ever just see a day that is so perfect you can't get enough? You just don't want anything to disturb it?"

"It is perfect."

"Thank you so much for the flowers and girly products." I move my feet to snuggle in against him and think this is the best feeling in the entire world. His shirt is soft against my cheek. The shirt and his shoulder smell like sunshine and pine trees.

Jealous, Jasper insists on snuggling between us. We laugh as Ford firmly puts Jasper on the ground at his feet.

"You're welcome for the girly products. I don't know what girls like, so I just bought the most expensive things and hoped for the best."

"Very kind of you." I grin.

Ford takes my coffee from my hand and sets it down, then he kisses me again. "You smell awesome."

"A change from the eau de locker room from yesterday!"

"I liked that, too, but this is nice. I could get used to this," Ford whispers against my neck.

"Me too," I whisper back.

He pulls a blanket over my legs because of the morning chill. Two people walk by to get to the hot spring in my mother's yard. Ford frowns at the lack of privacy and hands my coffee back to me.

I sip it as I look out past the forest to the lake. "I didn't expect you to be here this morning."

"Yeah, visiting hours aren't until ten, so I'll leave soon. Derek texted last night and said he caught the red eye. He'll be in Calgary this morning, and he'll come for Zoe. I told him she was fine and we could keep her until he's rested. I hope that works."

"Yes, absolutely."

"Good, I have to check on Melinda, then meet with the lawyers for the cay arrangement as Carter restructured the legal team. Then I have paperwork to draft for Leif."

"Why?"

"Leif and Jet are buying my restaurant, and since I'm working on this deal for your dad, I can't do both. I'll be back and forth from Belize all year."

"Really?" I sit up straight.

"I'll go back and forth until this deal goes through, then I'll reevaluate."

"That's a big decision!" My stomach flips.

"I just decided this week."

"I thought they wanted me to decide about Belize?" I was waffling about it because I'd never been there, but now that the decision doesn't rest on me at all, I feel put out, which is ridiculous. I decide to write it in my healing journal so I can

CHAPTER THIRTY-THREE

process it with Summer. I suddenly think it would be helpful to take her with us if we relocate.

Us!

"I can't reveal a confidence, but a big investor wanted in on this island on the ground floor. So. Belize is going ahead. If you are going back to Brandon, Truth said she might want to head it. So, once the deal is firmed up, the board will decide about Truth if you decline."

"Wow!" I'm stunned.

"I was holding back, and when I went to the Valley of Loss, this time, I felt different. I miss Madison. My heart is still broken. That will not change, but I thought about some things last night. I watched Melinda weep about the baby she might lose, and I realized as I stood by her that she was brave enough to live again. Stopping my life and every good thing in it won't bring Maddie back. Melinda knew that. I didn't fully grasp it until last night. She has a man who loves her enough to take a red eye to Calgary, and he should be at the hospital now. You probably can't relate to that."

"I totally can." The coffee is hot and I sip it slowly. "I know exactly what you're talking about."

"Really?"

"Yup. We're both emotionally stunted and terrified to live in case we get hurt again." I sigh and sip more coffee. Then I turn on the couch and face him. "Okay, let's get into it."

Ford turns to face me.

"Biggest fear?" I watch his reaction to my question.

"Losing another child in death. Can't deal with that."

I put my hand on his arm. "I'm so sorry."

"Your turn."

"Poverty." I say it so quickly it surprises me.

"Just that?"

"Spoken like someone who has never faced it." My eyes narrow slightly.

"You're right. That was insensitive and privileged of me. Sorry. Poverty. Anything else?"

"Living with a person who has an untreated mental illness, which in my experience, results in poverty or abuse or both."

"Full disclosure; I struggled with depression after Madison."

"It would be weird if you didn't." I adjust the blanket across my lap.

"But I did. I completely fell apart." Ford's honesty is refreshing.

"But you have doctors and therapists on your team?"

"I have a complete team of specialists," Ford says dryly.

"When was your last depressive episode?" I scrutinize him.

"When Melinda got married. I started spiraling, thinking of how badly I had failed her."

"But you were sick," I reason with him. Those words stop me in my tracks. I never made allowances for illness before. Ever. How could I change perspective this much in the short time I've been here?

"You are a woman of childbearing age. That is a massive risk." Ford grins at me.

"That is why I practice abstinence," I say primly and take another sip of coffee.

Ford runs his fingertip down my right arm and smiles as the entire arm covers in goose bumps. "I think your arm disagrees."

I catch my breath as he moves to kiss me. Jasper immediately gets between us in the space Ford created when he turned to face me.

CHAPTER THIRTY-THREE

"Looks like Jasper is firmly in camp abstinence and determined to protect your virtue."

I laugh so hard I almost spill my coffee.

Ford leans forward and kisses me—softly at first, as if testing things between us, then the kiss deepens. I forget what we were talking about, but I try to move Jasper out of the way, and he won't budge. Jasper keeps moving between us, so we have to break apart.

"Jasper, you're irritating," Ford growls.

"With the worst morning breath—ever."

"I've never seen Jasper sleep with anyone else." Ford grins and scratches behind Jasper's ears.

"I think he knew I was raw. Emotionally."

Ford's gaze meets mine. "I'm proud of you for doing hard things. It hurts, but it's all part of the process. You've changed so much here."

"I feel a complete lightening of the spirit here."

"I think that's the best compliment this place could get."

Ford moves to kiss me again, and I place my hand on his chest.

"Maybe this should slow down a bit. Until I decide about Belize. Can I look at the paperwork and see the projections?"

"Of course."

"And you should think about this, too. You might need to find a woman who has gone through menopause. Then you're safe."

"How far are you from menopause?" Ford tilts his head to the side.

I laugh. I can't help it, and I can't stop. "Far. Like ten years."

"That's a long time to live with your vow of abstinence." Ford frowns, then grins.

"Who said it's a vow?"

I laugh as Ford drags Jasper out from between us and pulls me closer. "Just one last kiss, then I have to go."

"But you want a relationship with a woman of childbearing age?" I won't leave anything unsaid. We're hashing it out in full.

"Yes. I do. And do you want a man with a team of specialists?"

I hold his gaze so he can see the fears buried there. "Yes, with no risk of poverty or untreated mental illness or abuse."

Ford doesn't look away or blink. "I can guarantee that."

"Really?"

"Really."

"So, just the pregnancy concerns." A smile pulls at my lips.

He presses his lips to mine. "Yeah. As soon as you're safely through menopause, we can go on that date." Ford laughs and kisses me again.

We grudgingly pull apart as his phone goes off.

"Sorry. I have to have the sound on..." His eyes skim the text. "Derek is held up. His flight got delayed. Melinda asked me to come in. Are you all right here with Zoe?"

"Of course. That's what I'm here for."

Ford gets to his feet. "If you need anything, shoot me a text. I can pick up supplies for supper."

"I can cancel the group supper if you want."

"Hm. Let me handle that. I'll ask if someone else wants to host. Prairie will jump at the chance. I'm leaving you Melinda's car. She told me there's a stroller in the trunk if you want to take Zoe on your walk. Do you mind leaving your sound on? That way I can get a hold of you. Derek should be here this afternoon. Then we'll know our next step."

"Of course. All good here. I have an appointment with Summer this morning, so I'll feed Zoe, and she and Jasper can come with me." I smile. "Let Melinda know Zoe is in good hands."

"Text me a list for supper supplies or whatever you need."

He tilts his head to kiss me, but Zoe starts crying, and we both mobilize. I enter the spare room to pick up Zoe from the playpen. She stops crying when she sees me.

"Good morning." I don't recognize my voice. I don't know where this gentle tone was hiding. When I pick her up, her arms go around my neck. I fall completely in love with her. "Oh, darling. There is a lovely day planned. We are going to get you all cleaned up and fresh, then we'll have breakfast, and we'll walk to the clinic. We'll have a swim in the salt pool and lunch on the deck. Would you like that?"

Zoe, of course, doesn't answer.

I get started on our plan and realize quickly that children slow everything down. Way down. There's no booking in fifteen-minute increments with a toddler. Life moves at their pace, and that pace is glacial. I check my phone and realize I'll have to walk quick to get to the clinic on time for Summer. I drag the jogging stroller out of the trunk and settle Zoe in the stroller with a bottle, then I set off for the clinic. No time to tidy up, I leave my usually neat house in an absolute disaster.

The house is a mess, sure, but the people in it aren't. We're a team. Together, we can tackle anything. Armed with that knowledge, I strap Zoe into her stroller and take off for the clinic.

Chapter Thirty-Four

Therapy

At the clinic, I wheel the jogging stroller right into Summer's therapy room. Jasper comes in with me.

Summer raises her eyebrows. "Look at you!"

She grins as I plop down on a chair. I drag a headband over the worst of my hair as Jasper lies at my feet. As soon as this session is over, I'll have a big lunch and take Zoe to the salt pool to play in the sunshine.

"What is happening?" Summer smiles brightly at me.

The thing about Summer is she makes therapy feel like a talk with a trusted friend. I think that's what I love about her so much—until she drops a question like a bomb—but as I answer her questions, I'm proud of myself. Up to this point, I have ditched Ben, been open to the idea of writing, could enter my mother's house, and have supported a friend in the Valley of Loss. Plus shed a couple of sizes and feel like a new person with a new outlook on life. Changing my diet to

CHAPTER THIRTY-FOUR

nutrient-dense foods and no processed foods has changed my body, but I realize the books she prescribed and the therapy changed my outlook. I can't recommend her enough.

The approach to whole body healing is something I understand now. I get it. I also completely understand why every approach I took before failed. Nothing was sustainable, and I never actually did the hard work of tackling my feelings around why I reached for comfort foods and alcohol. Specifically, wine—which I still love, but it isn't the life raft it was before.

"Well, my life has completely changed." I grinned back at her.

"A toddler and a dog. A toddler that belongs to Ford's ex-wife, mind you. A dog that also belongs to Ford. How do you feel about it?"

"I feel like things escalated quickly." I can't stop the smile from creeping across my face.

"Let's get into it. How are you?"

I take a deep breath and let it out slowly. "I went into my mother's house."

Summer's eyes light up. "How was that?"

"It wasn't planned." I quickly fill her in on the potential miscarriage, having Zoe for the night, and needing a playpen.

"So, there I am, standing on the deck and pouring my heart out to Jasper."

"This from a person who didn't like dogs only a few months ago."

"Yeah, I know, and there's more to that! Anyway, I am telling Jasper about the night I left my mother and how, when I walked in, finally, she was alive, and I broke apart. That's when my father and Truth came around the corner of the verandah, and my father said everyone has a breaking point and there's no shame in a fifteen-year-old finding hers."

Summer nods and adds her thoughts. "It's completely normal for someone with caregiver burnout to react the way you did. It's nothing to be ashamed of."

My eyes fill with tears. "I'm starting to believe that."

"At fifteen years old, to deal with a parent who can't cope—even grown adults who have autonomy fall apart. There is no shame in it. That was a normal reaction to a traumatic situation. You may be interested in other therapies. You were a child of an alcoholic, and there are programs for adult children of alcoholics. I have a list of them here."

I take the list from her.

"There is also a therapy called EMDR. It's trauma therapy and is very helpful in dealing with trauma where you can pinpoint the specific event that you are having a hard time getting past. These are options for you. Obviously, you can make that decision yourself."

"Right. I'll look into both."

"Anything else come up?"

"Last night, Ford and I had a conversation about the possibility of dating." I laugh as I pet Jasper's head. "We kissed, and we talked about what we both want in life. Ford doesn't plan to have children."

"What about you?" Summer asks.

"I think something's wrong with me."

"In what sense?"

"Not once have I yearned to have children."

"Do you know why?"

"I don't."

"What is your first thought about a child?"

CHAPTER THIRTY-FOUR

"My first thought is I feel tired just thinking of it. Isn't that the worst—"

"Why do you say isn't that the worst? Why do you think you should want to have children?"

"It's normal."

"If you don't want children and it's a decision you've made in a healthy mindset, that is a perfectly valid decision."

"I never thought of that. I always just thought something was wrong with me. Like some days I'm sure are great, but an exhaustion settles on me at the thought."

"So, the first thought is this will involve caregiving."

"Yes." A lightbulb clicks on in my head. "I guess I hadn't thought of that."

"Explore that."

"Um." I shift Zoe in my arms and kiss her forehead. I place her sleeping body in the stroller and tuck her in. "I took care of my mom until it broke me, then I was in business with Estee, and I took on way more than my responsibilities because I was scared of failing. There were a lot of loser boyfriends in my life. Now, I just want to take care of myself for a bit. Is that selfish?"

"Does it feel selfish?"

"No. It feels like I'm speaking my truth." A weight lifts from me as I say it. "Up to this point, I was just constantly in reaction-and-survival mode. Since I got here, they have encouraged me to explore my relationships with food, alcohol, exercise, sleep, people, writing, photography—it's the first time I have ever just wanted to let go of plans and constantly caring for someone. I want to write and take pretty pictures and see what happens. Is this madness?"

"It's healthy."

Summer grins, and something in me shifts.

I feel free. "It's okay if I don't want kids. Nothing is wrong with me?"

"I read lately, 'Look at all the things you love to do, and picture doing those things while parenting.' Does that appeal to you? Or would you prefer to do those things with no children?"

"I feel like I just now have the opportunity to explore what I really love in life, and I have changed so much in the last few months that I just want to get to know myself better. That sounds insane."

"No. That sounds completely healthy." Summer gives a big smile of encouragement. "Lots of women choose no children, and they are very happy. Lots choose children, and they are happy."

"Before, I thought I might ruin them because I would be like my mom or something. I don't feel like that now."

"Perfect." Summer nods. "Have you started writing?"

"I have."

"You could write your version of events. When you entered your mom's house at fifteen, what happened, how you felt, and contrast it with entering her house now. Writing is incredibly therapeutic."

A new thought crashes through my mind. Writing as therapy. It doesn't matter who reads it. It just matters that I pour out my heart on paper. "I never thought of that."

"A lot of writers say that writing happens for them on a very subconscious level. Like they write, and the story takes them into areas they never expect, and suddenly they laugh or cry or have an emotional release. That is why your mom invited so many writers to help others write their truths. I think you should write your truth before our next session."

CHAPTER THIRTY-FOUR

Zoe moves in her stroller. I quickly start rolling the stroller, but to no avail. Her eyes pop open, and she looks at me. Jasper raises his head.

"I think we'll need a shorter session today, but I will try writing that before next week."

"That sounds great."

After lunch, Zoe loves exploring the salt pool. She gets completely immersed in trying to stop the water from coming out of the jet. As she laughs and plays with the water, my heart sings with happiness as I watch her.

I suddenly understand why Estee rearranges her days to go fishing with her boys. I'm glad she had the option, honestly. She used work to create the life she wanted. What I had previously thought of as frivolous is healthy. My heart shifts toward Estee and her decisions as I watch the pure sunshine and happiness of Zoe's smile.

After the salt pool, the front desk staff find us a playpen, and I try to get Zoe down for a nap. I have some reports to check on and some orders to place. I just lay her down, sighing with relief, as a blue text lights up my phone.

Derek will pick up Melinda today. He's coming to get as soon as he can. I'll be there in half an hour so you can do your orders without interruption.

Even when dealing with Melinda and Derek, Ford remembers my schedule, and it makes me feel very cared for. I quickly texted back that Zoe is sleeping—there's no rush. I can do both.

I'll get supper then. What would you like?

My fingertips pause as I read that text and contrast it with all the texts from Ben asking me to bring him supper after my very long day of work for me, and a day of sitting on a couch, playing video games for him. I get a lump in my throat. We are a fantastic team.

I have never had a man in my life who pulled his weight. With this one text, I realize what I missed out on. I settled. I suddenly see the light.

I would like a chicken Caesar salad.

Done. I'll meet you at your place?

Yes, I want to let Zoe have a big swim before supper.

Is it okay if I give Derek directions to your home?

Of course.

See you tonight. I'll meet you at your place around four. I'll start supper.

My hands tremble with excitement that this is my life now. I can't stop the smile from breaking across my face.

Chapter Thirty-Five

Reconcile

Ford meets us at my place and takes Zoe as soon as I get in the door.

"I know, this place is a disaster!" I look around at the disorder, and it doesn't bother me.

"We'll clean it once we get this little muffin back to her dad." Ford nuzzles Zoe's neck so she squeals. "I should shave. Is it too picky?"

"Funny that she gets a vote on facial hair that wraps right around your neck—"

"It's growing on you." Ford grins as he kisses Zoe's cheek. She reaches out and grabs his chest hair.

I go change into my bathing suit, and as I come out of the bedroom, I spy the camera on the table. It hits me suddenly that it would be great to take some pictures for Melinda and Derek?

"This is crazy." I say as Ford looks up from helping Zoe get into a swim diaper. "But could we do a photo shoot?"

"Stop starting every sentence with 'this is crazy.' You're a talented person! Why not do a photo shoot?" Ford smiles.

I put the camera to my eye and hope I do it right as I take a picture of Ford kissing Zoe's temple. Placing her in different spots near the pool and am thrilled to catch her facial expressions as her pudgy little hand explores the texture of grass near the Hot Pools of Healing. I catch a great photo of the sun shining on the spray of water as she investigates the jets in the pool. I wish my mom could step out here to see the fun we're having with her pool. That thought gives me pause. I have so many things to thank my mom for. I get a lump in my throat and file that thought away but resolve to write it into my scene tomorrow.

Right now, it's lovely to watch Ford and Zoe play together. I couldn't be happier, and I decide to stay firmly in this moment. I lie down on the hot stones with the camera against my eye and take pictures of Ford and Zoe exploring a salt pool, including the nooks and crannies of the rocks. I catch the look on their faces as a butterfly drifts down onto a flower by the pool.

I put the camera down a fraction of an inch as Ford looks at me over the top of Zoe's head. He smiles, and I smile back. I close my eyes, then open them again. The same perfect scene is in front of me. My only regret is that I can't sit down with my mother and thank her sincerely. This is my perfect life, and I can't wait to see what tomorrow holds.

All the fear, anger, and darkness is replaced with the bright, shiny hope in Zoe's eyes and the promise in Ford's smile.

CHAPTER THIRTY-FIVE

Later, Ford grills our chicken while I feed an exhausted and fussy Zoe her supper. I give her a bottle and hold her until she falls asleep in my arms.

"She had a very big day," Ford whispers as I lay her down in her playpen.

"She did."

"How are you holding up?" Ford holds out my chair on the deck.

"I'm exhausted in a great way," I say honestly.

He pours me a Clemon, then places a lemon wedge on the side of my glass. He hands me a plate of Caesar salad with two grilled chicken breasts on top.

My mouth waters. I dig in. "What makes this so incredibly good?"

"Capers." Ford dives into his salad.

"My goodness, they are amazing. I need those."

"I bought you an extra bottle. They're in your fridge."

I meet his gaze. "Thank you for this. I—"

Ford takes a gulp of his Clemon and waits for me to speak. "What were you going to say?"

"It's ridiculous."

"I've noticed that you often say 'this is crazy' or 'this is ridiculous' when you're about to try something new or speak your truth. Just say it. I want to know."

"I have never in my life had a man make a meal for me until yesterday and now. Never. Not once."

"Really?"

"Really," I confirm. I carefully place a caper on top of my forkful of food.

"I'm sorry to hear that. Really sorry that you had that experience. You deserve better."

"Thankfully, I have Summer to help me process things."

Ford puts down his fork and leans back in his chair. "Anything you care to talk about?"

"I hadn't given a lot of thought to having a baby until you brought it up last night. I wondered why I wasn't concerned to hear you have no interest in more children. I wanted to be sure I wasn't just agreeing because all of this is really new."

"And?" Ford braces himself.

I adjust the candle between us. "If I had to choose between a positive pregnancy test and a plane ticket, I would pick the plane ticket."

"Really?" Ford's breath comes out in a whoosh.

"Yeah. I feel like my entire life has revolved around looking after my mom, then my business with Estee, and now I feel like I'm breathing for the first time. Like I suddenly had someone say, what do you want? And as a hairstylist, I don't ask clients what they want. No one really knows. I ask them what they don't want."

"Really?" Ford's eyes widen in surprise.

"Yeah. So, I've been asking myself what do I not want? The answer surprised me. I don't want to take care of anything right now. Just myself. That's what I need. My mom gave me six months, and I'm not sure it's enough. I have never had time to just be. Can you understand that?"

A few fireflies light up the pine trees near us. I watch them and feel a contentment I've never felt before. "I had a lovely day with Zoe. Absolutely lovely. But even as I held her in my arms and fed her bottles, I searched my heart, and I don't yearn for my own. I talked to Summer, and she had good advice. She said, 'look at what you enjoy doing, and do you want to do all that while parenting?' Until now, I have never actually got to decide what I like. Do I still love writing? Yes. Do I want to learn photography? I think I do! I feel like this is the first time in my whole life I am finding out what I'm passionate about, and I don't want that to stop. I need to be sure, though. So, I really don't want children now, and I am pretty certain that won't be my hope in the future, which surprises me."

"It could change." Ford scratches his chin.

"Maybe." The "I doubt it" hovers between us but isn't expressed.

I truly don't know, and it doesn't matter. I don't have to constantly live life like a catastrophe is right around the corner—I'm just going to live.

"So, we just see what happens." Ford squints at me.

"Yup. We just live in this moment and expect the best."

Our gazes meet across the table, and we smile at each other. We've both been through a lot, but we're still standing. We don't have to wait for the other shoe to drop. It had dropped, and we eventually got up and kept going. Banged up around the edges—sure—but we're not interested in perfect. We're both pursuing healthy, happy, and fun. You can't pursue that if you dread the future.

"A few months ago, that would have terrified me," I whisper.

Just as we nod on the truth of those words, headlights appear in the driveway, and a text lights up the screen on my cell phone.

Chapter Thirty-Six

Treachery

Ford cranes his neck to see who's coming up the driveway as I read the text from Estee.

Elle has left and rescheduled all your clients to her new salon. Please call me.

My stomach drops.

"What's wrong?" Ford asks.

I open my mouth, but no words come out. My hands shake as I reread the text.

A very disheveled Derek jumps out of his car and makes his way to the deck, where we're having supper.

"Derek. Good to see you. Sorry we are meeting under such difficult circumstances." Ford gets up to shake Derek's hand.

"Melinda is ready to go home. We're looking forward to getting settled."

Derek looks from me to Ford.

CHAPTER THIRTY-SIX

I am quiet, my body goes hot and cold trying to process the text from Estee.

"Zoe's in the spare room. She was tired, so we laid her down. Come on in. Are you hungry, Derek?" Ford offers to make him a salad for the road.

"You know, that's a great idea," Derek says gratefully.

"I had a photo shoot with Zoe. I would love to send the pictures to your email so Melinda can see how things went with her while she was in the hospital."

"Oh, that is so kind of you." Derek's eyes are red, like he might be on the verge of tears.

"Have a seat, and we'll get everything packed up for you."

Ford whips up a salad while I gather Zoe's clothes and personal items.

Ford packs the supper to-go in a brown paper bag, then we follow Ford to the spare room, where Zoe's sleeping after her big day swimming and exploring.

"I don't know how to thank you both for taking her and looking after Melinda." Derek leans over and picks up Zoe from the playpen. She immediately snuggles into her dad. I look at Ford and notice his face looks nostalgic.

He knows what it feels like to snuggle a baby girl in his arms when she's warm and heavy from sleep. I'm happy Zoe knows this feeling of safety and protection. Derek carries her to the car and places her in her car seat.

"Absolutely anytime, Derek. I mean it. How is Melinda?" Ford asks as we put all of Zoe's equipment in the trunk.

"She's on bed rest," Derek answers truthfully. "I took a leave of absence."

A look crosses Ford's face. What is it? Regret? My heart seizes in my chest. Does he still love Melinda?

"That's exactly what she'll need. You're wise to put your family first." Ford's voice is soft.

Why is his tone so soft?

Panic wings through me.

Derek nods. "Thank you. I have to get going. Thanks so much again."

Ford and I take a step back as Derek backs his car out of the driveway.

Ford waves, then turns to me.

I tell myself to say nothing. I can't. The words tear out of me, out of a place I didn't know I had in my heart. "Are you still in love with Melinda?"

Ford opens his mouth to speak, then closes it.

I take a step back. "I need to know."

"Melinda and I shared an impossible-to-deal-with tragedy. We fell apart, and I'm happy that she is happy. I will always love her because she was the mother of my daughter."

"Love her as in if she were single again, you would marry her?" I can't stop myself. I have to know.

Am I trading one kind of dysfunction for another?

Ben was a mess and couldn't keep track of his rent payments, but is this relationship codependent, too? Just differently? Am I with Ford because he's actually emotionally unavailable? Am I with him because he can't fully commit to me and I can justify staying a shade of single with him? With him but somehow able to protect myself from being disappointed and let down. I take another step back.

"Indi, I have no intention of living life like that."

"That didn't answer my question," I whisper.

"I—"

I feel the old hairdresser instincts coming out in me. That prickling in the back of my neck that makes me call a person

CHAPTER THIRTY-SIX

out on their lies. What do you want? No one actually knows that, but they know what they don't want. I don't want a dysfunctional relationship with a man who would leave me broken and vulnerable. I had that with my mom, and I can't risk it.

Pain stabs through my heart. I'm losing my business and my boyfriend. I need Summer and a plane ticket back to Brandon. I was foolish and reckless to trust this new life, to trust this man who is obviously too good to be true. It's time to go home, get my business back and—And what? I don't know, but I'll figure it out as I go. All I know is this was all too much, too fast.

Just as panic sets in, Ford's screen flashes in the dim light of night.

His face hardens as he reads the text. "Your father is holding an emergency meeting—tonight."

I don't speak. I can't handle one more thing.

"He wants the board on-site in the next twenty minutes. We'll have to come back to this conversation."

I hand him my phone with Estee's text beaming at him.

"But she's signed a non-compete, right? No problem, you just serve her with—"

I burst into tears.

"Serve her with the papers..." Ford reaches for me, and I take a bigger step back.

My tears fall so hard I can't wipe them away fast enough.

"Hey, Indi, I'll tell your father you aren't available. You need a business meeting with Estee."

"No. I'll go. I'll sign away my rights to this clinic. I'll be on the next plane back to Manitoba." I choke on the words. Here I thought I had processed all my craziness with Summer, and I'm still a loon.

I never expected this sudden betrayal from Elle. Why now? Why not at the very beginning? I worked with her for years. I can't stop my thoughts from spiraling into absolute darkness and disaster.

The only thing I know is I can depend on my hands, my scissors, my foils, and Perfect Blondest Blonde—that I know. This, this creating a spa on a private island is a pipe dream, thought up by a confirmed lunatic.

"Please don't make a rash decision, Indi. Think this through. This clinic is millions of dollars in your pocket. Don't turn down millions for thousands." Ford holds out his hands to me.

Anger whips through me at his entitled comment. I step back farther. "We better get to the meeting."

"I am not in love with Melinda as a romantic interest. I am her friend. She will always know she can come to me, as she did in this crisis. That won't change." A muscle jumps in his jaw.

It's the same tone he used with me when we disagreed about my mother. He's honest. I'm scared to death. Ford drags his hands through his shaggy hair. All I can think is I'm jumping out of the frying pan of dysfunctional Ben into the fire of still-in-love-as-a-friend—whatever that means—Ford.

We don't speak on the way to the clinic.

Chapter Thirty-Seven

Behind the Chair

The boardroom is quiet when we arrive. Everyone's assembled. Truth's face is a thundercloud of fury. My father's eyes narrow as he rereads the letter in front of him.

"Thank you all for coming." His tone is hard. "Ford, as legal counsel, you should read this."

Ford takes the letter from my father and skims it. His jaw tightens.

"Do you have the rest of the paperwork?" Ford's voice holds no emotion. He's in barrister mode.

Carter hands a file to Ford. He sits down beside me and grabs a pen, and if the pen moves as fast as his brain, he's thinking very quickly.

"My real estate agent in Belize sent this paperwork marked urgent—an hour ago. Ford, I need a counter offer immediately."

"Yes, you'll also need me on-site." Ford checks his watch. "Call the pilot."

"Already did."

I sit by Ford like a stone. Suddenly, I understand with startling clarity how Melinda felt. I'm facing complete disaster—Elle stealing all my clients and putting Blyss and Bloom into possible bankruptcy—and he's putting his work first.

My voice shakes. "Before we go too far, I should tell you my assistant has stolen my entire business, and I am needed in my salon to figure out what to do next."

"Oh, Indi, I'm sorry." Truth shakes her head.

"Surely there is paperwork and non-compete—" Carter's gaze meets mine.

I drop my eyes to the table. "Unfortunately, all of this happened so fast. I didn't insist on that. You can imagine how stupid I feel! I never dreamed she would do this!"

"Non-competes are tricky to enforce, anyway. Don't feel too bad." Ford puts his hand on my shoulder.

I shrug him off. "I'm going back to Brandon. I will return to take my mother's ashes to the Cliffs of Consolation, but this is all way too much change, too fast. I'm sorry." I choke on my sentence. "It's been life changing, but I am not ready to change this far. I know hair. I don't know how to start a wellness clinic in a foreign country. A country I have never even been to."

"I do, though. I would be right by your side." Ford sits down and turns my chair to face him. "Lark is moving too."

"If I don't go take my clients back—" I take a deep, shuddering breath.

Truth comes around the table and pulls up a chair. She takes my hands in her own. "Indi, you need to do what is right for

CHAPTER THIRTY-SEVEN

you. You didn't use any of your weeks that the will allowed for you. Go with our blessing and do what you need to do."

"We'll table the decision about you operating the clinic in Belize," Carter says quietly.

Truth squeezes my hands with hers. "Do you need me to come with you? I can fold towels."

The thing I love about Truth is her ability to look at a situation and pitch in to help.

"No rash decisions. Go home. See how things are. Save Blyss and Bloom. Once you're back behind that chair, you'll know what you want. You have a month and a half to decide."

I nod. Truth is so reasonable. I hug her and hold on hard.

"I'll take you home." Ford gathers the paperwork.

"I can walk."

"I will take you home." Ford doesn't take no for an answer.

"I need a haircut."

I look at Ford and blink in surprise. "A haircut?"

"We're professionals, Indi. I need to go to Belize, and I need to look like a shark. Sharks don't have neck hair. You're a hairstylist, and you can be disappointed and devastated by someone, but still give them an awesome haircut."

"I wouldn't say—"

"No need to say anything. We'll talk privately."

I take a deep breath and let it out slowly.

Carter comes around the table and gives me a very hard and quick hug. "The pilot will be ready in two hours."

"Perfect. I can be there in good time." Ford moves to the door. "Indi?"

I hug my father and gulped back tears. "I'll let you know when I'm back safe."

Together, Ford and I leave for my cottage. I try hard not to look at Ford as he pulls off his shirt and washes his hair in the sink of my bathroom. I swallow as the muscles in his shoulders tense as he towel dries his hair. At the sight of him without a shirt, I tell myself to get a grip on my emotions.

"I'm sorry." Ford sits in a chair with an old towel around his broad shoulders.

I push down my feelings of attraction for him as I comb his hair into sections.

"I'm sorry too."

"When you asked me that, I hadn't even thought about it. When Melinda left, I was gutted. But I was already such a mess from losing Madison that I wasn't super clear about my feelings. Honestly, men don't think much about it. We just spiral and try to crawl out of it. I could lie and say I have no feelings for her, but obviously, she was the mother of my child—"

"Would you marry her again?"

"No. I wouldn't," Ford says firmly.

I take a razor to the longest pieces of his hair and rough cut it. Then I go in and comb out the perimeter. I work fast. Both of us have planes to catch and emotions to process. I double-check the number on the guard and slid it onto the clippers. Swiftly, the salt and pepper hair falls onto his shoulders. I cut the corner of his hair that connects the top to the sides, then stand in front of him. His eyes meet mine.

"Close your eyes," I whisper.

"What are you going to do to me?" Ford squints.

"I'm going to trim your eyebrow hair."

Ford grins. "Why is it that every time we have a romantic moment, it's interrupted by a snake, a crying toddler, or eyebrow hairs?"

CHAPTER THIRTY-SEVEN

"Maybe we aren't meant to be together." The thought makes my throat close with tears. "I saw Melinda. She is absolutely perfect—supermodel beautiful."

Ford's eyes fly open. "What?"

"I feel very less than her." I wipe my tears on my shirt. "Keep your eyes closed. This is a big job. The last thing we need is an eyebrow hair sticking into your eye and slowing us down."

"I'm swooning," Ford says dryly.

Finally done with his eyebrows, I double-check the top of his ears for any stray hair and am satisfied he looks perfect. Too good to be true.

I take my place behind the chair and run my fingers through his hair, testing to be sure everything on top is even. I press a hot cloth to the back of his neck, take a dollop of conditioner, and spread it over his neck. Changing my blade so it's super sharp, I razor his neck with a straight blade so it's perfectly smooth. Within minutes, I'm done. It took all of fifteen minutes to transform him from a person who looks like he lives in the wilderness to someone who's ready to take on a boardroom and make lesser lawyers shake with fear.

Even with stubble, Ford looks fierce—sharp, hard, and ready for battle. Ford looks like a man who would attract every supermodel in sight, like a man who wouldn't notice a broken-down hairdresser with a sore neck caused by old pain that is suddenly flaring up! *Ugh.*

He could have his pick of anyone—anywhere. If I lived on kale and dust for the rest of my life, I could never compete with the supermodels that would fling themselves at him when he gets to Belize.

My traitorous knees buckle at the sight of him. He needs to shave, but somehow, that stubble looks incredible against the perfect haircut. Yes, the haircut's perfect. Not bragging—but it is. In a world where everything is upside down and crumbling with betrayal, the haircut is on point.

"Indi. You're beautiful. If you think I'm comparing you to Melinda and thinking she's better, you're mistaken."

My chest tightens. "I think I can see what you had, and we'll never have that."

Ford stands, and my breath freezes in my throat. I stay safely behind the chair.

"I am not interested in what I had. It doesn't exist anymore."

His deep voice makes my stomach flip.

"What do you want, Indi?"

"I don't want to feel single in a relationship, Ford."

Ford nods. "That is perfectly reasonable."

"When you hesitated, I panicked." I place my razor on the table, keeping the chair between us.

"Indi, if this land deal weren't so time sensitive, I would go with you to figure out your salon situation. But I can't. I work for your dad. Let me figure this out in Belize. Then can we have one conversation before you decide anything?"

"That's fair." My throat ached with tears because in all honesty, I feel abandoned.

"There is only one island for sale. If we lose this deal, it's gone forever." Ford's tone pleads with me to understand that he has no choice.

"I understand." I fuss with my scissors and comb and take the guard off the clippers.

Ford checks his watch, the big one for scuba divers. "I have to go. My plane leaves in an hour, and I haven't packed."

"Right."

"Don't sign anything or make any big decisions until we can talk."

CHAPTER THIRTY-SEVEN

"I'm fine." After that lie, I take a deep breath and release it slowly. "I scare easy."

"So do I," Ford says quietly.

"No, you don't. You look like you're ready for the front lines."

He really does. He is stop-your-heart gorgeous.

Ford pulls me out from behind the chair and into his arms. He hugs me hard. My head wants to resist, and my traitorous heart is ready to pool at his feet. But in the battle between them, my head wins. When Ford leans in to kiss me, I pull back and put space between us.

"I need some time." My voice is hoarse with emotion.

My heart hardens as his phone blows up with messages.

He reads the texts quickly. "I'm so sorry. I have to go. I have a meeting with the estate agent on Ambergris in exactly twelve hours. I am sorry."

"I'm sorry too." My tone sounds very final.

It's the same tone I used as Phyllis tried to hand me the phone when my mother called, frantic, from a police station, on the night I left. I said no that night, too. I wonder if I'm going to say no for the rest of my life.

Chapter Thirty-Eight

New first

Truth and Carter are in my house, helping me pack, within minutes. "I got you a flight out of Calgary right to Brandon."

"When does it get in?"

"At two p.m."

Immediately, I text Estee to let her know we can meet in person at three p.m. She texts back a heart and a travel safe.

After my long flight, Phyllis waits for me in the airport parking lot.

"Indi, you look amazing!" Phyllis's jaw drops in shock as I hug her. "You're half gone!"

"No, I am certainly not. I still have some weight to go."

"Not much. Let me look at you. Goodness, this is an incredible change."

"Thanks. How is Estee holding up?"

CHAPTER THIRTY-EIGHT

"She said we can take until five because the accountant wants to be at the meeting and she had a client she couldn't move."

"Good, that lets me get showered and changed. I feel like I need a minute."

"Are you hungry?"

"Not really."

"We're having family supper after the meeting, if that works for you. If you aren't too tired?"

"That sounds great."

"Truth told me about that Mediterranean chicken bake you like. Low-carb, I think she mentioned."

"You don't have to do anything special for me, Phyllis."

Phyllis frowns. "Of course, I do. I love you."

With that, I burst into tears.

Phyllis pulls over and hugs me with all her strength. "You have been through so much. You're grieving. It's healthy. It's normal."

"I'm sorry. I can't pull myself together."

"You don't have to. You're home."

Home. Yes, I'm home and with people who have long track records of caring for me.

Once I sob my heart out to Phyllis and the storm subsides, I finally pull myself together.

Phyllis drops me off at my condo, where I take a hot shower, then pull on my robe that hangs off me now. I blow-dry my hair perfectly straight and spend a full fifteen minutes on my makeup. I need a haircut, but it's okay. I style it carefully into a sleek look that I haven't seen in months.

I look through my clothes for something that will fit and find a pretty sundress that's sort of one-size-fits-all. I have to adjust the shoulder straps, as I lost so much weight in my arms and shoulders.

I drink some water to calm down and pace my condo. I can't believe I'm home and feel so restless. Months ago, I didn't want to leave.

In May, I would have been thrilled at the requirement of being on site getting waved. My home was a place to eat and sleep and get ready for work the next day. No laptop to write at, no camera, no Hot Pools of Healing, no deck overlooking a lake and mountain. My deck looks out over a supermarket parking lot. Ford is on his way to Belize and is certainly not a half mile away from this sterile condo.

Finally, it's time to go. I arrive at Blyss and Bloom early. I want to see the stylists before they leave for the day.

The salon is a buzz of talking and blow-dryers. The front staff is trying to get towels washed, and the backbar restocked for the next day. Blyss and Bloom runs like a well-oiled machine without me.

My chair and Elle's are empty. Unfortunately, I know exactly how much money that empty chair is losing.

I take a deep breath and immediately regret it. My nose prickles from the ammonia hanging in the air. A colour correction is happening at the sink. I make my way over, trying to ignore my watering eyes from the ammonia that wafts from the sink as I get closer to the source.

Estee places her hand on the handle to the back room. "Ready?"

I wipe my eyes again and nod. "You know how I love math and accounting."

"As much as I do." Estee groans as she opens the door to the accountant—and Ford.

CHAPTER THIRTY-EIGHT

"Ford!" I gasp in shock. I wipe my eyes and try to focus on him at the same time.

"Hey." Ford grins at me.

My heart flips in my chest. "You're supposed to be in Belize. What are you doing here?"

"Putting you first." Ford stands and holds his hand out to Estee.

"Estee, this is Ford."

"Nice to meet you, Ford." Estee stumbles over the words.

I knew Estee like a sister, and I can feel her swoon at my side.

Ford with a proper haircut, a fresh shave, and a bespoke suit takes my breath away—Estee's too.

"I am so sorry. Could we have a moment?" I ask Estee and Brian, the accountant.

They quickly exit the back room, and I turn to face Ford.

"Here's what's going on. When faced with a crisis, I work, and you run. We're not doing that," Ford says firmly. "The last time the woman in my life faced a crisis, I went to work.

As I got on the plane to go to Belize, I realized I was doing it again, and I will not do that to you. What's between us is new, Indi, but I like the direction it was headed until it hit hurricane Melinda and Zoe.

Melinda left me and had children with another man. We're completely done. I hold a place for her in my heart, as you saw. If she's ever in a life-threatening situation, I'm there. Same way I would be there for Lark or Carter or Truth. This is how I operate for anyone that I know in crisis. So, that's the truth about that.

To prove it, there is a multimillion-dollar deal on the table in Belize, but it will just have to wait until I know what is happening here." Ford takes a step forward and places his big hands on my arms.

"You built this business from the ground up. It is your heart and your soul. You love the people you work with, and you love your clients. That makes you who you are. So, I want to apologize for saying such a tactless thing to you before. That you are facing a business where you stand to lose thousands or millions. I am so sorry.

That was the wrong way to look at it. I tried to see it from your perspective. You face losing a business that has been your only security and safety. I see that. I see you. Indi, you are my first priority. Not an island in Belize and not a wellness clinic built by someone else. Whatever has to happen here, whatever you need, we'll face it head-on together." Ford takes a tissue from the box in my hands and carefully wipes away my tears.

"I hope these tissues are biodegradable," I whisper.

Ford throws back his head and laughs.

He smiles at me, and I blow my nose and smile back.

"You're not the only one reverting to old patterns."

Ford's gaze meets mine, and he waits for me to elaborate.

"This is the only thing I truly trusted after I left my mother, because I never felt worthy of Phyllis and Al's love. I always worried I would mess it up. My value came from other people, like Estee, needing me to swoop in and fix a mess. I could work harder and keep things afloat so I would have value." I press the tissue to my eyes. "So, I bolted, and this gave me the perfect excuse, but I would have run, regardless."

Ford nods and opens his mouth.

I hold up my hand. "I'm not done. I ran instead of having a conversation and trusting someone other than myself. So, from now on, I'm not running anymore. We'll fight it out or talk it out or whatever."

Ford lets out a deep breath. "So, we're going forward?"

"We are officially a dating couple." I reach for the tissues.

CHAPTER THIRTY-EIGHT

"Then why are you crying?" Ford asks.

"I'm allergic to ammonia." My eyes are streaming. "I'm allergic to my salon." With that admission, I burst into tears. Just like when I was on the floor with Ariana stepping over me, my body has decided, and I'm forced to accept it.

"Really?" Ford's face creases with concern.

"Yeah. Really."

"So, what do you do about that?" Ford wipes my tears away with the tissues.

"Suffer. Take lots of medication to get through a day."

"That's not sustainable."

"Yeah. So, I have to change an entire salon to ammonia free, which is a nightmare I can't even think about, or I have to quit hair. That's what I know for sure. But right now, we have to meet with the accountant." I open the door. "Sorry to keep you waiting. Please, come in."

"Everything all right?" Brian asks cautiously.

"Everything is fine." I take two more tissues out of the box. "It turns out I am allergic to ammonia. I didn't know."

Estee takes a deep breath and lets it out slowly. "Oh, Indi."

"I haven't needed antihistamines in months. I don't even have any on me—but you need me back here, Estee. I'll get a box—"

Estee puts her hand on my arm. "Indi, we can't go ammonia free. We just can't. It would take—"

"I know." I lean back in my chair, defeated. "I can take pills until I get the clients back, though. You're cutting back for your kids, and that's important. We built this together, and I can't let you down."

Brian clears his throat. "That's why I'm here. Let's look at the numbers, shall we?"

I reach for Estee's hands, as I always do when the accountant talks. It's ridiculous, holding hands like preschoolers when faced with our financial information, but numbers terrify me, both of us actually.

Ford notices our clasped hands and smiles encouragingly. But the smile drains from his face as he pulls out a yellow legal pad and jots down numbers too. Suddenly, the terror filling my heart shifts. We will figure it out. We're going to fix it.

"I will stay and call every single client, explain what's going on, then rebook them with the stylists who would be the best to accommodate them."

"I'll get your client list." Estee goes to the front desk, and within minutes, I hear the printer. She pulls out the appointment book and looks over the columns for a six-week booking block. "Alli could take half of that."

"She's stable?"

"As stable as anyone, honestly," Estee says cautiously. "She's dropped that boyfriend, and she's working two jobs to make ends meet. This is an excellent solution for her."

"I'll work every other day to give my nose a break."

"Monica is just getting back from maternity leave. She could take the rest. Her clientele hasn't started booking back in with her yet. She'll start with half—"

"Right. We'll have a meeting with her and Alli and see which clients they think would be a good fit for them. Maybe Monica wants to come back a little early."

"Yes. She might in order to have her income at full tilt. She would be foolish not to."

"I think my work here is done." Brian stands. "I wish you all the best. Let me know if you need any further information."

"I think we can take it from here." Ford stands and shakes Brian's hand. "Great to meet you."

CHAPTER THIRTY-EIGHT

"You too." Brian pats Estee's shoulder. "You know, you've done great work, ladies. You don't have to hold hands anymore for the financial reports. Even if you lose these clients, in a year, that will all smooth over."

"We stand to lose a lot."

"But it's just money, Indi. It's just money, and we'll be fine." Estee squeezes my hand and lets it go. "Your eyes are swelling shut."

I smile at Brian. "Thanks, Brian. I guess this is our last financial report together. It's been a pleasure."

Brian hugs me. "I wish you all the best, Indi."

When Brian leaves, we sit at the table again. I blow my nose. Then I look down at my list of clients. My heart aches because I love them so much. I can't imagine doing their hair for the last time.

How would I do it?

I see the names and think of so many appointments where we bared our souls, hearts, fears, and triumphs. Many of the women on my list I think of as family. Some are like replacement sisters and moms. They're an amazing group of people.

Estee's phone lights up. "It's Mom. Supper is ready."

"Right."

"Would you like to meet my family, Ford?"

"I would love to." Ford smiles, and I smile back.

Chapter Thirty-Nine

Family

Watching Ford meet my family for the first time is the sweetest experience of my life. He blends in, even though he's wearing a suit and tie in a family that doesn't wear suits during leisure time. He's respectful to Al, charming with Phyllis, and he offers to grill the supper on the barbeque. Estee's husband and Al go out with him, a beer in hand to talk.

"He's lovely." Phyllis has tears in her eyes as she hands me the homemade salad dressing. "Really lovely."

"Yes, he is." My throat tightens.

"You deserve this, Indi." Phyllis puts her hand on my wrist to get my attention.

My eyes fill with tears as I look at Phyllis. All of her, including her tight perm, wrinkles she refuses to Botox, and skin she doesn't ruthlessly exfoliate. Her steadfast eyes that

CHAPTER THIRTY-NINE

see through me. I get a glimpse of the strong Phyllis from the night I ran. How she held me. How she and Al cared for me.

"How do I ever pay you back, Phyllis? I don't know how to."

"Some children occur to us. We don't have them ourselves, but they were meant to be in our family. You were that child." Phyllis says simply.

"What do you mean?" My breath catches with the emotion of those words.

"You're living. You're happy. You are out from behind the chair. That's all we want. Happy kids. You are our kid." Phyllis's gaze holds mine.

"Why, though?" My throat is tight with unshed tears. "Why did you step in when I was fifteen?" I hold my breath, waiting for the answer. "I never understood it."

"No one did for me." Phyllis places a steaming-hot casserole on top of the oven, then she turns to me. "I saw myself in you. I know that someday, you will do this for someone else. Tansy almost quit speaking to me, you know?"

Her words caused me to think of Hailey. I wondered if she was okay. I snapped my attention back to Phyllis. "When did she stop speaking to you?"

"When I let you chart your own course until you went too far."

"Ben."

"Yes. Ben was the final straw. We had to join forces."

I nodded. "Thank you."

Phyllis smiles and hugs me hard. "Go to your man and check on the meat. We're almost ready."

At the end of supper, Ford and I settle onto the porch swing with hot tea.

"I can't tell you how much I appreciate you being here today. When I watched you jotting numbers on a legal pad, I have to be completely honest. I swooned."

Ford laughs. "When I watched you take over Zoe with a bottle, I swooned, too. We're a good team."

"A little broken, but yeah. A good team."

Ford's eyes softened with sympathy as he spoke the next sentence. "Sorry you're allergic to your work."

"Yeah, thanks. There are ammonia-free alternatives, but we can't ask the salon to switch it's too much change too fast. Besides, I'm curious about what will happen next."

Ford nods. "A private island in Belize. It's going to be a lot of work. What do you need me to do to make this transition smoother?"

I put down my tea and snuggled into him. I settled my head on his shoulder. "I'm fine. I am dreading the phone calls to the clients. How do I say goodbye to these people?"

Ford presses his feet into the deck boards, and the swing moves. "What will you say?"

"I'll say that for health reasons, I can't continue, but I have two stylists I recommend. I will be there for the transition appointment so they feel comfortable that they will receive the same service. It means I'm here for six weeks at least."

"I can't do anything to help? You're sure? I can fold towels or—"

"You can help me by telling me straight. Did you agree with the numbers the accountant showed us?" I straighten and look at Ford. "Numbers seem to slip around the page, and I can't figure them out. I always look at people who can figure out numbers with a certain awe. I never could. That's why I hold Estee's hand. We both fear numbers."

CHAPTER THIRTY-NINE

"Numbers are your friend." Ford squeezes my hand. A completely different experience from Estee's grasp earlier.

"They are not." I refuse to be swayed.

"The numbers he presented were very conservative. You're in good shape even with half of what he suggested comes back to your salon. Do you think you can get half?"

"Yes. I can get half."

"You sound very confident. I like it." Ford grins at me.

"I know my clients." I grin back.

"Then it will work. What do you need from me?" Ford asks.

"I need you to go to Belize and secure a property that will let Salt and Citrus expand."

"I'd rather do that with you."

"I trust you to do that for us."

"What if that cay is gone?"

"Let it go."

"What?" Ford blinks in shock.

"Let it go. What are the alternative properties?"

"Are you sure?" Ford gasps.

I squint a little as I think about it. "I had some reservations about an island."

"What reservations?"

"An island sounds lonely. What are the alternatives?"

"You really are an extrovert."

"Guilty."

"I have some on my phone."

Ford takes out his phone and I lean over him. I can smell his aftershave, and it makes my heart flip in my chest. When I glance up, every single member of the Bloom family is watching out the kitchen window. I wave at them and they leap away and pretend to dry dishes.

"That's the one." I look through beachfront properties and try to think back to what I loved about my first and only beachfront vacation. "What is the reef like on this one?"

Ford quickly searches it. "Reviews say the reef is in good shape."

"What is the eel population?"

"Zero."

"I think that's the one," I say.

"The rooms are abysmal. Like really terrible."

"Doesn't matter. Not being on a private island, it's easier to bring in supplies. We can keep our costs down."

"True," he agrees.

"And we don't have to house our staff on sight. Except Lark, of course. We're a package deal."

Ford sighs at that declaration. "She sings. Constantly."

"I know. I love her, but all that singing. Ugh. I'll talk to her," I say.

"Okay."

"What I love about this is that we have the airport at Ambergris right there, and we have a water taxi from Chetumal. It's a win-win."

"I've always just taken private jets and never thought about it," Ford says so offhandedly I stiffen beside him.

"Good thing we have a blue-collar girl on staff to keep our heads out of the clouds." I nudge him.

"You're likely allergic to clouds."

"Probably." That comment makes me pause. "What are your parents going to say about me? How are they with working class?"

"They are terrible, which is why we will be two countries away." Ford laughs.

I frown. "I am *very* charming."

CHAPTER THIRTY-NINE

"Yes. You are."

"But you are spoiled. I can tell you ooze privilege."

"Sorry. I know. It's terrible."

I don't press him about his family; instead, I launch into my take on the expansion. "I prefer if our clients can get there without a zillion connecting flights or water taxis. This is my colour vision for this space and the feel that I want to convey."

I pull out my phone and show him paint swatches and linens.

"You're sure this is the one?" Ford asks again.

"When you go, take your GoPro and show me the reef. Sign nothing until I see that reef."

"I wish you could come." Ford caresses my cheek.

"I can't. I can't leave Estee here with this mess. I would love to, but—"

"This is your family, and family is first."

"Right. I think that is going to be our new motto, right?" I move closer to him.

"Yes. It is." Ford agrees. "I want to be clear, though. Six weeks is a long time."

"I'll meet you at the trailhead for the Cliffs of Consolation," I whisper.

"I'll be there."

"And from there?"

"We head to Belize. Everything will be finalized financially, and we'll start the expansion."

"I'd kiss you, but the entire Bloom family is looking at us again. You're the first guy I brought home that wears a tie."

"You'll be the first girl I bring home that has flown economy."

I laugh so hard I think I might fall off the porch swing. When I calm down, I kiss Ford. I kiss him in such a fashion that the Bloom family averts their eyes.

"Six weeks is a very long time," I agree.

"It'll be worth it." He promises as he kisses me back.

Chapter Forty

Transition

As I do the transition hair appointments with the stylists who will take my place, I go through sixty antihistamines and walk over sixty kilometers to get ready for the Cliffs of Consolation and my mother's ashes. I don't understand why we aren't hiking into the Valley of Loss. It seems odd to me, but it's what Tansy wanted, and I'm learning to trust her. It's a bittersweet thought.

To trust a woman who's dead and can't benefit from that trust. The great thing about mothers and daughters, though, is we can stand on each other's shoulders. Tansy wouldn't benefit from my trust, but I would benefit from the exercise of building it. I'm recreating my life with new tools, new coping skills. Whether I stay in Belize or in Snow—or wherever—I'm moving forward.

Within six weeks, eighty-five percent of my clients came back to Blyss and Bloom.

Ariana stays with Elle in her new salon. To say I'm not hurt would be a lie. But she doesn't owe me anything, really. There's no need to fight with Elle. There is no reason to be negative. For over twenty years, I worked on these clients, and more than Ariana would go where they needed to. I know I gave Estee and the girls at Blyss and Bloom my best. I could do nothing more.

It's way harder than I expected to say goodbye to my clients. Honestly, so many tears as I hug clients that I shared every triumph and tragedy with. Every time I waver on my decision to quit the salon, my nose and my neck remind me I can't do it anymore. My heart reminds me, too, with every text and video from Ford. He found the perfect place I hadn't expected in a stretch of coast where we hadn't looked before.

What we agreed on at the beginning isn't as perfect as this estate. The real estate agent had been holding it for a select client, but that client had a fortune reversal.

"Indi, it's perfect. It checks every box," Ford says excitedly over the video conference.

"Let me see the reef again."

He screen shares the reef on the conference call. A baby octopus moves across a beautiful reef. A myriad of fish dart around healthy coral.

Tears pool in my eyes as I watch the ocean wildlife on the reef. "It's perfect."

"So, purchase it?"

"How far is it from the airport?"

"Twenty minutes, and a water taxi comes and goes from Ambergris every half hour."

"It's only half an hour to get across?"

"Fifteen minutes."

"It's the one."

CHAPTER FORTY

"You don't want to see the rooms?"

"We can fix all that. Is there an airstrip?" I stop myself and mouth those words soundlessly. I can't believe I just asked that.

"No. We would have to commission that."

"Can you set that up before you return?"

"Sure. Anything else?"

"No. Just come back. I want you to go to the Cliffs of Consolation with me. I—"

"I'll be there." Ford's voice is warm and deep in my ear. "I wouldn't miss it. I wish your mom could see this place. It's exactly what she wanted."

"The financing is in order?"

"Yes. I put the proceeds of my restaurant into this property. I'm an investor. I wanted someone on the ground who liked numbers."

"Oh! Perfect!" I laugh. "I'll pick the paint, and—"

"You handle the people, and I'll handle the numbers."

"Deal."

"I'll see you at the trailhead."

"See you there."

"Indi?"

"Yes, Ford."

"I'll bring the biodegradable tissues." Ford says softly.

"I'll need it," I whisper.

I really will. My mother gave me my life back and not just a regular life. I never dreamed this high. Ever. But this will make every dream I could have envisioned come true. Even dreams I had never considered. I never could have conjured up the possibility of a wellness clinic in a beautiful new land or man like Ford. I wish she were alive so I could say thank you. Carrying her ashes to the Cliffs of Consolation will have to do.

Chapter Forty-One

Cliffs of Consolation

The Cliffs of Consolation take my breath away. Mist hangs heavy over the cliffs, giving the entire area an ethereal feel. This ceremony of saying goodbye couldn't happen anywhere else. The place where Tansy chose to rest is absolutely perfect.

We hiked hard and wept on the way. We talked about all the good and all the bad, and with every step, we healed each other. I look around at the people in the group that are now my best friends. The day is so bittersweet because I love every single one of them, and Tansy will never know what she's given me.

Carter takes a deep breath and opens a letter from Tansy. "Tansy insisted on having the last word." He smiles at us all.

I smile back at my dad, and I wait to hear what the letter says.

"We are gathered here today at the Cliffs of Consolation, not the Valley of Loss, because losing someone who has lived a long life is different than the loss of someone taken far too soon. My first letter is to Ford."

Ford stiffens beside me, and I take his hand in mine.

"You will carry your tragedy with you forever, but if I'm right, I think in Indi you will find someone to lighten that load. She will keep you busy, engaged, and tangled in clients, and for that, I am grateful because you will keep her safe. She's terrible with numbers, but super with people. You should likely handle the money, but I don't want to interfere. It's not my way."

We all laugh through our tears.

"Never let her go hungry, as I did."

My heart breaks at that statement. My eyes fill with tears as Tansy speaks of her pain and her truth. So simple and yet so honest.

"Don't let her worry about you. Be strong for her, as I was not. Ford, don't let the electricity go out. Keep my girl in the light. Do not let my girl live one day in fear. There will be sadness, and there will be joy, but there cannot be fear between you. Keep her heart safe. Keep her spirit free and her bank reconcile balanced."

We laugh at that last parting shot.

"Truth." Carter's voice shakes.

We all stop laughing as we brace ourselves for Tansy's last words to her twin.

"You are my soul in another body."

I close my eyes because there are no truer words than those.

"There are no words for you except thank you, and you know why."

CHAPTER FORTY-ONE

We all have tears in our eyes, but as I move to Truth, we weep together.

It takes a long time, but somehow, it doesn't matter. The Cliffs of Consolation seem to be suspended in a land where time does not exist. Only hearts, love, and longing linger here.

"Indi."

I hold Truth's and Ford's hands.

"Indi, you are my heart."

I bow my head as those words wash over me.

"Do you remember that day in the park with the lovely sun shining down through the oak trees? All the other mothers had nice, neat sandwiches wrapped in wax paper, and I had a macrame bag of oranges."

Carter walks forward and hands me the aromatherapy blend of Sunshine in a Bottle. I unscrew the cap and smell it as he speaks. The scent intensifies the memories the letter evokes.

"I am so sorry, Indi. I was so sick, and we lost all that life together. But I love you, and if the process has worked as it is supposed to, you should be on the cusp of a new life. A life full of actual bliss. I love you. Every molecule of you. When you smell the blend, I want you to remember how much I love you. Have the happiest life, my love."

Tears spill from my eyes, and my dad steps forward and scoops me up.

"I love you too," he whispers as I weep into his shoulder.

I wish I had reconciled when she asked before. I curse myself, then I realize she would hate that, so I decide to let it go.

"She wants you to read the rest." Carter hands the letter to me.

"How?" I weep.

"It takes as long as it takes." Carter brushes his tears away and hands me the letter.

I wipe my eyes and take her letter in my shaking hands.

"Carter," I start then can't finish.

They wait for me to pull it together.

"Carter," I start again. "You gave me Indi and then a whole new life. Thank you doesn't seem like enough." I take a deep breath and let it out slowly.

Ford comes to stand beside me. I can feel the solid strength of his arm against mine.

"Take care of our girl." My voice cracks. "I know Ford will treat her right, and I know you will love her enough for both of us. In the meantime, you absolutely must tell Truth what your feelings for her are. Honestly. It's gone on long enough. You love each other, and I'm out of the way. Life is short. Seize it."

My eyes widen as I look at Carter and Truth. She tentatively slides her hand into his, and he brings her fingers to his lips and kisses them.

"I think that's what you would call interference, which she just assured us she would never partake of," I say dryly.

Everyone laughs, and the tension that had been building since May breaks. Sweetly. Perfectly.

"I love you all. Continue to help those who need it. Love each other. I need you all to know that my life was richer for all of you being part of it. Tansy."

I almost can't get that last sentence out. It hurts to say the words—her last words to this group of people I had grown to love.

Ford picks up the spade and digs the hole for the oak tree. Once the earth is removed, I open my backpack and take out the scene of the night I left, which I wrote in my mother's

CHAPTER FORTY-ONE

house. I wrote that scene from a place in my subconscious that I didn't know existed. I settle my account of that night and the contrast of entering her home now in the ground. I also developed pictures of my new life, which I place in there, pictures of Jasper and Ford, but the second-to-last picture is Ford kissing Zoe. My heart nearly stops as Lark moves forward with a picture of Ford kissing me. Finally, I place the picture of our new venture—Salt and Citrus Belize. I add a picture of the baby octopus that sold me on the property.

It feels right that Tansy started this work, and it's up to me to finish it. I can't believe that at one point, I was going to sign it over. I take a moment to think about what anger and resentment could have stolen from me. What forgiveness had given me back was immeasurable.

Finally, I take a deep breath and place the essential oil Sunshine in a Bottle on top of all the writing and photography. I weep as I pour her ashes into the earth. My eyes meet Ford's. He dashes tears away, leaving a streak of dirt on his face.

I reach for him and press my forehead to his. Finally, we put the oak sapling on top of my writing and photos and the bottle that encapsulates the one perfect day.

Sometimes, that's all we get.

Carter and Truth, Ford and I place dirt around the tree. All four of us have a part in planting the oak tree in her memory.

Once we're done, I sprinkle the scent of Sunshine in a Bottle at the base of the tree. The scent of mandarin, oak, and warm summer sun mixes with fresh-turned earth. I move my hands through the scent and the soil and cry. I really weep for her, for all that we endured, and all we missed.

Jet comes to me and places her hands on my shoulders as I close my eyes and breathe in the light and out the dark thoughts. Lark kneels beside me and slides her arm around my waist. Tamsin kneels on the other side of me. I catch a glimmer of sun off her diamond bracelet. But my eyes finally lock with Ford's because he kneels on the other side of the tree, facing me. He gently takes my hands from the earth and holds them. It's a silent, gentle way to say it's okay to take my hands from the soil.

Is it? My eyes ask him silently.

"You never let it go, and you never get over it. You just cope as best as you can," Ford whispers.

"She loved you, honey," Lark murmurs.

"You saved her, and she saved you right back." Tamsin puts her hand on my forearm.

"Breathe in the light." Jet rests her fingertips on my neck.

I close my eyes, and I breathe in the light, the scent of Sunshine in a Bottle mingled with the soil. I weep as take my hands from Ford's, and I press the scent and the earth together for the last time.

I focus on the memory of Tansy handing me the orange slice. I let every emotion wash over me from the day that inspired Sunshine in a Bottle. Someday the sun will shine through the leaves of this oak tree.

Who knows what mother and daughter would share an orange under the boughs of this tree in the future?

As I open my eyes, all that's left is a realization that if Tansy had been well, every day—most days—would have been like that perfect day.

That thought is my truth.

That knowledge is my peace.

Epilogue

Fresh Start

Wearing a yellow bikini, I stand in front of the full-length mirror in my room in Belize.

My reflection surprises me. I don't know what my weight is, but I'm at my goal life. I'm physically healthy, no longer insulin resistant, no longer on the verge of type 2 diabetes. Emotionally, I'm happy—ready to start this new venture with Ford.

Having Salt and Citrus Belize renovated and ready for guests by February first will be an enormous task. But we aren't worried about that tonight. Lark is in Belize City to pick up some supplies, and we have a date.

A proper one!

After we snorkel the reef, Ford is serving us supper on the beach—with a tablecloth, candles, and napkins.

He's determined to keep his word from the night we had Zoe and handled a crisis instead of a first date.

I can't wait to swim out to the corals and see if I can find that baby octopus.

Grinning, I reach for my fins and snorkel. Making my way through the courtyard, I wave at Ford, who has his fins on already.

Together, we stand on the white sand beach. I slide my hand into his. We walk into the water, keeping our backs to the surf so our fins stay flat. The warm, salty Caribbean Sea swirls around our feet.

"Before we go in, I have something for you." Ford rummages in his pocket.

My heart zips with anticipation.

In his hand is a gold necklace with a tiny gold octopus and a coral-coloured bead.

As soon as I see that bead, my heart melts at the sentiment. I notice he still wears his original bracelet as a memory of his daughter, but he has a new piece of leather with the same coral-coloured bead.

My breath catches at the sight of a new bracelet beside the old one.

"I thought it would be a great idea to mark this occasion with a piece of jewellery." Ford's eyes search mine. "The octopus, because that's what sold you on this place. The bead because we're starting a new life here together, and instead of documenting all the hurt, now I want to document all the joy. Creating this venture with you is exciting, and I can't wait to see what happens next."

My heart skips a beat as he places the necklace on my neck. The octopus and the bead settle in the hollow of my collarbone.

EPILOGUE

I press my fingertips to the bead.

Ford smiles, his eyes search mine. Finally, he dips his head, pressing his lips to the bead at my throat, then he kisses me gently, reverently, as the waves of the Caribbean push us even closer together.

"Thank you, it's beautiful."

"You're welcome." Ford kisses me again, and I see a flash of light on the top knuckle of his pinky finger.

"What is that?" I try to grab his hand. "I saw a glimmer of something."

"You mean this?" He holds up his hand and there is a beautiful diamond engagement ring glittering in the sun.

"What is happening!" I gasp and try to pounce on his hand so I can get a better look, but a wave takes me to my knees.

Ford drags me up and kisses me. "It's for tonight."

"I don't want to wait." I pounce on him again.

"I promised a proper date!" Ford protests as he tries, with great difficulty, to hold us both upright as the sea tries to knock us off our feet. "When you don't have seaweed in your hair." Ford laughs as I drag his hand close to me so I can inspect the ring.

"Right here. Right now." I crow as I try to wrestle the ring off his finger.

"Indi." Ford pulls me against him. "Can you be serious? There's a proper procedure!"

"It's beautiful!!" I gasp at the sight of the ring. I take a step closer and *trip on my fin*.

Ugh!

Ford catches me for the second time and he's holding onto me so tight; I can feel his heart pounding in his chest.

"Yes." I kiss him as hard as I can.

"Indi, I didn't ask yet." Ford laughs as he shakes his head, pulling me close as the waves tear at us.

"I said yes!" I am squealing with delight and I can't stop.

Ford laughs as he slides the engagement ring onto the fourth finger of my left hand.

It's perfect. I admire the gleaming diamond. I look up at him just as a wave blindsides us, breaking us apart. We give up fighting the surf. Swimming past the turmoil; we find each other in the gentle swell of the sea. Ford smiles at me as he picks some seaweed out of my hair.

I am loving the feel of our arms, legs, and fins tangled together. It's more perfect than anything I could ever imagine. Beyond anything I could have hoped for. With love and gratefulness in my heart, I kiss him again. And again. And again...

The End

Acknowledgments

Wow! There are so many people in my health and wellness team to thank, it's hard to even know where to start.

First of all, my husband Peter. Thank you for supporting my dreams.

I want to thank Ashley Collier (*Summer*) of Wildflower Counseling for her help as my therapist. Without her sessions, I couldn't write chapter Thirty One. I was stuck there for about a year! Thank you from the bottom of my heart.

A big thank you to my primary care physician, Dr. David Cram. Once I was properly diagnosed by you, I wrote 100 hundred pages of this book. Thank you so much.

Also, Dr. Blake Denbow, my chiropractor, (*Dr. Barrett*) I was happy to write you into Chapter Sixteen. Every hairstylist has a 'back going out' experience and thankfully Blake (Dr. Barrett in the book) was there for mine. Thanks Blake!

Thank you Roxanne Scraba for your hard work as my massage therapist!

A big thanks to Li Lin (*Tao*) my acupuncturist from Brandon Acupuncture.

Also a big thanks to *all my clients* who have shared triumphs and tragedies in my chair.

***Not one of you are in this book*.** *That is my gift to you!*

And to my friends: Jet (Amber), Tamsin (Tammi), Prairie (Lezlie) and Lark (Kari). Thank you.

To my friends (the ya ya sisterhood in particular) I couldn't write in because I had a limited amount of slots for secondary characters, I am grateful for your love and friendship. My life is better because of you.

Thank you, Becky Jo for always reading the first pass.

Thank you Wendy for doing last minute proof reads!

Thank you to my parents Kelvin and Debi Jenkins who gave me a fantastic childhood.

I love you all. Thank you for supporting my best life!

Big hugs,

Beck

Afterword

Reference Material / Bibliography for Sunshine in a Bottle:

The Obesity Code: Unlocking the Secrets of Weight Loss (Why Intermittent Fasting Is the Key to Controlling Your Weight) by Doctor Jason Fung.
  Publisher: Greystone Books; Illustrated edition (March 1 2016)
  Complete Guide To Fasting: (Heal Your Body Through Intermittent, Alternate-Day, and Extended Fasting) Paperback – Oct. 18 2016, by Jason Fung and Jimmy Moore.
  Victory Belt Publishing; 1st edition (Oct. 18 2016)
  Codependent No More: How to Stop Controlling Others and Start Caring for Yourself Paperback – Jan. 1 1992 by Melody Beattie
  Publisher: Hazelden; 2 edition (Jan. 1 1992)

Afterword

Clemon

A clemon is simply carbonated water (I use a soda stream and natural spring water) and lemon juice (to taste) and lemon wedges and ice.

I love it.

I serve it in a big wine glass. There is no sugar and it takes a bit to get used to it, but it's fantastic and refreshing.

You can use limes instead or lime and lemon together.

Jet Fuel

To be honest, it's kind of *grainy* Jet Fuel!

Jet's Super Seeds take all sorts of variations in my life and food plan.

This combo is one of my favourites (40 ish grams/ fat blend (50 ish grams):

1 Cup full fat unsweetened coconut milk (I buy this by the crate. I love it. In everything. Everyday.) I quit drinking milk two years ago and don't miss it.

1 scoop of your preferred protein powder (around 26 g of protein)

3 tbsp of hemp hearts

2 tbsp chia seeds

2 tbsp flax

I grind up the hemp, chia and flax in a coffee/seed grinder. You don't have to, but I do.

Blend with an emersion blender and enjoy.

About Author

I'm a veteran hairstylist (25 years behind a chair with no end in sight) who wanted to write books and had no idea how that was going to work out but here I am *loving every minute of it.* My husband and I love to travel and we hope to exit out of here in February!

My favourite thing in this world right now is being bossed around by my six year old niece—Meika. She is where I got the phrase: Right here. Right now.

You can follow me at Carolyn Finch Writes on Facebook, it's my private readers group and I share all in there. If I get to the Caribbean to research Castaway... you'll see my journey there.

Or check out my website: CarolynFinchWrites.com

Made in the USA
Columbia, SC
26 September 2022